By Samantha James

Samantha JAMES

The SECRET PASSION Of SIMON BLACKWELL

AVON BOOKS
An Imprint of HarperCollinsPublishers

AVON BOOKS
An Imprint of HarperCollins*Publishers*
10 East 53rd Street
New York, New York 10022-5299

Copyright © 2007 by Sandra Kleinschmit
ISBN-13: 978-0-7394-8037-3

Printed in the U.S.A.

The Journal of Simon Blackwell
August 1843

The physician visited today. He is pleased that my pain has begun to abate. But the pain he speaks of is of a different sort. Fortunate, he declared me yet again. Fortunate to have survived.

I grow weary of those words, for he cannot know the wrench of despair that tears at my very soul. The stillness that plagues each night in endless darkness.

No one can.

Yet perhaps it is only right. Perhaps it is only just.

Perhaps it is no more than I deserve.

Each night I wonder if the time has come to cease my entries in this journal. Yet I know I cannot. Not now. Not yet. For all I have left of those I loved so dearly is this record.

And my memories.

Perhaps someday it will not hurt so to think of them. Perhaps someday it will be easier.

But when? I ask myself. Dear God, when?

One

It appears Aunt Leticia desires my presence on the occasion of her seventieth birthday. She and I are the only ones left of my mother's family. Despite the fact I detest London in the summer—indeed I detest London at any time—I am obliged to humor her. I shall depart in the morning.

Simon Blackwell

London, 1848

Lady Annabel McBride slowed her stride as she strolled west through Hyde Park, accompanied by her cousin Caroline and Caro's two young children.

"Lud, but I must look a fright," fretted Caro. "The heat is particularly abominable for July, don't you think, Annie?"

Anne peered at Caro from beneath the round brim of her bonnet. Overhead the sun poured down in brilliant radiance. The hour was well before noon; nonetheless, Anne was aware of droplets of sweat gathering between her breasts. Her striped silk walking gown was de rigueur for the day, the bodice tightly fitted, trimmed with ribbons and lace; of course Mama saw to that. But beneath, trussed up in stays, numerous layers of stiff petticoats and ruffled skirts, Anne felt much like a package to be tossed to and fro upon a ship and heaved to the farthest reaches of the sea.

Caro, on the other hand, despite her complaint, appeared fresh as a dew-laden flower, on this, surely the hottest morning of summer thus far.

How Caro managed to maintain her svelte trimness after two births in such close succession was a source of both envy and annoyance among society's ladies—a tiny waist, after all, was a thing much coveted by all.

Anne, of course, knew it had much to do with Isabella and little John, aged three and two respectively; there was but a scant year between them. Both resembled Caro, with sun-gold hair, deep blue eyes, and dimpled cheeks. Lively and vigorous did not even begin to describe the pair, known to the family as Izzie and Jack. Add to the mix a decidedly impish bent—along with a child's eagerness to explore each nook and cranny of the world within view—the little ones were, in sum, a handful. Many a time their antics dictated that Anne hastily bite back the urge to laugh, lest the two be inclined to repeat whatever mischief had brought it on.

"Oh, pooh," Anne announced with a quirk of her lips and a sidelong glance at her companion. "You are divine, cousin, and well you know it." Anne was reminded of the myriad pins scattered throughout her hair. Already she could feel her coiffure drooping, thick and heavy, down the back of her head. Had she been at home in Scotland, she'd have dispensed with her bonnet, shucked off her petticoats (in the privacy of her chamber of course), and restrained her hair with a simple ribbon at her nape before venturing outside. But this was London after all, and admittedly the heat was much more bearable with her tresses swept high and off her face and neck. Oh, to be back at Gleneden, back in the climes of Scotland with a cool breeze swirling fresh from the waters of the loch.

A carriage clattered nearby as they advanced along the walkway. The warmth of the morning had not kept Londoners behind shutters and doors, closed tight against the heat.

Izzie and Jack had taken to scampering through the grass beneath the shade of a tree. Jack began to chase Izzie around and around the base of the tree trunk; Izzie squealed her delight. Caro sank down on a nearby bench, shielding herself with her parasol and feverishly fanning her cheeks.

All at once her fan rapped shut. "Isabella!" Caro called out sharply. "You are not to wander off. Come now. Come to Mama!"

Anne saw that Izzie was skipping toward the Serpentine. Izzie flashed her mother a beatific smile over her shoulder, then began to run full-out as Caro rose to her feet.

"Come chase me, Mama!" the child sang out.

Anne laughed aloud, watching as Izzie uttered a high-pitched shriek and darted just beyond her mother's reach. Caro, of course, was hampered by the bulk of her skirts. Anne's gaze slid back to Jack.

But Jack was no longer there.

Her smile vanished. Anne dropped her parasol and was on her feet in an instant. "Jack?" Anxiously her gaze encircled the grassy area before her. The imp! Where the devil was the little scamp?

She caught sight of him then. He had taken his cue from his sister—but he was sprinting in the opposite direction, running for all he was worth. Anne called his name, but his legs pumped furiously; he raced as fast as his chubby legs could take him.

"Jack, stop!" He looked back at her, for it was a game to him now. Anne lurched forward to give chase. Alas, her petticoats snagged between her legs and she nearly pitched forward onto her face. Again she silently cursed the unwieldy burden of women's clothing. Righting herself, she glanced frantically toward the place where she'd last seen Jack.

Once again Jack had disappeared. Then she saw he'd nearly reached the broad, sand-covered track of Rotten Row.

A horse and rider were bearing down fast.

Panic enveloped her. Heedless of anyone who might chance to see, she grabbed handfuls of her skirts and dragged them high.

It all seemed to happen in a swirl of sound and motion. Someone shouted; the rider's hands twisted in the reins and jerked back. His mount screamed and reared high; powerful hooves slashed the air. Terror closed Anne's throat, for Jack was almost directly beneath the steed!

A horrifying dread clutched at her insides. God. *Oh, God.* Little Jack didn't know the danger he was in. And she would never make it. She couldn't reach him.

Anne was well aware what the force of powerful hooves could do to a man. A man could be maimed, crippled. Killed.

A child stood no chance at all.

From very far away, she heard a garbled scream—her own, she realized dimly.

And Jack . . . the boy had finally halted abruptly. He'd turned back toward Anne, his round little face looking faintly perplexed.

But there was something else. Some*one* else. She had no sense of who or where or even when he'd appeared. But in the blink of an eye came a flash of movement. A figure charged forward; the little boy was snatched high and away, just as the massive animal's front legs hurtled down, mere inches from little Jack's head. Anne was so close, the very earth beneath her slippers thundered and shook.

The rider called out his apologies. "No harm done now, eh?"

Anne barely heard. She rushed forward toward man and child. Her heart still thudded wildly in her chest. She was quivering from head to toe, both inside and out, shaken to the core by the close call.

Her gaze climbed upward, to the man who now held Jack in one arm, one hand curled protectively on the boy's back. Anne's lips parted as she sought to muster her wits about her. But before she could say a word—

"By God, madam, have you no sense?" Eyes the color of storm clouds raked her from head to toe. "What the devil is wrong with you? A good mother would never allow her child to be placed in such danger. Why the blazes weren't you aware of your son's whereabouts?"

Anne sucked in a breath, already breathless from her mad dash after Jack. But it wasn't lack of air that held her tongue. It was shock. Sheer and utter shock.

And indeed Anne was, quite literally, stunned beyond speech. There was no denying the anger that fed the words. She could only gape at him, shocked by the force of his anger, stung by his bluntness. He was rude. Rude beyond measure—why, nearly beyond comprehension. Clearly he'd left his manners at his doorstep.

Her lips pressed tightly together. Anne had inherited her mother's wealth of rich chestnut hair, her ivory complexion, and her warmth and generosity. But as the rest of the family well knew, her impetuous nature and her lightning temper were undeniably Scots—undeniably her father's, God rest his soul.

Oh, how she longed to acquaint this man with the sting of her palm; for that matter, her fist. But such behavior was hardly ladylike, and she would spare this gentleman—ah, but she was exceedingly inclined toward generosity, it seemed, for his scathing tone did not warrant such restraint. It most certainly did not proclaim him a gentleman.

Her eyes narrowed. "Now see here," she began.

"No, madam, you see here! The boy could have been killed because you, his mother, did not keep him in hand, like a proper parent should. You are singularly unfit for your role as mother!"

And, Anne thought, he was singularly grim. Singularly an ass. Singularly a tyrant—certainly as fierce as one, if the thinness of his lips and his glowering countenance were any indication. By Jove, if he insulted her again, she *would* hit him. She *should* have hit him already. And Jack (oh, but the little fellow was surely a traitor of the worst kind!) was amusing himself with the shiny gold buttons on the man's waistcoat. Jack was usually most fussy with strangers, but he appeared quite content with this one, which only inflamed her further.

"I am *not*," Anne stressed through thin lips, "his mother."

The man made a sound of disgust. "His nanny then. By God, you should be dismissed."

Anne sucked in a breath. How dare he speak to her so!

"My boy! Please let me have him! Oh, *please!*"

It was Caro, breathless from her flight across the grass. She thrust Izzie into Anne's arms. "Dearest, are you all right?" With a cry she fairly plucked Jack from the man's hold.

"He's fine, Caro," Anne said quickly. "Not a scratch, thanks to the . . . gentleman." It was all she could do to force the word *gentleman* past her lips.

Caro clutched the boy close. "John Ellis Sykes, you've given Mama such a fright." She buried her cheek against Jack's plump neck. Her eyes squeezed shut, wet with tears.

The man's gaze had narrowed on Caro. His severity began to ease. Not that Anne was surprised. Caro's fragile, dimpled beauty had always had that effect on men. But Anne was still spitting mad at this man's outburst. Despite the fact he was obviously a gentleman—his clothing and bearing declared him such—Anne was not given to call him one. And when he bent to retrieve his top hat from the ground, displaying a rather well-formed derriere, a most childish notion took hold of her. Oh, but what she wouldn't give to place a well-aimed kick at his—

Sniffing, Caro raised her head and slanted the brute a watery smile. "Sir, I am indebted." She held out a hand. "I am Mrs. Caroline Sykes. And you are . . . ?"

"Simon Blackwell." Ever so briefly, he pressed Caro's gloved fingertips. "A pleasure, madam."

Caro laughed lightly. "I see you've already met my cousin, Lady Annabel McBride."

Anne did not offer her hand; Jack's rescuer didn't seem to expect it. He inclined his head, and the good manners ingrained by her very proper English mother dictated she acknowledge in turn. Anne did so, albeit rather stiffly.

Yet in that very same instant, she found herself swallowing, struck by several things in turn. His height, for one. He was tall, taller than she'd realized, as tall as her brothers. And despite his size, his reflexes were remarkably quick. His hair was like the darkest hour of the night, the same thick black as his brows. The brim of his hat cast a shadow over square, angular features. But then he turned his head ever so slightly, and she saw his eyes. It was almost jarring to see they were a pale gray, a shade darker than crystal. And unsettling, in a way she could not discern—in a way that had nothing to do with his rebuke.

All at once, she wanted nothing more than to depart immediately. Now. She didn't like Simon Blackwell. She didn't wish to participate in niceties. The sooner she and Caro took their leave, the better.

It appeared Caro was not of the same mind.

"I should welcome the opportunity to thank you properly, sir. Indeed," Caro was saying with that brilliant smile that her husband, John, declared had snared him on the spot, "I should consider it an honor if you would join us for supper. Aunt Viv won't mind, will she, Annie? I adore Aunt Vivian, and it has nothing to do with the fact she's always called me her favorite niece. Aunt Viv brought a bit of English decorum and elegance to the family, my father always said. My father and Annie's father were brothers, you see, both big, brawny Scotsmen. And Alec will no doubt join us for supper, I suspect. Annie and Alec are my cousins, as you've probably gathered, along with their brother, Aidan, who's off with his regiment in India. Now that their father has passed on, Alec is the head of the family, but he maintains lodgings elsewhere. And Aunt Viv has been generous enough to let me and my husband, John, stay with her while our town house is being restored."

How Anne managed to stop her jaw from dropping, she had no idea. She *did* know she could have cheerfully throttled Caro. Granted, it was true her mother wouldn't mind a guest. But why on earth had Caro regaled this stranger with a goodly portion of the family history?

Her expression must have displayed the nature of her thoughts, for suddenly Caro stopped short. "Annie? Is there something you wish to add?"

Anne stifled a groan. Instead she said lightly, "Caro, you allow no time for the gentleman either to accept *or* decline. Indeed, you make it rather difficult for him to say anything."

"Oh, do forgive me." Caro laughed prettily. "I'm running on, aren't I? I'm sorry, I'm still a bit overwrought. Annie, you should have stopped me." And yet again, she allowed no time for speech. She addressed Simon Blackwell. "Will you join us tonight, sir?"

Simon Blackwell shook his head. "It's very generous of you to extend the offer, but I assure you, it's quite unnecessary. I've no wish to intrude on your evening."

So he wasn't completely without manners, Anne admitted grudgingly, shifting Izzie to her other hip. But his polite refusal went unheeded by Caro.

"Oh, but it is necessary!" she burst out. "I should never be able to forgive myself if John and I didn't convey our gratitude. If anything had happened to my little angel, why . . . I don't know how I could bear it!" She hugged Jack fiercely, blinking back tears.

It appeared Simon Blackwell was not impervious to them. "I should hate to be an imposition," he said slowly.

"Oh, but you will not!" Caro cried. Her beaming smile reappeared as she cited the address just off Grosvenor Square. "We generally dine at eight. Dinner is usually quite an informal affair, just the family. And if you fail to appear, sir, why, we shall send out the Runners to hunt for you. After all, we know your name now. And now, sir, until this evening, I bid you good day. Shall we, Annie?"

Anne, who was rarely at a loss for words, stared at her cousin as they left Simon Blackwell behind. "Caro," she said, once they were out of earshot, "what have you done?"

"I just invited my son's rescuer to supper," came her cousin's breezy reply.

"But—he's a stranger!" Anne was still rather aghast. "I mean, really, what do we know of him?"

"We know all we need to know! It's hardly like you to be so tiresome, Annie. It's obvious Simon Blackwell is a most pleasant gentleman. I know a man of good character when I see one."

A gentleman, Anne conceded darkly as they crossed the street, but hardly a pleasant one.

"Oh, yes, a most pleasant gentleman," Caro mused as they continued the walk north toward her mother's town house.

Anne pursed her mouth. "Caro, if I didn't know you were madly in love with John, I could almost believe you were playing the coquette with that man."

"I was not. I was being polite, something that seems to have escaped you, dearest. And his looks are rather dashing, in case you hadn't noticed."

Anne was annoyed. "Well, of course I did. But—"

Caro laughed out loud. "Excellent," she nearly chortled. "Most excellent!"

Anne raised a brow. "And why is that?"

"Oh, come, Annie, you needn't sound so prim. I know you better than anyone. You've had your share of suitors in the past. Why, I do believe Lillith Kimball has never forgiven you for stealing away Charles Goodwin."

Anne scowled. "You know very well I did not steal him away."

"Well, you cannot deny you had quite the *tendre* for him."

Alas, it was true. In her first and only Season out—because of her father's subsequent illness—Anne had been rather smitten with Charles Goodwin, a man whose blond, godlike countenance had many a miss, Anne included, vying for his attentions.

And it was Anne upon whom Charles had settled his attentions for the latter half of the Season, while Lillith Kimball had captured his attentions for the first half. But one single evening at the opera had cured Anne's *tendre*.

Charles had managed to secure the box next to her, Caro, and John. He'd proceeded to boast about the vastness of his holdings in England, his *appartement* in Paris, the fact that he was heir to his father's earldom. Anne had never met a man so full of himself as Charles Goodwin. As relayed by the man himself, the list of his accomplishments—and his opinion of himself—was limitless. Anne was scarcely able to enjoy the performance for the way Charles prattled on about himself—and not a word about *anything* else. It had taken Anne but scant minutes to recognize her mistake—and acknowledge that there were more important facets to admire in a man than simply a handsome face.

Then, during the intermission when Caro

and John had gone to seek refreshments, he'd even tried to kiss her! It was the most acutely awkward moment of Anne's life when she turned her face aside and lurched to her feet, mumbling an excuse about finding Caro and John. Moreover, Charles had called on her for some days afterward. It was Alec who had informed him rather cuttingly that there was little point in continuing to do so.

Anne glowered. "Oh, come," she said rather crossly. "I certainly did not steal Charles away from her. In point of fact, after that horrid night at the opera, I'd have liked to steal away myself!"

"Well," Caro said with a chuckle, "I rather suspect you'll never convince Lillith Kimball of that. I do believe she still carries a torch for him. She has yet to marry, you know. And neither has Charles."

"That is hardly my fault," Anne said stiffly.

"Yes, I'm aware of that, love," Caro continued breezily, "which brings me back to one Mr. Simon Blackwell. Need I remind you that you have no other suitors at present? After all, this is your first visit to London in nearly two years."

"I fail to see what that has to do with anything," Anne declared.

"Oh, but it has *everything* to do with it. I daresay Jack and Izzie would just adore having a little cousin to play with."

Anne blinked, too stunned to say a word. "For pity's sake, Caro!" she managed finally. "Are you listening to yourself?"

Together they began to climb the steps toward the shiny black-fronted door. Caro cast her a sidelong glace. "What's the matter with you, Annie? You act as if you're . . . oh, I don't know. Afraid somehow."

"Afraid? Hardly!" For all her bravado, at the memory Simon Blackwell's piercing gray eyes, Anne felt a curious shiver run through her.

" 'The lady doth protest too much,' " Caro quoted. "Come now, where is your pluck, my dear?" Caro sailed through the door, which had been opened by a footman. They handed the little ones to a maid. "You've always been the daring, adventurous one, unafraid of anyone and anything. I'll never forget the way you once convinced me we should hide behind the screen in Alec's room when he slipped Veronica Brooks inside."

Anne bit her lip. Though Caro was a year older, it was Anne who had always taken the lead in their escapades. "Nor will Alec," she admitted.

Caro chuckled. "That was wicked of us, wasn't it?"

"And quite revealing. Oh, but it was Veronica who was revealed, wasn't it?"

"Oh, but do not flutter those angelically wide

blue eyes at me, love! Those who know you are aware you are as feisty as ever!"

"How can you say such a thing?" Anne fought hard to suppress a smile and didn't at all succeed. "I've reformed. Truly. And I would remind you, I'm hardly the one who invited that man home for supper. Your hero was quite rude to me, Caro!"

"John is my only hero, love. And while you say you've reformed," Caro said lightly, "I know you, Annie. You'll always be the same inside. You're the vibrant, fervent one—that's why we love you. Everything you do, you do with all your heart. Alec will always be as secretly devilish as you are, and Aidan, I'm sure, will ever be the man of adventure."

Quite so, Anne admitted silently.

"Now, back to Mr. Simon Blackwell, love." Caro's eyes were alight with laughter. "Please don't forget his name when he comes to supper."

Anne's nostalgic smile ended in a most unladylike snort. "If he even puts in an appearance. And if he does, well, then perhaps John should like to know that you were flirting with that— that *man*, Caro!"

Caro laughed. "John adores me as much as I adore him," she pronounced cheerfully. "But you're right. It wouldn't do to behave in such an outrageous manner. Therefore, I shall be perfectly happy to leave the flirting to you, dearest." With that, Caro blew her a kiss.

Anne sank down on the stairs with a moan. How divine, she thought dismally.

It appeared she must resign herself to supper with the tyrant after all.

Two

The light in my life has gone out. I fear I will be forever in the dark.

Simon Blackwell

Precisely at eight o'clock, the knocker at the front door sounded.

The household was in a bit of an uproar. Izzie and Jack had just been bathed, but had escaped the clutches of their nurse and scampered downstairs. From the parlor doorway, Caro heaved a sigh and crooked a finger at Izzie. Just as the maid opened the front door, Anne scooped up Jack from the stairway, where he appeared intent on leaping from the last stair as his sister was so fond of doing. Anne gave him a quick squeeze, loving the feel of his small body. Fresh from the bath, his round cheeks still glowing and rosy, he was adorable as always.

And then Simon Blackwell stepped inside.

Caro flashed a beaming smile. "Mr. Blackwell! How wonderful to see you again—and right on time."

"I'm a man of my word," Simon murmured with a faint lift of his brows. "It would be quite rude to be tardy."

Would it have killed the man to smile? *It would be quite rude to be tardy*, Anne mimicked in her mind. She felt suddenly rather cross.

She wasn't exactly pleased that Caro had been right—he had shown! And now that he had, it would be quite rude to claim illness, Anne admitted to herself, particularly when she was already here in the flesh. Well, no doubt Caro would be chortling later this evening.

He acknowledged Anne's presence with a faint bow. "My lady," he murmured. His countenance remained unsmiling, his tone utterly noncommittal.

Anne withheld a glare. The memory of his arrogance earlier in the day washed over her in full force. Nonetheless, she would show the grace and civility he had not.

Izzie, who had been closest to the door—and to him—turned suddenly shy. When the child slipped behind her mother's skirts, Anne wanted to grin wickedly. *Yes, poppet, you've decided he's quite the tyrant too, haven't you?*

"Isabella, don't be so shy, duckling! Don't you remember, we met Mr. Blackwell in the park today."

Isabella peeped out at him warily. Meanwhile, Jack had mashed his face into Anne's shoulder, only to pop up an instant later. His eyes sparkling, he extended chubby hands toward Simon and leaned forward.

The gesture was unmistakable.

But Mr. Blackwell didn't want to hold him. In the instant before he took the little boy, she spied it on his features; she sensed it as well. It was not distaste that flitted across his face, nor could she deem it reluctance.

She was suddenly indignant. What the devil? she wondered. He'd had no qualms about holding Jack when he'd rescued him; there had been something about his hold on the boy earlier today that indicated a familiarity with little ones. Perhaps that was why it suddenly seemed so odd now when it appeared he didn't want to.

It might have been different had the little boy been dirty and sticky. But he wasn't. His body was soft and sweet-smelling, and all at once, Anne was brimming with fire.

Her mouth opened. Anne was fully prepared to smite him with the sting of her tongue.

"Well, I see Jack is determined to make a pest of himself again."

It was John, Caro's husband, fair and ruddy-cheeked and ever jovial.

Simon turned his head. "Jack?" he repeated. "Isn't his name . . . isn't it John?"

Anne glanced at Simon sharply.

"It is," said Caro with a chuckle. "But my husband John here"—she offered up her cheek for the brush of her husband's lips—"has called him Jack since the day he was born. And despite my most ardent objection, nearly everyone in the family has followed his lead in calling our son Jack—even me," she said with a laugh.

"Papa!" Jack squealed in delight.

"Here, I'll take him," John said easily. John scooped up his son and ruffled the youngster's hair before handing him over to his nurse.

Vivian McBride, who had been napping, had descended the staircase to join them. Caro made the introductions, and then Alec strode in as well. Alec playfully chucked Anne beneath the chin, then turned to their mother.

"Mother," he murmured, bending low to kiss one parchment cheek, "you're looking particularly lovely tonight."

And she did, Anne decided with a twist in her heart. Of course, Vivian McBride would have looked exquisite in a flour sack. Her frame was slight, her features porcelain and delicate. She wore a gown of pale lavender silk; it was only recently that she had come out of mourning. Her husband's ravaging illness had been long and difficult, but throughout, Vivian was cheerful and strong—and scarcely more than a few footsteps from his bedside.

Not until she'd said her private good-byes to the man she had loved throughout the course of thirty years and six births—though only Alec, Aidan, and Anne had survived—did she finally break. Only after his passing did the duchess close her eyes and weep, with only her children as witness. Yet when the duke was laid to rest, Vivian handled it as she did all else, with the utmost dignity and poise.

"Alec," said the duchess, "may I introduce our dinner guest, Mr. Simon Blackwell? I understand Mr. Blackwell made a rather dashing rescue of little Jack today in Hyde Park. Mr. Blackwell, my son, Alec McBride, Duke of Gleneden."

The two men shook hands. "Ah," drawled Alec. "So Jack was being a mischief maker, eh? I confess, I'm not terribly surprised."

Anne was scarcely listening. She was still pondering the moment when John had appeared and called his son Jack. She wasn't certain what had just happened, but *something* had.

What lay behind Simon Blackwell's query? *I thought his name was John.* His voice had been so odd when he spoke Jack's name. Rather hoarse and . . . well, just so peculiar. And his expression had been strange as well. It was as if, for a hairbreadth of an instant, everything—

including the ability to breathe—had frozen solid. Caro didn't appear to have noticed, nor did any of the others. Was she mistaken? Anne stole a glance at his profile.

He appeared completely recovered.

Vivian directed her smile at Simon. "Mr. Blackwell, would you be so kind as to escort me in to dinner?"

"Your Grace, I should be honored."

No one would have called Simon Blackwell a man of lighthearted folly. From her place directly beside him—oh, but she had the feeling Caro was responsible for that!—Anne considered him ever so discreetly. His jaw was square and angular, cleanly shaven to the skin. He was deeply tanned; clearly he did not spend all his time in the pursuit of leisurely endeavors. There was in his demeanor a presence so strong she felt it like a jolt, an undercurrent that was almost overwhelmingly elemental.

Clearly he was a man of means. It wasn't only his clothing that declared him such. Neither his pose nor his manner had suggested that he was uncomfortable in either their home or their presence.

He'd shed his morning coat for other attire. The collar of his shirt was high, nearly touching his cheeks, his cravat precisely tied. But for his shirt, he was garbed entirely in black. The cut of his jacket was several years behind the fashion, plainly tailored, but hewn of the finest material. Still, the cut was dark and severe, a bit like the man himself, Anne decided with a touch of wryness.

But it was his size that sent her pulse skidding oddly. The fabric of his jacket was stretched taut; beneath, his shoulders seemed enormously wide. The span of his wrists was in similar proportion, the length of his fingers curled around a delicately fragile wineglass, strong but not meaty. The backs of his hands were liberally sprinkled with a netting of hair as dark as that on his head. All combined to make the contrast even more pronounced.

Anne was not a particularly small woman. In her younger years she'd been thin and awkward as a cat without fur. As her father had liked to tease, that was no longer the case. Yet the man beside her made her feel quite small and petite, a feeling most unusual to Anne.

He was hardly old, and yet . . . She pondered his age, most suddenly—and most curiously. At his temples gleamed a smattering of silver. She glanced between the three men. Alec was seven years her senior, and John the same age, yet thus far neither displayed any sign of gray.

Considering her dislike of him, she didn't expect to find him—drat it all!—so handsome. And not just handsome, but quite exquisitely handsome. Drat! Why had Caro pointed it out?

And why did she even notice? inquired a silent voice in her head.

It was most vexing. And she was decidedly short of breath. Had Agnes laced her up too tightly? Surely that was it. Still . . .

"Damnation!" she muttered, her fingers clenching her napkin in her lap.

Her mother turned large blue eyes upon her. "Anne? What did you say, dear?"

Anne swallowed. "Nothing, Mama."

Vivian turned her regard back to their guest. "Is your primary residence in London, Mr. Blackwell?" she inquired.

"No, Your Grace." He paused. "Actually, I rarely visit London. I spend most of my time in the country. The north country, to be precise."

Anne reached for her wine. "In the country? What, sir? Are you an eccentric?" The question slipped out before Anne thought better of it.

Vivian had merely to raise a finely arched brow and fold her hands in her lap to display her displeasure. And now Alec was glaring at her in that disapproving way he sometimes had, she noticed with annoyance. He was her older brother, and he was a duke, but she certainly would never quail before him!

Anne could not deny she had erred. She couldn't precisely say what had come over her. At some other time she might not have been so stubborn. But tonight . . . *What?* she wanted to shout. *What?*

It did not lessen when she felt the scrutiny of their guest settled on her. Their eyes met. A curious tension seemed to hum between them. "What makes you think that?" he asked pleasantly.

Her chin came up. Anne took a sip of her wine before glancing his way. "Well, sir," she pointed out, "you did say you rarely visit London. Perhaps you're a recluse then."

Alec interjected. "You must forgive my sister's forwardness," he said lightly. "Our only excuse is that we come from the wilds of Scotland where manners occasionally fall by the wayside."

Anne longed to give an unladylike snort. Alas, her mother continued Alec's unwanted rescue.

"London can grow tiresome, can't it? I'm always glad to go home to Gleneden."

"I can imagine it is, Your Grace. But actually Lady Anne's assumption is correct. I would probably not have come to London were it not for the occasion of my Aunt Leticia's seventieth birthday."

Vivian's fork poised in mid-air. "Leticia," she repeated. "Leticia Hamilton? The Dowager Countess of Hopewell?"

"The very same, Your Grace."

Vivian made a sound of pleasure. "Why, she was my patroness at my come-out years ago.

Indeed, her birthday celebration is the day after next—at Lady Creswell's."

"Precisely why I'm here, Your Grace."

Oh, but she should have known. What had begun as a pleasant enough day was continuing its descent. Of course Anne was aware that her mother and the countess were dear friends. They called upon each other whenever they were in London and corresponded regularly.

Gritting her teeth, Anne disguised her annoyance.

It wasn't just Caro. Now it appeared Simon Blackwell had succeeded in winning over the heart of her mother—and with scarcely any effort at all!

But it was Caro who said brightly, "Forgive my presumption, but did your wife accompany you, Mr. Blackwell?"

Anne was mortified. Beside her, she could have sworn Simon Blackwell was uncomfortable as well.

Caro practically cooed her satisfaction. Anne longed to slink beneath the table.

"No," he answered. "I live alone."

It appeared John had been studying him as well. He tipped his head to the side. "Do we have a previous acquaintance, Mr. Blackwell?"

"I was thinking the same as well," said Alec. "You look familiar. And your name as well. I thought perhaps we'd met before, but I don't believe we have."

"Nor do I, Your Grace—"

Alec waved a careless hand. "No need to stand on formality, man. Call me Alec."

"Very well then, Alec. I'm certain I'd remember if we had."

"Perhaps not. But you attended Cambridge, didn't you?" Again John spoke.

Simon's brows shot high. "So I did."

"By God, you were an oarsman, weren't you? The year the colors were chosen."

He referred, of course, to the annual boat race between Cambridge and Oxford, and the colors of the crew. Oxford wore dark blue, Cambridge a lighter hue. John and Alec were mad for the race that was now an annual event; both made it a point to be in London every year since they'd left Cambridge.

"It was my second year at Cambridge. I always aspired to the Blue Boat, but I was told I had no technique," Alec said.

"That, gentlemen, was eons ago." There was a hint of amusement in Blackwell's voice. "Though I do believe Cambridge will ever have the advantage."

"Hear hear." John raised his glass high for a toast. "Indeed."

Anne made a faint sound. Three pairs of male eyes turned her way.

"My sister," Alec said dryly, "is no longer fond of rowing. She and Caro were once stranded for hours in the middle of the loch at Gleneden, our home in Scotland."

Anne sent Caro an arch look, for Caro was biting her lip, clearly struggling to hold back a laugh.

"I don't believe I've heard this particular story before," John remarked.

"It was after dark when they were discovered," added the duchess. "A storm had blown in and drenched them to the skin. I recall the poor dears suffered quite a fever for some days afterward."

Alec's eyes gleamed as he glanced at Anne. "We laugh about it now, but my mother and Caro's were quite frantic."

"I can only imagine."

"Of course it might have been averted somewhat if they had told someone their intentions."

"True," Caro agreed, "but I expect it wasn't Annie's intention to lose both oars either." Anne's cousin maintained her silence no longer. She wiped tears of laughter from the corner of her eyes. "I shall never forget the look on your face, Annie, when you scrambled after the first oar, only to hear the splash of the other as it fell into the loch. Though you made quite the heroic effort to retrieve it," Caro amended on seeing Anne's baleful expression.

"Ever the intrepid adventurer, our Annie." Alec smiled mildly.

"And yet another McBride with no technique," John observed.

Anne was vastly annoyed. Oh, traitors, all! she decided. Rising, she dropped her napkin on her plate. "Well," she said lightly, "it seems you are all rather easily amused." She pushed back her chair. "Mother, perhaps it's time we took the entertainment to the music room."

Vivian rose gracefully to her small feet. "An excellent idea, Anne. Mr. Blackwell, you'll join us, won't you?"

Moments later Vivian was running her fingers nimbly across the piano keys. But Anne seized hold of the opportunity now afforded her. Before her mother could begin a melody, before any of the rest of them had even take a seat, she held back. "Oh, dear," she said with a forced laugh, "I fear I must beg my excuses. I suddenly find I've developed quite the headache."

Vivian looked up at her in silent question. It wasn't like her to be sickly—ever. And Caro's mouth formed an "O" of surprise. Alec's ice-blue eyes sharpened, and even John was frowning. As for Simon Blackwell, well, she knew the instant his regard settled on her; she felt it with every pore of her being. It was vastly annoying, she thought, wondering what the devil had come over her. Yet was it any wonder she felt like a bug beneath a glass? She kept her gaze trained on her mother—and away from him.

Vivian inclined her head. "Of course, Anne," she said. "Feel better soon, darling."

And with that, Anne bobbed a curtsy—and once she was out of sight, she nearly ran to her room.

An hour later, Anne had just thrown back the coverlet on her bed when she heard a faint cry from down the hall. She paused, one knee perched on the bed. Footsteps scurried by; she spied their shadow beneath the door. Reassured, she slipped beneath the covers, then picked up the book at her bedside, intending to read a short while. A scant minute later there was a light tap on her door.

Caro opened it. "Annie?"

"Come in, Caro." Anne set aside her book. "Jack?" she inquired.

"Izzie. John went in to her." Caro stepped into the room and closed the door. "Are you feeling better?"

"Yes," Anne lied.

Caro looked at her closely. "You do seem a bit pale. Are you sure you're all right?"

Anne picked up the other pillow and settled it against her chest. "I'm much better, Caro. I think perhaps it was the heat." She didn't dare say it was the company . . .

Caro peered at her earnestly. "We didn't mean to make sport of you, you know."

"I know."

And it was true. It wasn't their teasing. It wasn't that at all.

It was he.

Simon Blackwell.

But it had been a cowardly thing to do—to flee the way she had. Already she regretted it. But it was done and—

"I didn't mean to worry anyone." She patted the place beside her. "Come sit, love."

Caro settled herself next to her.

"Mr. Blackwell made an early evening of it as well. He left a scant half hour after you went upstairs."

"Did he now?" It was a statement, not an inquiry.

"Oh, Annie, don't look like that! I know you do not care for him."

"You're right. I do not. Indeed, he struck me as quite the . . . unconventional sort."

Caro winced. "Unconventional? What, now you've decided to temper your words?"

"What?" Anne queried, knowing full well what Caro meant.

"Annie, why, you all but called him an eccentric! And merely because he chooses not to frequent London. Why, *you* much prefer the country to London. Yet you dared disparage him for it."

"I did not disparage him. I did not *call* him an eccentric. I merely made an innocent query."

"Innocent? Annie, it was quite apparent to everyone you think him an ogre!"

Anne secretly smiled her satisfaction. Simon Blackwell was . . . well, exactly as she expected.

"Annabel McBride! Do not look like that. He's hardly a beast! I stand by my initial impression."

"And mine is but confirmed. I think he's the stuffiest man I've ever had the misfortune to meet."

"Anne!" Caro injected. "I cannot believe we're discussing the same man."

"And I cannot believe you had the audacity to inquire as to his marital state!"

"I did not inquire. I merely made the discovery that our Mr. Blackwell is unwed."

"He is not *our* Mr. Blackwell." Anne longed to throw up her hands.

Caro was wide-eyed and demure. "Oh, do forgive me. *Your* Mr. Blackwell."

"Caroline Sykes! I tell you now, Simon Blackwell and I would never suit."

"You don't know that."

"Oh, but I do." Anne was adamant. The idea of her and Simon Blackwell . . . Why, it was ridiculous. More than ridiculous, really. Whatever was Caro thinking?

"Why do you find him so objectionable?"

"Caro!" Anne shot her what she hoped was a quelling look. "Either way, it's not worth arguing over."

"Oh, come. We never argue." Caro smiled. "Well, almost never." Which was very true. Anne was reminded of days gone by. So often, she and Caro need not say a word to know what the other was thinking.

Though Caro was eyeing her curiously, it appeared Caro was reminded as well. "Annie," she said softly, "do you remember when we used to stay up almost the whole night through? We'd throw open the window and gaze into the night wishing on stars." She smiled wistfully. "There's nowhere in the world that has more stars than Gleneden, is there?"

Anne tacitly agreed.

"We talked . . . and talked more, didn't we?"

"Yes," Anne said dryly, "that's mostly what I remember." She paused. "The last time was the night before you married John." She grinned. "Caro, I've never seen anyone so excited!"

"I've never *been* so excited. Too excited to think of sleep!"

They both laughed. Caro sighed. "I miss those days."

Anne arched a brow.

"What, Annie, you don't?"

"Well, yes, of course. But we're both older now and—"

"And I know what you're going to say, Annie. I have a husband and children. So yes, it's different, yet as I sit here now, it's just the way it used to be. Why, it's just the way it's always been. And . . . Annie, oh, Annie, I have a secret!"

Anne leaned close. "What?" she whispered.

Caro whispered back. "Annie, I think that I . . ." She laid a hand on her belly.

Anne's eyes widened. "What, again?" She hastily amended her words. "Oh, Caro, I didn't mean—"

"I know, love. Oh, I know! But"—she bit her lip—"oh, my, I haven't even told John yet! I shall have to rectify that tonight."

"Yes, I rather suspect he'd like to know," Anne injected wryly, then smiled. "He'll be thrilled, won't he?"

"He will," Caro admitted. "And this is another girl, I just know it."

"Do you now?"

"I do," Caro insisted. She paused, then reached for Anne's hand and sighed. "Oh, Annie, if we were wishing on stars, do you know what I'd wish for? I'd wish for you to be as happy as I am."

Anne tipped her head to the side, a faint smile on her lips. "But, dearest, I am happy."

"Oh, yes, yes, I know, but . . . oh, you'd have a bit of catching up to do, but Annie, wouldn't it be grand if—if you had a little girl, too? And someday the two of them . . . why, they'd stay up all night the way we used to."

"Like sisters," Anne said softly. "Like us."

And all at once a vivid picture appeared in Anne's mind—the image of two little girls whispering and tiptoeing barefoot across the floor, then erupting into giggles as Nurse threw open the door and scolded, sending them scampering back to bed and ducking under the covers—only to emerge the instant the door closed.

Suddenly there was a gigantic lump in Anne's throat. Oh, how she loved Caro! They hugged each other, each wearing a sloppy, sentimental smile, but neither cared.

"Well, dearest, I suppose it might be wise to find a husband first before the children come." Anne's laugh held a breathless quality.

Caro still clutched her hand. She squeezed her fingers. "Above all, I want you to have what I have," she said softly.

"Someday I will," Anne said.

And in that moment, there was never a doubt in her mind.

Three

His name is Jack. Dear God, the boy's name is Jack.

Simon Blackwell

Simon knew, the moment he stepped into the McBride residence, that he shouldn't have come. He knew it as soon as he crossed the threshold.

The McBrides were a close-knit family. He liked them. Truly he did.

All but the girl. All but Anne. And it wasn't that he disliked her.

But she disliked him. She disliked him intensely.

Yet still she occupied his mind the entire way home.

What was it that made him so uncomfortably

aware of her? Was it her spirit? An adventurer, her brother had called her. Yes, he could see that trait in her. He'd sensed it this morning.

All at once Simon's memory was suddenly far sharper than he wished. In his mind's eye, he recalled every detail. She had dark slivers of eyebrows. Her eyes were a deep sapphire, but darkened to midnight when she was displeased. Her hair was like sun-drizzled honey and chestnut all melded together.

And—God above—but he could not help it. When she'd turned toward him, he'd glimpsed the sweet swell of her breasts where they peeped above the scalloped lace of her gown. There was a luminous, almost pearlescent quality to the fairness of her skin. It looked supple. Firm. He'd had to stop his gaze from dwelling long and hard on the rise and fall of her chest.

What was it? he pondered. The scent of warm flesh and vibrant woman? The faint scent of roses? The scent of *her*? He thought of the way she moved, her long, leggy stride—a stride that bespoke confidence, yet not vanity.

Why couldn't they have seated him next to her cousin, the married one? he wondered impatiently. Of course, if he'd refused the invitation in the first place, there would have been no problem. Never mind that it would have been the height of rudeness. What did he care? What did he care about anything?

Stepping into his lodgings, he strode straight to the bedside table, where he splashed a liberal portion of whisky into a glass. He downed it quickly, welcoming the burning as it slid down his throat, the hazy fuzz that began to surround his mind.

It did little to still the questing in his being. Indeed, it only made it worse.

Moving to the bureau, he untied his cravat and dragged it loose. Dear God, what was wrong with him? Yet even as the question slid through his mind, he knew the answer.

One night had forever changed him. *That* night.

It was then he had turned to solitude. It was then he shut himself away. *To hide,* sneered a voice in his soul. But within him was a heartache too painful to reveal—to anyone.

If only he could feel numb. But five years of widowhood had changed him. Five years of widowhood had made him distant. Perhaps even hard. God, he thought disgustedly. Was it any wonder that Anne disliked him?

He'd always regarded himself a most astute observer of human nature. He'd always been sensitive to the moods and feelings of those around him.

But he wasn't the man he used to be.

Absently he rubbed his right shoulder. Beneath the cloth of his shirt, the skin was tightly drawn and puckered. He'd learned to live with the near-constant ache, accepted it for it was now a part of him as much as his memories. Yet if he was honest with himself—as he usually was—the ache in his heart was a thousand times worse.

And tonight the door to the past had been flung wide open.

"Is there anything I can do for you, sir?"

It was Duffy, whose rheumatism had begun to slow his gait. Simon glanced up at the stoop-shouldered man who had served him since he was a boy. The old man had come in and turned down the bed and he hadn't even been aware of it.

"Duffy," he said, "do you find me difficult?"

Duffy ran a head over his bald pate. "Sir—" he began.

"For pity's sake, you needn't mind your tongue," he stated gruffly. "You know damned well I won't dismiss you. Come now, out with it."

Duffy cleared his throat. "What I think, sir, is that you've suffered too long already. And I wonder how much longer you will continue to make yourself suffer."

Brave words. True words. Well, Simon thought with a twist of his heart, he *had* asked.

"Will that be all, sir?"

Simon inclined his head. It was Duffy who saw that he was clothed and fed. If not for the old man, he wondered with a touch of cynicism, what would have become of him?

"Very well then." With a quickness that belied his age, Duffy stepped up. "I'll just tidy up a bit first," he said cheerfully. He reached for the bottle of whisky.

"No," Simon said. "Leave it."

Duffy's faded gaze came up questioningly.

Almost defiantly, Simon curled long fingers around the neck of the bottle.

"Good night, Duffy," he said.

When he was alone, Simon made his way to the desk near the window.

Slowly he reached for his glass—and then his journal. It was habit, he supposed, rifling through the pages. But he reasoned that even in his disordered mind, there must be some sense of right.

And all at once, his rage at God, his rage at the world at large surged to the surface. A tearing rage ripped through him. A rage he had not felt in weeks. Months. Just when he'd thought the hurt had begun to fade . . .

Once again, he was bleeding inside. His lungs burned. To have so much, all that a man could treasure—and then in an instant, it was gone. Everything. How could it be?

He wanted to scream. To cry. He thought of Rosewood. Of Ellie. Of Joshua and little Jack, ever the bright-eyed, mischievous sprite. Of cherub cheeks and dimpling smiles. And for long, horrifying moments, he felt himself locked in torment. Locked in time—plunged back into the midst of a nightmare.

He'd let them die. He'd *made* them die. Their lives forever gone.

And his forever dark.

He slumped in his chair.

Oh, God.

All because of the blasted girl, he thought bitterly. Anne. Damn her, he thought. *Damn her.* She'd seen his reaction. It was almost as if she'd known . . .

Damn her to hell for reminding him.

Pray God he did not see her again. Pray God he did not want to.

Pray God it did not happen.

Again and again the neck of the bottle dipped into the glass. Again and again he raised it to his lips.

The pages of his journal flipped open. Then the quill was in his hand, scratching across the paper. When he was finished, he stared at the words he'd written. His writing—his name—so neat and precise, so unlike the jumble of his life.

He stared until his eyes were burning and dry, until they began to blur, whether from tears or drink he did not know. And he could not forget.

His name is Jack.

* * *

Anne was in the habit of walking daily. Even at Gleneden, when the Scottish winds blustered and squalled, only the fiercest of weather kept her indoors. If she was not walking, she was riding. Admittedly, as she ambled toward Hyde Park, the notion of crossing paths with Simon Blackwell again cropped up in her mind. But that was silly. She wouldn't allow anyone to keep her from her pleasure, certainly not him.

The day was not as hot as the previous day, but it was still very warm. Anne rested her parasol on her shoulder, quite enjoying her stroll. She passed a man angling in the Serpentine—and then she saw him.

Oh, no. It could not be. It simply could not be.

Their eyes tangled. He stopped short—or was it she?

Anne had the oddest sense he didn't know what to do as well, or what to say. But it appeared there was no help for it.

"Well, well, my lady, I see your dilemma. You are uncertain whether to acknowledge me or ignore me."

His bluntness took her aback, but only for an instant. "And I see you're as eager to see me as I am to see you."

He accorded her a faint bow. "I trust you've quite recovered from your headache?"

His tone was politeness itself. He knew, damn him, he knew it had been a lie!

But Anne was ever one to take up the gauntlet. "And I trust that your dashing rescue has left you none the worse for wear?"

They eyed each other. The oddest thought shot through Anne's mind. He was dressed entirely in severe black. No one would ever accuse him of being a peacock, that was for certain. And just as she had last night, she sensed power and strength beneath the clothing.

Her heart was pounding oddly as well. Anne swallowed. "There is no one present," she said. "We need not stand on pretense as we did last night."

"Pretense? Is that what it was?"

His gaze had sharpened along with his tone.

"The truth is, I didn't expect that you would come to supper last night." The confession emerged before she could stop it.

"My dear Lady Anne, I was invited."

"So you were."

"And if I hadn't come, would that have made me a coward in your eyes?"

"Of course not," she stated shortly. "It would simply indicate that you've a mind of your own."

There was a sudden glint in his eye. "Some might take that as a challenge, my lady. But perhaps we should adopt the facade of good manners now. For the benefit of those around us, of course. Shall we walk?"

His tone was utterly pleasant, but Anne was

not of a mind to trust him. "Must we?" she muttered.

"I beg your pardon?" Now there was a faint edge to his tone.

Anne lifted her chin and said nothing.

He offered his elbow. "Shall we?"

If it hadn't been for the presence of a young couple passing not three feet away, Anne might have refused. No, she *would* have refused. Instead she smiled and laid her fingertips on his sleeve.

"I gather," he remarked, "that you're a rather outspoken young woman."

"I suppose I am. Do you criticize or do you commend?"

"Neither. I merely wonder what I've done that you malign me so."

Anne compressed her lips.

"You need not hide it, you know. You don't like me, do you?"

God rot it, did he have to sound so reasonable? And why did she feel so suddenly *un*reasonable?

"Lady Anne," he said gently, "why don't you simply admit it? You don't like me."

Anne pondered her dilemma. If she agreed, it would be most impolite. If she disagreed, well, it would be a lie, yet another one!

Her chin rose a notch. "I do not know you, sir. Nothing but the little I learned last night," she said stiffly. "What I do know is that upon our first encounter, you were not particularly polite to me. If you recall, you gave me quite the dressing-down . . . why, almost in this very spot!" Their stroll across the grass had brought them nearly to the track of Rotten Row.

He stopped short. "Ah, so that's it. And now you seek to even the score, is that it? You wish me to grovel."

"Somehow," she retorted tartly, "I don't believe you're the groveling sort."

"That's quite a statement for a woman who says she does not know me. And I suspect that's not all, which leads me to ask what other grievous misdeed I've performed."

What approach should she take to *that*? "Are we inclined to be frank?" she asked sweetly.

He inclined his head. Beneath the brim of his hat, his eyes were a dark pewter. "By all means."

"Despite your gallant rescue of Jack yesterday, I am given to wonder why you even bothered, for I rather suspect you dislike children."

He stiffened. "You're mistaken," he said curtly.

"Am I?" His reaction but confirmed it. "I did not imagine your distaste in holding Jack last night?"

He stepped back. The movement dislodged her grip on his elbow.

"My dear Lady Anne, you are correct in your earlier assessment. You do not know me. But if it is an apology you seek, I shall endeavor to give it. I apologize."

His delivery was clipped and abrupt, almost staccato-like. Anne was more shocked than hurt. She could not help it. Her jaw fell open.

"And now," he concluded with a tight smile, "I shall rid you of my presence and bid you good day. That should please you, will it not? Or perhaps you wish my escort home?"

Anne was too stunned to say a word.

"No? I thought not." A stiff bow, and he strode away.

Anne stared after him, still openmouthed . . . and suddenly fuming mad.

The man was no more than she presumed, no less than she expected. He was detestable. Disagreeable. Unbearable. She could think of a dozen other ways to describe him, none of them particularly flattering.

Her pleasure in her walk had vanished. She proceeded home. The door slammed as she stepped inside, her skirts whipping as she turned toward the drawing room.

Caro had just descended the stairs. "Well," her cousin observed mildly, "you're in a bit of a tizzy today."

Anne yanked at the ties of her bonnet. "It's him. That dreadful man."

Caro paused on the last step. "Oh, my. Dare I ask who this man is? Or are you having secret assignations without my knowledge?"

"If I were having secret assignations, it would not be with Simon Blackwell!"

A hint of a smile flirted at Caro's lips. "Ah," she said.

"Do not look like that," Anne said crossly. "Caro, this is not amusing!"

"Dearest, I don't believe I've ever seen you so passionate about any other man."

"Passionate is hardly the word I would use. He is a most crusty man, Caro. So much so that I wonder he does not splinter into pieces. I vow that should I ever see him again, I shall tell him so."

"Hmmm. That may happen sooner than you think, dearest. Though I would advise you to bite your tongue, considering that he will be a guest in your mother's home."

"Never tell me you have invited him to dinner again!"

"No. But your mother has."

Anne nearly shrieked. "What? . . . When? . . . Why?"

"The Dowager Countess of Hopewell's birthday fete will be held here instead of Lady Creswell's. She's fallen ill, I'm afraid. And your mother insisted on hosting it." Caro paused. "And Annie—"

"What, there's more?"

"No. But do you know what I think?"

Anne didn't know whether to laugh or cry.

"I suspect you're about to tell me. Indeed, I know it."

"You say he's stuffy. Crusty. But there's something almost sad about him." Caro hesitated. "Annie, I know you may not agree, but I think he's lonely. John thought so as well."

Caro was right. She didn't agree. "Well, if he is, I do not wonder why," she muttered.

"Annie," Caro chided, "it isn't like you to be mean-spirited. As the countess's nephew, of course he will be present. And Aunt Viv is so excited about hosting the fete. You know this is her first entertainment since coming out of mourning."

And that was what held Anne silent. Caro was right. Before her father's illness, her mother loved nothing more than to entertain. And Anne would never—ever—do anything to deprive her mother of her pleasures, or dampen her happiness in any way.

She could not cry off. Very well then. For her mother's sake, she would welcome Simon Blackwell. For her mother's sake, she would be gracious, and pretend her dislike of him did not exist. No one, save Caro—and the man himself!—would know otherwise.

Yet again, it seemed she must endure his presence. There was simply no help for it.

Four

It's said that I am a man grown bitter. But it is
not bitterness that fills my soul to the dregs. I've
lost my way. And I know not how to find it.

Simon Blackwell

Anne had resigned herself to her fate. There was
nothing she could do to avoid it. She must deal
with it—or him—as best she was able. Should
her path chance to cross Simon Blackwell's, she
would react with the decorum instilled in her by
her mother. She would not embarrass her family
with small-minded behavior.

No, Anne would never have deprived her
mother of this night. Ever since her mother
had offered to host the Dowager Countess of

Hopewell's birthday celebration, her dear mama had been flitting to and fro like a butterfly. Though she was fatigued at day's end, Vivian was gay and glowing. Not until then did Anne realize how much her mother had missed her social activities. There was a lightness in her that Anne had not seen in many a month. Both Caro and Alec had noticed as well.

And indeed the affair was a lively festivity. The ballroom had been scrubbed and dusted and aired and was now filled with the lingering scent of roses. Dinner was scrumptious. A quartet had begun to play, and the dance floor was already filled. Vivian, animated and radiant, was making the rounds of the guests. The Dowager Countess of Hopewell beamed.

At dinner, it was Simon Blackwell who rose and offered a birthday toast to his aunt. When he smiled—oh, but there was no denying it!—he was so strikingly handsome, Anne's breath stopped in her throat. She discovered herself mulling the oddest question.

He infuriated her. He disturbed her. He distracted her. So why, when all was said and done, did she find him the most attractive man she'd ever met? Why couldn't she stop thinking of him? Why couldn't she put him from her mind? It should have been easy.

Heaven above, it wasn't.

She'd thought of him nearly every moment

since they'd met. Not particularly pleasant thoughts, but she'd thought of him nonetheless.

It was highly disconcerting, and certainly something she would never divulge to Caro. Caro would surely cackle with delight at such a confession. And it was not, Anne assured herself as she managed to strategically place herself at the opposite end of the ballroom, an effort to avoid him. It was simply the desire to be wherever he was *not*.

Which was, she decided, rather silly. It was ridiculous to allow him to unsettle her so. And with that thought fixed securely in her mind, she laughed and chatted and danced.

But fate did not favor her tonight. As if Simon Blackwell's presence wasn't enough for her to contend with, Lillith Kimball was here as well. Lillith was off to the side of the ballroom, standing near the musicians, watching the dancing. Anne knew the precise moment Lillith saw her, too.

Ann nearly groaned. Instead she summoned a smile and inclined her head; Lillith adopted no such courtesy. Her expression was cold. Quite deliberately, Lillith turned her back.

So. Caro's words the other day at Hyde Park flitted into Anne's mind. For whatever reason, it appeared Lillith had neither forgotten—nor forgiven—her resentment over Charles Goodwin.

How silly. How stupid, for it had been two

years. But should she chance to encounter Lillith, Anne was determined to be pleasant.

Just as she swung away from the punch table, Anne saw Simon. Off to the side near the double-paned doors that led to the terrace, a tall figure clad in dark evening clothes that set off his height to full advantage. His waistcoat was a deep, rich brown, his frock coat a dark hunter green—it was the first time she'd seen him garbed in clothing other than black. He'd turned his gaze to stare through the glass, into the darkness that lay without. Anne studied his averted profile, her steps inadvertently carrying her closer.

Despite the distance that separated them, she sensed something odd in him, something like the first time he'd heard little John called Jack.

The thought that flooded throughout her mind was startlingly strong—that he was not aloof, but alone.

At precisely that instant, he raised his head. Their eyes met. And held, for an indiscernibly long stretch of time.

Strangely enough, Anne couldn't look away. Even more strangely, she didn't *want* to.

The moment was broken only when he tipped the edge of his glass toward her, a silent acknowledgment.

She could have avoided him. Ignored him. Turned away and pretended she had seen neither him nor the gesture, for why did she care?

Why did she bother? But Caro's words suddenly spilled all through her.

I know you may not agree, but I think he's lonely.

She was scarcely aware of her feet moving beneath her. Almost before she knew it, she was standing before him. What lay behind her movement, she could not say. She did not *know.* Her heart suddenly foundered, then recovered its rhythm, and now it was a wild knocking that thumped throughout her breast.

"Lady Anne. Fate contrives to bring us together yet again. Forgive me if I do not ask you to dance. I fear we would both be placed in an awkward position when you refuse."

Anne caught her breath, stung without quite knowing why. Why? Why? She shouldn't have cared a fig!

But she did. Oh, how she did!

She eyed the glass in his hand. "Are you unwell, sir?"

"No," he said curtly. He raised the glass to his lips and drank.

"Pardon me for making the observation, but you seem rather out of sorts. Therefore, I ask again if something is wrong?"

His eyes flickered. "My dear Lady Anne," he said coolly, "I pray you, stick to your own affairs and refrain from meddling in mine."

Anne's temper began to simmer. "It's no wonder you're a recluse if you're always so disagreeable. Or is it only me whom you find so distasteful?"

"My lady, I could well say the same to you."

"Yes, I can see where you might." She took a deep breath. "But what if I said you have misjudged me, sir? What would you say to that?"

He gave her a long, slow look. "I would ask what is behind this sudden change of heart."

Anne flushed. "It occurs to me that my opinion of you may have been hastily formed." He made no comment, and Anne found herself rushing on. "It is my cousin who chided me, who made me reconsider. Caro—well, she thinks you're lonely."

He had gone very still. "And you, Lady Anne? What do you think?"

"I don't know what to think. Truly. But it occurs to me that I may have been petty and small. And I should hate to think of myself that way."

He eyed her, then said slowly, "You do not mince words, do you?"

"What is the point? My brothers consider me impulsive and spirited, though that is my own choice of words. I admit, I am quick to judge. Perhaps sometimes too quick, for my tongue has occasionally been known to land me in trouble."

A brow climbed a fraction. "Why am I not surprised?" he murmured.

His voice was low. *Raspy*, some might have called it. *Husky* was the word that came to Anne's mind.

He lapsed into silence, raising his glass to his lips once more.

Anne garnered her courage. "It is your aunt's birthday," she ventured further. "A joyous occasion. Therefore, I propose a truce for the night." Taking a deep breath, she held out her hand.

He stared at it. There was a hollow silence. His gaze flitted to her face, then returned to her outstretched hand. He did not want to touch her. She knew it instinctively. The temptation to withdraw her hand was almost overwhelming. She didn't. Instead she found herself holding her breath, a curious tension sizzling the air between them.

He said nothing for the longest time. Then he took her fingers, squeezing them briefly. "Forgive me," he said very quietly. "Your opinion of me has not been unwarranted. And for that, you have my apologies."

Just that quickly, between one heartbeat and the next, something changed. What it was, why it was, Anne wasn't certain. She knew only that it *was*, and with the dawning realization came a barrage of questions about this man.

A man passing by jostled his elbow. The portly fellow wore a bright green waistcoat and yellow jacket that clashed horribly with his thinning red hair. Simon gazed after him with a faint frown.

"Do not take affront," Anne said quickly. "That is Lord Calvin. He has the air of a peacock, and dresses like one as well, does he not? He stuffs himself like a sausage into his clothing. It's rumored the only way he manages is by donning a corset. I daresay it's true, judging from the way he walks."

Something she never expected graced Simon's lips—a smile. A genuine one, at that. Then he glanced away. Raising his glass to his lips, he nearly drained the contents.

Anne watched him, the strong tendons in his throat working as he swallowed. "Are you always so fond of spirits?"

The question was both imprudent and impudent—and too late to recall. Anne bit her lip. Whatever on earth had possessed her to say it?

His gaze swung back to her. His eyes narrowed, pale and silver. His smile vanished. Something that might have been anger passed over his features. To her surprise, he set the glass on the tray of a passing servant.

"I could use some air," he said abruptly. His tone was low, his manner rather strained.

"This way." The terrace was but a few paces to the left. Anne led the way. She did not stop until the voices in the house were but a faint murmur.

"God, but I hate London," he muttered.

"If you hate it so, then why do you not quit it altogether?"

"I intend to. Tomorrow, in fact. And then you need suffer my presence no more."

She ignored this last. "Tomorrow?" she heard herself ask. "So soon?" Oh, heavens, what was she doing? Surely it wasn't dismay in her voice!

"After Aunt Leticia's birthday party tonight, there's no reason for me to stay."

Anne forced herself to look away. Up to the heavens. High above, a half moon peered through a hazy veil of clouds. Nearby, the clang of church bells tolled the hour.

"A pity there aren't more stars," she said wistfully. "But that's London, I suppose. Too many buildings, too many people. Caro and I were musing about it just the other night—how there's nothing like the night sky at Gleneden."

"Gleneden," he echoed. "Your home in Scotland, isn't it?"

"Yes. It's north of Sterling. Nestled on a point of the loch, with several others nearby."

"It's much the same at my home," he said after a moment. "Though we're given to fierce storms from the sea." He paused, then said, "You and your cousin seem very close."

"We are," Anne said simply. "Caro is as much a sister as my own might have been."

"So you have no sisters?"

"No. Well, actually, yes."

He looked at her questioningly.

"I had a sister once," she explained. "A younger sister who died, actually, when she was a year old, along with an older brother, during an outbreak of influenza. I'm afraid I don't remember her. Another was stillborn before my mother gave birth to me. So whilst we were growing up, it was Alec, Aidan, and me. And oftentimes, Caro."

Silence cropped up between then. Through the darkness, she could feel his eyes on her face. He had shifted slightly, so that his sleeve brushed the bare skin just above her glove. Over her shoulders she wore a white stole. She shivered, but not from the evening breeze that swirled through the air. No, not from cold. She felt heated. Hot. Almost feverishly hot.

"Sir," she said, "you are looking at me."

"My dear, we are in the midst of conversing. Where else am I to look?"

Anne fell silent. All at once her pulse was clamoring.

Nervously she wet her lips. It was a struggle to hold herself upright. She didn't know what to do with her hands. She wanted to clutch at his forearms, for the world was suddenly all awhirl. He stood near, so near she could see the intricate folds of his cravat, each fine gold thread stitched on his waistcoat. A faint sound caught in her throat. When she looked up, he was even closer. Closer than was proper.

His expression was solemn, his mouth unsmiling. But not hard. Beneath his brows, his eyes were clear and pale. Unsettling, in a way she could not explain.

His gaze had drifted to her lips. It wandered lower, lower still . . . her gown was of pale peach, cut daringly low yet the very height of fashion. His proximity was unnerving. Disturbing. Yet Anne didn't retreat. And all at once, she didn't want to.

His eyes had returned to settle on her mouth.

"You should run, Lady Anne. Run away now."

He sounded so strange. And how odd that he should say that. For that was exactly how Anne felt. Out of breath, as if she'd run at breakneck speed from the lower floors clear to the rooftop.

An adventurer, everyone called her. What could be more adventurous than standing alone in the dark with a man she barely knew? Simon Blackwell was almost a stranger. She should have been alarmed, but she wasn't.

Nervous, oh, yes. And excited, in some way she couldn't fully define. A jumble of feelings swirled inside her. She felt as if her heart had come unseated in her breast.

Yet still she stood her ground.

Only an hour earlier, she'd have deemed it impossible. But now, everything inside her was churning. Clamoring. She knew instinctively what he was thinking—what he wanted. And she knew, with every pore inside her, that she wasn't going to stop him . . .

As soon as he was able, Simon had gone in search of a drink. Not the punch the ladies liked, but something stronger.

He hadn't been pleased when he'd learned his aunt's celebration was to take place at the Mc-Bride household. He loved his aunt, so he'd fulfilled her wish, made the obligatory appearance at her birthday celebration. But the sooner he left London, the better. He would not miss it. He did not like the questioning glances—the pitying glances—of those he'd known so long ago.

Anne's approach had caught him off-guard, to say nothing of her offering of peace. Lonely, Anne had said. God, if she only knew! he thought derisively. But she was right, he did drink too much. Of late it seemed the only way he could cope.

A recluse, she called him. And perhaps he was. His life had palled. No, more than that. It was a shambles. He had no wish to be around people. No wish for the world to recall his devastating loss.

Yet more than a hint of guilt needled him. He wasn't fit to be around decent people. His behavior was abominable. No less than churlish. And why? Because the very lovely Anne reminded him of things he'd rather not think of. A part of him wanted to shout at her to leave him be. God, but he wished she'd stayed away!

But the moment she came near . . . he could not help it.

It was damned disconcerting. Goddamned annoying. The scent of her was—sweet Jesus!— intoxicating. There was no other word for it.

And now . . . now he watched as she licked her lips. A white-hot jolt bolted through him. Simon knew it for what it was. Desire. Deep and molten. He could not stop it.

He paused and looked at her. Really *looked* at her, the way he'd not looked at a woman in a very long time. Sweet Christ, the way he'd not looked at a woman for five long years. The way he'd once looked at Ellie.

It was a mistake.

Her evening gown was cut in a deep vee, so low it revealed the rounded swell of her breasts, the cleft between, the tremor of each as she breathed. The nakedness of her shoulders emphasized the fragile length of her neck—it had tempted him all evening! Like her brother, she was of more than average height, with long, elegant limbs to match. Her skin was satin and cream, skin that made a man want to . . . The thought stopped him cold.

But *she* didn't stop him cold, he thought almost angrily. She made him feel hot inside. Hot and . . . oh, Christ. This was getting out of hand.

A scathing self-derision poured through him, even as a ravening heat coursed through his veins. Dear God, he was lusting after a woman with her entire family present just inside the house. What the hell was wrong with him?

A rending ache shot through him. She made him think of all he'd once had. Of all he'd lost.

In all the time since Ellie's death, no woman had tempted him. No woman had touched him. He'd touched no woman. But this one—Lady Annabel McBride—made desire claw through his vitals like a sword. Desire that was almost painful in its intensity stole over him.

For until now, he'd almost forgotten that he was a man. And Annabel McBride's presence was an unwelcome reminder that five years without a woman had fired his blood and made everything inside him collide.

Simon didn't like it. He didn't like it at all. Yet he couldn't stop it either. He should have left. Gone off and hired a woman for the night to relieve the floodtide of desire searing his veins. Yet even as the notion possessed him, he knew there would have been no true satisfaction.

"You should run, Lady Anne. Run away now."

And still his body betrayed him. Betrayed him most traitorously and most thoroughly! A familiar tightness gathered low in his belly, there between his thighs. God, he thought with a black, silent gust of laughter. Did the chit even have any idea of the effect she was having on him?

Or perhaps she *did* know. She didn't move. She just continued to stare at him, her head to the side, her hands twisting around the ends of her stole, those expressive eyes wide and dark, and faintly questioning.

A storm churned inside him. In his heart. His soul. And then everything came crashing down around him.

She was right, he thought hazily. He shouldn't have drunk so much. If he hadn't been drinking, he'd never have done what he was about to do next.

Five

Perhaps this is God's way of punishing me.

Simon Blackwell

There was a low vibration of sound. A sound of need. A sound of anguish. It was her name. Muffled against her lips. *Her lips.*

Strong hands closed around her waist. He caught her up against him; her breasts registered warmth and the hardness of his chest. She longed to reach up, to twine her arms around him in turn, burrowing her hands inside his jacket. But she didn't quite dare, for this was her first real taste of desire. Lord, her first taste of a man.

It seemed so impossible, so improbable. Simon Blackwell was kissing her. *Her.*

Never before had she been kissed—Charles

Goodwin's attempt certainly didn't count. She'd managed to avoid it, thank heaven.

But Anne was no different from any other woman. She had dreamed of it. Imagined the thrill of a man's lips warm upon her own . . . Wondered where it would be. *Who* it would be . . .

And her first kiss—*this* kiss—did not disappoint.

She felt as if she were tumbling. Floating. The sensations were incredible. Intense. Her hands came up to curl against his waistcoat. Instinct was her guide. Her feelings were her guide. It was as if some powerful force had taken over her body. Tilting her head back ever so slightly, she parted her lips, granting him license, unwittingly deepening the kiss.

When his tongue touched hers, a little shock zinged throughout her body. Did men kiss like that? A silly question, to be sure. Anne did not consider herself a missish schoolgirl. She was well traveled, well read, well spoken. Yet she'd never dreamed of such a thing. But it seemed so right, so natural. She wanted to cry out when his mouth left hers. She felt the flutter of his breath across her skin, the pressure of his lips against her cheek. But then his mouth returned. His hands, strong and warm, swept her stole from her shoulders. He caught her up against him. His lips ground against hers, harder, conveying a sense of hunger she didn't fully comprehend.

Nor did she care. God, it felt so good. The world seemed to cave in all around her.

So lost was she in the fever of the kiss that she failed to hear the gasp and flurry of movement that came from behind her.

And so did Simon.

The slam of a door was jarring. Anne felt him stiffen. Slowly he raised his head. Eyes narrowing, his gaze stabbed into the haze of lights that burned from the house.

"Good Christ," he cursed.

Anne's lips were still throbbing. Her head whirled dizzily. She stared up at him dumbly. "What?" she said faintly.

He yanked her stole up over her shoulders. His tone was grim. "There was someone here."

Comprehension was slow to arrive—but her brother was not. By the time Anne had gathered her wits, Alec was there, with Lillith Kimball beside him—smirking! Anne knew then—knew that Lillith had done this on purpose, followed her and Simon on purpose . . . then run back to Alec.

Alec said something to Lillith. She gave a slight nod, pouting, then gathered up her skirts and headed back toward the house.

Alec's gaze went from Anne's flushed cheeks to Simon's, and back again.

"What the devil is this?"

Anne stood as if frozen. Simon's fingertips hovered almost protectively on the small of her back.

Alec's eyes narrowed. "I'll thank you to remove your hands from my sister."

Silence descended, a silence like no other.

Simon's hand fell away.

"Alec? Alec, what's going on?"

It was her mother. And now Caro was here too.

Dear God, had Lillith told anyone else? The notion flashed through Anne's head.

She shouldn't have looked at them. Any of them. But she couldn't help it. Yet when she did, her face grew scalding hot.

"Anne," Vivian said faintly. "Oh, Anne."

What little aplomb Anne possessed began to crumble. It took a supreme effort of will not to cry.

Alec was stony-faced. Caro and her mother were still stunned. All but Alec. He was scowling at Simon in thin-lipped disapproval.

Indeed, it almost appeared a contest as to which would break the stillness. It was Simon who said in a voice of deadly quiet, "I believe we should have a word, Your Grace."

"And we shall. We shall indeed, sir. But this is a social occasion. Neither the place nor the time to discuss this . . . matter."

"I quite agree. Tomorrow morning?"

Alec nodded. "My town house," he said tersely. "I shall send my carriage round."

"There's no need." Simon was just as curt. But he made no attempt to leave. Anne was aware the instant his gaze slid back to her.

He cleared his throat. "Lady Anne—"

Anne couldn't breathe. She couldn't move. She certainly couldn't look at him.

"I shall take care of my sister," Alec cut in. "You need not concern yourself."

She could have sworn she heard Simon's jaw snap shut. She was distantly aware of the two men confronting each other. She had the oddest sensation they were only a hair away from blows.

Alec's jaw locked. "If you please, sir."

Finally Simon executed a low bow and was gone.

Alec bestowed on her a glare from icy blue eyes. He had laced his hands behind his back. Anne thought half hysterically that it was the only way he could stop them from curling around her neck.

She lifted tear-bright eyes to his. "Alec," she said helplessly. "Mama—"

"I believe you've said enough, Anne. I believe you've *done* enough." Alec glared at her.

Anne longed to sink through the earth and disappear into its depths forever. Red-hot shame consumed her.

It was Caro who stepped forward and took her hand. "Come, love," she said gently. "I'll help you to bed."

In her room, Caro dismissed the maid and helped her from her clothing. Anne did not speak. But when she slipped into bed, the turmoil of the last hour caught up with her. "Caro," she said desperately. "Oh, Caro—"

She did something she never expected, something she did but rarely.

She burst into tears.

Caro's arms closed around her. "Hush, Annie," she soothed. "It'll be all right. It will."

If only she could believe her. But all at once Anne wasn't sure that *anything* would ever be right again.

It was early when a rap on the door sounded. Anne roused as Vivian stepped inside. Pink-cheeked, her hair tucked up beneath a cap, her mother looked surprisingly well-rested, Anne almost grudgingly decided. Anne, on the other hand, was bleary-eyed and exhausted. She'd slept barely a wink.

Vivian plumped a pillow behind her back. "Take your tea, pet, while it's nice and hot. Oh, and I brought those croissants you're so fond of."

Anne accepted the cup, sipping from it gingerly. She didn't want tea. The thought of food made her want to retch. How could her mother act so normally? Would that the last evening had been a dream! Oh, how she longed to crawl beneath the covers, never to emerge.

Anne had never deemed herself a coward. But, oh, how she wished she could be numb.

Vivian flitted around the room, straightening the curtains, neatly folding her bath towel and summoning the maid for her bath.

Anne set aside her teacup. "Mama," she said.

"Yes, poppet?" Vivian perched on the edge of the bed and reached for her hands.

Anne stared at her mother's fingers, so slim and dainty and fine, curled firmly around her own. How was it possible there was such strength harbored in this small, tiny woman? She thought of her father, of the way her mother had bathed his brow and comforted and cheered him when his spirits were lowest. How had she remained so unfaltering and strong throughout the darkest days of his life . . . of *hers*? But hers was a resilience that could not be seen, Anne suddenly realized, a staunchness of spirit and faith . . . and dwelled solely within.

She swallowed. "Mama," she said, her voice very low, "I should like to explain—"

"There is no need." Vivian squeezed her hand. "I know what you're going to say, dearest. Well, perhaps not to the letter, but I've an idea and . . . We can't change what has happened, Anne. Yesterday is gone, and will be forever gone. We cannot reclaim it. We cannot *change* it. And so we must take heart that the days ahead will be better. We must trust that the days ahead will be brighter. We must do what we can to *make* it so."

Anne bit her lip. In her mind, it wasn't so simple to banish all doubt and summon such certainty. "Mama—" She stopped, unable to go on.

"Anne. *Anne.* Do not fret, dearest. Know that I love you. Know that Alec loves you, and Aidan as well. And know that nothing or no one will ever change that."

A tremendous ache filled Anne's throat.

"Now, pet, why don't you get dressed? I expect your brother will wish to speak with you this morning."

Anne gave a watery smile. "Mama," she whispered, "I'm so very lucky to have you."

"Ah, love," came Vivian's soft rejoinder, "I was about to say the same to you."

Vivian was right. Even before she'd finished dressing, she received a summons that Alec wished to see her at ten o'clock. His town house was not so far that she could not easily walk the distance. But Helmsley, his coachman, stated that his master was most insistent that he deliver her safely. Anne was annoyed. What did Alec think? That she would bolt?

So it was that she was feeling rather rebellious when his butler ushered her into his study. Alec was already there, seated behind the great mahogany desk that had once belonged to their father. He was busy signing some papers. He didn't look up when she entered, but the quill continued to scratch across the surface.

At length he finished, setting aside the sheaf of paperwork.

Leather creaked as he leaned back in his chair and surveyed her. Anne and her brothers had always engaged in good-natured banter; it was rare that she was truly at odds with either of them. But in this moment, she envied Alec his ease. She envied him his station. It wasn't fair, she thought resentfully, that she should be made to feel like an errant child simply because he was older. Because he was a duke. Because he was *male.*

She pretended to flick a thread from her gown. Tucking her feet beneath the chair, she raised her chin.

A dark brow arose. "Well, Anne," he said smoothly, "what do you have to say for yourself?"

His superior, autocratic air seared her temper. He could be quite haughtily imposing when he chose, but Anne would not be cowed.

"Oh, bother!" she said irritably. "Who are you to talk to me so?"

"I am the man who is striving to keep his sister from a scandal that may well dash her reputation to bits." His tone was as icy as his glare.

"Do not take that air with me!" she cried. "You are hardly a saint and I know it!"

"I am not the one under discussion here, Anne. You are."

His glower was fierce. Anne hated being at odds with her brother. When they were young, she was always one step behind Alec and Aidan, always trying to keep up with them. But Alec's sharpness stung.

She transferred her gaze to a point just beyond his ear and compressed her lips.

"Anne, are you listening?"

His censure cut deep. A part of her longed to clamp her hands over her ears. "Must I?" she muttered.

"Annie! I know you can be reckless. You've always been one to charge off into the unknown. But I never expected this from you! I thought I'd have to fend off countless marriage proposals. But this has put you beyond the pale!"

She set her chin. "I'm not a child, Alec. Pray don't treat me like one. Besides, this only happened because Lillith has no liking for me."

"No," he said very quietly. "You're not a child. But surely you understand the gravity of what happened last night. There are consequences to such behavior. You were careless. And you were caught. I've requested that Lillith maintain her silence, but I do not trust that she will comply. Indeed, it may be too late already."

Anne fought a surge of dread. Lillith Kimball would delight in maligning her.

Alec paused. "Annie," he said gently, "I can't rescue you this time. I can't make this disappear. This cannot be swept under the rug. It must be remedied before it becomes a full-blown scandal. Can you accept this? Can you accept *him*?"

Anne looked at him, her eyes huge. A half-formed suspicion winged through her mind. No, she thought dazedly. Surely it could not be. Surely he did not mean . . .

Her mouth opened, then closed. "Alec," she said desperately, "I will not lie. I . . . we . . . I swear . . . it was but a kiss. No more than that . . ." Her head bowed low. She could look at him no more. She could *say* no more. Her chin began to wobble.

She was dimly aware of his rising. "Annie." He dropped a hand on her shoulder. "Oh, God, Annie, don't cry. I take no pleasure in this, but there's no other way! If there was, you know I'd move heaven and earth to see it done."

There was a rap on the door. It opened a crack. "Your Grace, Mr. Blackwell has arrived."

Oh, Lord. It was true then. Anne battled a surge of panic.

"Annie," said Alec, "would you like to wait in the salon?"

There was no need for him to ask again. Anne

was already on her feet and bolting from the room.

The duke was civil when Simon entered his study. Simon hadn't expected otherwise. Alec appeared relaxed, but Simon wasn't fooled. The pleasantries they exchanged were forced, the tension in the air thick and ripe.

Simon had no desire to postpone the inescapable. He faced the duke squarely. "Let us be direct, Your Grace. My conduct with your sister last evening was most reprehensible."

Alec leaned back in his chair. His expression was hard.

"You have my most sincere apologies," he said.

"More than apologies are due, sir." Alec's tone was clipped.

Simon did not back down from his unrelenting regard. What could he say? What *was* there to say? Even now, he didn't know why or how it had happened. It should *never* have happened. But it had, and there was no turning back. He'd dallied with a lady, an unmarried woman. Sweet Lord, the sister of a duke! And beneath the very roof of her home!

She stirred him. She stirred him in a way he hadn't thought possible, in a way he'd never dreamed might happen. The truth was that he'd gone—for a brief spate of time—a little mad.

Deep in his soul, he knew it wasn't Anne's

fault. She was young. Inexperienced. He, on the other hand, had no excuse.

"I cannot countenance the disgrace of my sister," Alec was stating. "I *will* not. This is not the way I would have had her find a husband. But I cannot allow her name to be sullied. I cannot allow the humiliation and embarrassment of my mother. Of my entire family. The situation must be remedied. Only you, sir, can do that."

Simon eyed him, keeping all expression under rigid control.

"You are a gentleman," Alec continued tightly. "I trust you will act as such?"

Simon remained very still, but his mind was churning. He was well aware what Alec was saying—indeed he'd expected it. But it hadn't seemed real until now. To wed her . . . His mind tripped on the thought. It was unthinkable. Impossible.

And inevitable.

He sat with his hands on his knees. He had to stop himself from balling them into fists. Inside he was seething. He'd known this was coming. Yet now that the moment was here . . . There was a bad taste in his mouth.

Were the circumstances reversed, Simon would have demanded the very same. He understood Alec's protectiveness. He supposed Alec had no recourse. Still, it stuck in his craw. He didn't have to like it. No man liked having his hand forced.

He felt compelled to make his feelings clear. "I have no wish to marry."

Alec's eyes narrowed. "You should have thought of that before you laid hands on my sister."

"Allow me to finish," Simon said coldly.

"Certainly." Alec's tone was pleasant; his icy glare was not.

"However much I did not anticipate the possibility"—his mouth twisted in a black smile—"it appears I have no recourse but to enter into marriage with your sister."

He was aware the duke neither liked nor appreciated either his tone or his choice of words.

The duke inclined his head. "I will, of course, see that you are given a generous dowry—"

"I want no dowry." The words were bit out. Christ, he did not want *her*.

Alec's tone was cool. "I assume you'll be returning to your home in the north?"

Simon gave a terse nod.

"I have your assurance you will treat her well?"

Simon stiffened. His lips barely moved as he said, "You offend me by suggesting otherwise."

Alec nodded. Some of the tension had drained from his features. "Of course. Forgive me. It is just that . . . this is most unexpected. I did not expect to have to contend with this situation."

Nor had he, Simon thought bitterly.

"There is one other thing," Alec said slowly. "I've only just realized why your name is so familiar." He paused. "Please be assured I have no desire to make you uncomfortable," he said very quietly.

Darkness burned in his soul. Simon felt his entire body grow taut. He knew what was coming. He *knew* what Alec was about to say. Damn, he thought. *Damn.*

"Belated though they are, please be assured you have my sympathies."

"Thank you." Simon nearly bit out the words.

There was an uneasy pause. "Does Anne know?"

"No." The word was flat and uncompromising.

"She should," Alec said quietly.

"And I will thank you, Your Grace, if you leave that particular undertaking to me." For all that he was thin-lipped and grim, Simon was faultlessly polite.

"As you wish then." Alec studied him a moment. Then, rising, he came around the corner of his desk and extended his hand.

Simon could not have called himself a gentleman if he'd refused the gesture. It was not intentional, but he was the first to withdraw his grip.

"Well," said Alec. "Anne is waiting. May I send her in?"

"Certainly," Simon said curtly.

Alec exited the study.

Left alone, Simon closed his eyes briefly.

Unexpected, Alec had called it. God, he thought with a silent, black shout of laughter, but wasn't it the truth? He had not anticipated that his stay in London would be a lengthy one. At this hour yesterday, he'd thought to be well away from the city. Only now it appeared he wouldn't be leaving London today at all!

And when he did, it would be with the one thing he'd never expected in a thousand years . . .

A wife.

$\mathcal{S}ix$

Life is not sweet, but bittersweet.

Simon Blackwell

In all honesty, Anne reflected quite some time later, it was probably a blessing that it all happened so fast.

Simon was standing near the window when she entered, his booted feet planted slightly apart. He remained in utter stillness for a moment, and Anne had the strangest sensation he sought to resurrect some tremendous emotion from deep inside. He pivoted, his shoulders hitched ever so slightly, along with the tilt of his head.

So did Anne's.

She couldn't help but notice the taut fit of his

jacket. He was a powerful man. A proud man.

He indicated the small settee. "Perhaps you wish to sit."

Anne did not want to sit. She wanted to run, as far and as fast as she was able.

But she was made of sterner stuff, or so she contrived to assure herself. Cowardice was not her way. Silence was not her way. It was true there were times she had cause to regret something she'd said or done. Her feelings were something that she had never been able to constrain.

There had been no need.

Yet now there was a hollow silence. The moment seemed to stretch on into eternity. Anne discovered herself wholly beyond words.

"It appears we shall have to marry."

It was so far removed from what Anne had always expected that it didn't seem real. For this was not a proposal, she decided vaguely. This was but a moment of acceptance—of resignation—on his part.

And perhaps a moment of resignation on hers as well.

He didn't want to marry her. It was there in the coolness of his eyes, in the rigidness of his posture, in the clipped way he uttered the words.

They did not kiss. They did not touch. There was certainly no declaration of love . . . or anything else.

Anne couldn't help it. Seared in her mind was the feel of his mouth locked against hers. She couldn't help but recall—and vividly so!—what had brought them to this course. She remembered the way he'd touched her. The heat of his mouth, the breadth of his chest, the ache in her own, the way she felt as if she were grasping for something that hovered just beyond reach. The way she'd longed to touch him in return, to linger and explore.

Did he think of it too?

She sucked in a breath. No. *No.* She could almost believe it had never been. That their blazing embrace last night was but a figment of her imagination.

But nothing was as it should be. Her life was suddenly wheeling out of control, and there was nothing she could do to change it.

What*ever* had possessed her to allow him to kiss her? she wondered wildly.

Somehow, she never thought to wonder what had possessed *him*.

Anne had never thought herself fanciful. Not a dreamer.

Though to be perfectly honest, she'd never met the man who inspired such dreams. At least not yet. But she'd always been certain she would find him. Or that he would find her. She'd always thought it would happen, of course, for she did not think she was destined to spend her days a spinster.

It appeared she would not.

But not so soon. Not *now.*

And not with this man who seemed so distant and cold!

She didn't want to look at him. She couldn't help it either. He did not retreat from her scrutiny. She almost wished that he did! For when she gazed into his eyes, his features, she saw no welcome. No surge of joy. His expression held nothing of tenderness.

And she thought, in that moment, something inside just shriveled up.

"I'm so sorry"—her voice was half strangled—"that it came to this."

Something darkened in his eyes. "Do not blame yourself," he said very quietly.

Anne lowered her chin. She discovered it was the only way she could let enough air into her lungs to breathe again.

At length she raised her head. "When?" she asked levelly.

"I expect as soon as it can be arranged."

As soon as it can be arranged.

As it happened, the wedding preparations proceeded smoothly. Despite the swiftness of the upcoming ceremony, the gown she was to wear was very à la mode—of course Mama and Caro saw to that. Over the next week it seemed they dashed headlong from shop to shop, like bees in a frenzy. If Anne could have bowed out, she would have.

Perhaps the hectic pace was something to be thankful for. It left scarcely a moment to think, and therefore no time to dwell, either happily or unhappily, on something that could not be prevented. And while she could not adopt the pretense of joy at her nuptials, it gave her a measure of pleasure to witness the spirited zeal with which her mother and Caro approached the task.

So it was that the night before the wedding, Anne was exhausted.

Shortly after dinner, she withdrew to her room. Just before she was ready to crawl between the sheets, she heard little footsteps running in the hall. The door flew open, and Jack flew inside, naturally followed by Izzie. And just as naturally, Caro trailed after them.

The little ones could not contain their excitement over being a part of the wedding party. They bobbed about her room, like boats upon the seas. Their laughter was infectious.

Izzie scrambled onto her lap. "Mama says I shall wear my pretty new frock tomorrow, and I shall look like a princess, just like you." Her eyes glowed. "Will I be a princess like you, Annie?"

Anne caught her small body up against her, her heart turning over. There was something so precious about this moment, and she was loath to let it go . . .

She pressed her cheek against Izzie's. "Oh, yes, sweeting, the prettiest princess of all."

Lizzie's eyes glowed. "Will Jack be a prince?"

Anne looked at Caro over the top of Lizzie's froth of curls. "Ah, yes, a prince. Princess Izzie and Prince Jack."

"No!" Jack startled all of them by letting out a vigorous protest. "I shall not be a prince. I shall be king!" And puffing out his chest, he swaggered across the carpet in quite a princely—or rather, kingly—manner indeed.

Anne bit her lip. Her eyes met Caro's, who smiled weakly. Jack had vaulted into the middle of the bed. Lizzie squirmed out of Anne's arms and scrambled after her brother.

"I shall be king," Jack boasted lustily, his little voice rising higher and higher until it was more squeal than shout. Both were shrieking at the top of their lungs until Caro lunged after both and caught them mid-bounce.

Not until Caro had shushed the pair and gave them over to the arms of their nurse did Anne's laughter begin to subside. Oh, but she needed that. She hadn't realized just how much until it was over.

She was still smiling when Caro ventured back a short time later. Barefoot and clad in a high-necked nightgown, she looked scarcely old enough to be the mother of two, soon to be three.

She blinked when Caro proceeded to scuttle into bed beside her.

"You kept me company the night before I married John," she announced on seeing Anne's surprise. "I think it's only fair that I should return the favor."

Anne groaned. "John will miss you."

"So he will. But he knows I'll be back in the morning. After all, it's only once that my favorite cousin Annie and I get to share the night before her wedding."

Anne concealed a wince. And yet, foolish though it was, she was secretly glad that Caro was here.

Caro squirmed around a bit, settling herself before turning to Anne. "Are you all right?"

Had Anne sensed any hint of pity, or anything of the like, she wasn't sure she could have retained her composure. She steadied her breath. Despite her family's good-natured teasing, she was a practical and sensible young woman.

Which led to her next thought. Perhaps, she counseled herself cautiously, she should be counting her blessings.

Caro propped herself up on an elbow. "I have an idea," she announced. "I think we should weigh the advantages of your next adventure."

Anne wasn't surprised that Caro knew precisely what she was thinking. Of course, that wasn't exactly how Anne would have put it, but it would suffice, she supposed.

Caro continued. "You could do worse, you know."

Anne arched a brow. "How so?"

"Your soon-to-be husband is not a fortune hunter."

"Not that we know of," Anne pointed out.

"Oh, I'm fairly certain of that. He refused a dowry."

Anne had not been aware of that particular fact. It was, she admitted a trifle grudgingly, rather commendable. She'd always considered the practice unpalatable, as if women were no more than beasts to be bartered and sold to the highest bidder! Of course, that did not make her an admirer of *him*!

Caro went on breezily. "He's not old as the ancients. He's not overly padded in all the wrong places."

"Caro!"

"No, I should never call him a fop." Caro's eyes began to sparkle. "Though he is rather fiendishly attractive."

Anne was sorely put not to roll her eyes. "Yes, dear, you've made your opinion abundantly clear on that score."

"Well, imagine if he were not!" Caro stated as only she could. "You'd end up with children who looked like goblins."

The corners of Anne's mouth twitched. No, she decided rather naughtily. That would be her husband who looked like a goblin.

"I knew I could make you smile!"

Anne's smile, however, was extremely short-lived.

"Annie, what is it?"

Her eyes slid away from Caro's. She could not hide her uncertainty. "My life is suddenly . . . so bizarre," she said haltingly. "It's happened so fast. Caro . . ." She floundered. "I still don't know how it happened. I'm not even sure *why* it happened."

Caro was still watching her, her lips creased in the tiniest of smiles. "Sometimes it's just like that."

"What?" Anne asked. "What do you mean?"

Caro looked at her as if she were crazed.

"Love," she said simply. "Oh, Annie, sometimes it's just there and one can't explain where or how or why or even *when* it happened. It's just there."

Anne was stunned. "Caro, I—I don't love him."

Caro shook her head. "Annie, I know this is not the way you would have chosen to wed. But I think—oh, I do not know why!—I think it will be all right. That you and Simon . . . Oh, Annie!

I don't know how to say it other than I truly believe that the two of you somehow belong together."

Now it was Anne who looked at her as if she were crazed. Caro was such a romantic. There was a sweetness inside her that barred her from the truth. But Caro was wrong, Anne thought vaguely, cringing to the depths of her soul. Her memory allowed no mercy. *It appears we shall have to marry.* His statement ricocheted through her mind again and again. Caro hadn't seen the utter lack of emotion in Simon's eyes, the flatness in his voice.

She could not imagine Simon Blackwell even capable of something so tender as love.

Nor could she bear to tell Caro it would never happen—not with Simon Blackwell.

No, she couldn't bear for Caro to glimpse her distress.

She and Caro lay awake long into the night. But it was so very different than it had been when they were young, Anne admitted with a pang. When Caro's eyes finally closed, Anne slipped from the bed, careful not to awaken her.

Resting her hip on the windowsill, she gazed long and hard into the cloudless depths of the night.

Yes, she thought again. So very different . . . there was no laughter bubbling in her heart, no chorus of song bursting in her breast.

Instead, her every breath grew more bitterly acute than the last.

For there were no stars out tonight to wish upon.

And it wasn't excitement that held Anne from sleep.

It was dread.

The ceremony took place at nine the next morning.

A tepid sunshine shone weakly through the curtains in the drawing room. Simon had taken his place beside her, his carriage unbendingly erect.

Anne swallowed. She gazed through the gauzy veil at the minister—oh, God, her mother's veil, for Mama had so wanted her to wear it. She had come to her room this morning, carrying it like a treasure beyond price.

For indeed it was.

Only then did Anne realize that this particular aspect of her wedding attire had been neglected.

"Anne," she said with that tender little smile that had always wrought so much pleasure. "You are my only daughter. I want you to wear the veil that I wore the day your father and I married. May you be blessed as I was blessed. And God willing, perhaps someday your daughter shall wear it too."

"Mama—" The swell in Anne's throat closed off her breath and her words. She felt as if she would break into a hundred little pieces as her mother placed it on her head. With gentle reverence, Vivian tugged the wispy layers into place.

Mama, she cried brokenly inside. *Oh, Mama.*

To her credit, she did not cry. Nor did she waver as she spoke her vows.

And then the veil was being lifted away, revealing her face.

She knew she was pale. She could feel her skin whitening.

Her gaze veered upward. A jolt shot through her as she realized that Simon was staring straight at her.

Time hung unending . . . the man unbending.

Would he kiss her? she wondered wildly. Did she even want him to?

His head lowered. His lips brushed hers. The contact was polite, perhaps even respectful— and could scarcely be called a kiss, Anne decided almost lividly, for it was bestowed in such a manner that she was convinced it was accorded only out of requirement.

God, why did he even attempt to such pretense!

He turned and offered his elbow. She sorely longed to plant her own squarely into his ribs! It was *her* restraint, she decided, that was accorded only out of requirement.

As was the custom, Vivian had planned an elaborate wedding breakfast. Meals in the McBride household were never a laborious affair, particularly not when Jack and Izzie were so lively, and neither was this one. At the far end of the table, Vivian and Simon's Aunt Leticia were engaged in animated discussion.

She was not, she acknowledged, the first woman to marry a man she did not love; such was the rule rather than the exception. The acknowledgment was both painful and reassuring. No matter how it came about, marriage was intended to be a celebration of two lives joined together, hardly a funeral. What purpose would melancholy serve?

The dishes were scarce being cleared when Simon leaned over. "No doubt you'll wish to change into suitable clothing. We've several very long days of travel ahead of us."

Anne's gaze swung to his. "What?"

"It's time to go home."

Home, she repeated silently. *Home.* Despite her earlier self-admonitions, a part of her wasn't ready to relinquish so readily—or so soon. *This* was home, she thought dimly. Here and Gleneden.

Simon rose to his feet and addressed the assemblage. "I do hope you'll forgive our hasty departure, but we must be on our way."

Anne thought vaguely it was a good thing her

maid had already begun packing her trunks.

Anne didn't want to leave. In a few days, perhaps. Tomorrow, at the earliest. Couldn't he have consulted her? At the very least, informed her earlier? Not that he'd had to. But it would have been the courteous thing to do.

She could feel his gaze resting on her face. She pressed her lips together. She cared not that her dismay must have been keenly apparent.

"It's time I was home," he said with a lift of his brows.

Anne said nothing, merely dropped her napkin on the table.

A scant time later, they stood near the carriage. The horses stomped restlessly.

Pride and bravado had sustained her while she changed into traveling clothes. Jack and Izzie began to wail when they were told they wouldn't see Anne for a time. Their nurse took them back inside. Anne hugged John, and then Alec stepped forward.

He took both hands in his and kissed her forehead. "Take care, Annie."

Mama was next. Anne's heart caught. Anne wrapped her arms around her mother's slight form. Drawing back, Vivian touched her cheek.

"You'll write, won't you, dear?"

"You know I will, Mama."

Caro had been hanging back slightly. Now she came forward. It was then that Anne noted her eyes were bright with a betraying sheen of tears.

"Caro," she said helplessly. "Oh, Caro."

"Annie, I shall miss you so!"

A wobbly laugh emerged. "It isn't as if we'll never see each other again. It shall be soon, I promise." They clung to each other, neither wanting to let go.

Anne had little recollection of being helped into the carriage. But there was a pinch in her heart, a hollow ache in her chest as she settled herself so that she faced the back of the carriage. Throughout their farewell, she'd managed to conceal her true feelings. Indeed, she was even smiling as she gave one last wave.

It was all so fast. She hadn't expected that they were to leave so quickly.

Or that it would hurt so much.

The carriage lurched forward. Down the street, around the corner. Caro had taken several steps forward, as if to follow. And as her form finally receded into the distance, a slow-growing comprehension slipped over Anne.

She'd never been away from her family, not really, except for a few years of school when she was young. Not even then, truly, for Caro had been there as well. Throughout her entire life, her loved ones had been near to protect her, to shield and shelter her, to lend her strength, even when she hadn't known she'd needed it. Her parents. Her brothers, Alec and Aidan.

Now there was no one.

Despair slipped over her. A thought sprang to the fore and she was powerless to release it.

The man beside her was a stranger. Yet was she the outsider . . . or was he?

Anne was not the weepy sort. She'd always consigned such weakness to those who were faint of heart. But now, a tearing pain ripped through her. It was as if she were being literally—unbearably—divided in two.

Never had she felt so alone. Never had she *been* so alone, and the desolation that wound through her was crushing.

She struggled against it. She struggled with all her might. She told herself it was foolish, so very childish to feel this way!

It was no use. Two hot, scalding tears slid slowly down her cheeks. She tasted bitterness. She tasted helplessness, staring through the glass long after her family disappeared from view. She did not wipe them away. Such effort was beyond her.

Beside her there was a movement. She felt rather than saw her husband slowly reach out. The heat of his palm settled over her hands, there where her fingers lay so tightly twisted in her lap. She did not turn her head. She did not dare!

The contact was brief—oh, so brief! It was

over almost before it began. It was a gesture meant to comfort. To console. But it didn't make her struggle any easier.

Indeed, it only made it harder.

Seven

I recall the feel of her all too vividly. Why can
I not forget?

Simon Blackwell

Anne was sorely mistaken in her belief that Simon gave no more thought to the kiss they had
shared.

If he could have leaped out to ride the entire
journey with Duffy and his driver, he would
have. He dearly longed to shut her out, closet her
presence away where he need not think of her.

Perhaps he could have . . . if only he hadn't
glimpsed her tears. If only he could have paid
no heed and turned a blind eye.

If only she hadn't cried.

If only the journey home did not drag so endlessly!

It wasn't the confinement within the carriage that nagged at him, but *her*. Her closeness surrounded him. It was impossible to ignore her. Her scent—damn it to hell!—was that of sweet, delicate roses. How quickly it became uniquely her own—and intimate in some way he pondered long and hard yet could not define—nor did he like!

Their wedding night had proved particularly awkward—for both of them. It was late when they stopped at an inn. Anne picked at her meal, and Simon had a very good idea what was on her mind . . . There was no point in dawdling, he decided. As soon as she laid down her fork, he escorted her up the stairs and down the hall to her room.

Stepping into the chamber, she paused, then turned. She was nervous. Simon sensed it—he saw it as well. He had no wish to prolong her uncertainty.

"I shall send the innkeeper's wife to attend you," he said. "And in the morning as well. Have a pleasant night, and I shall see you at breakfast." He gave a slight bow and withdrew.

For that very reason, he began the next morning atop his mount alongside the carriage. He was quite certain that Anne was once again relieved—and, confound it, he wasn't sure if he should be pleased or affronted! Either way, he felt compelled to spend part of each day with her.

And each day, when he resumed his place inside the carriage, he positioned himself on the opposite seat, assuming an air as if it was of no consequence. Yet the size of the conveyance was such that there was no way an entire day could pass without their touching.

Her knee bumped his when she shifted restlessly (it was rather difficult to avoid, since her legs were surely as long as his, he suspected). It occurred rather frequently, he discovered, which led him to surmise that perhaps she was not a good traveler. Or perhaps she was not particularly fond of his company.

Neither of them seemed inclined toward conversation. When there was, the subject was confined to the weather. The food. The condition of the road. It was gentlemanly on his part, ladylike on hers.

Never had the journey been so long and arduous! He longed for it to be ended.

As for what would follow after that . . . Simon tried to dismiss it from his mind, a singularly foolish notion, he discovered. He did not want to think of her as an obligation. It was not fair to her.

Yet, God knew, it was difficult to think of her as his wife!

It was a dilemma, he suspected, that each of

them pondered. Which irritated him, yet for the life of him, he did not know why!

The journey to and from London usually spanned the length of several days. In deference to her comfort, they alighted for refreshment once during the day, and again to spend each night at an inn.

It was near the end of the third day that she sat up. She had been gazing rather absently through the window. But all at once she straightened, as if in sudden revelation.

"My God," she said faintly.

Simon quirked a brow. "Is something wrong?" he inquired.

"Nothing is wrong," she countered immediately. "It's just that—"

She broke off. She lowered her head, momentarily confining her attention to her lap. Then once again her gaze skidded to the window. It was then he noticed a smile, such that he had the sensation she was trying to hide it.

"Is there something on your mind?"

"Aye." In the back of his mind hovered the awareness that it was the first time her speech had revealed her Scottish heritage. "I mean . . . no."

"Forgive me if I fail to comprehend," Simon remarked, "but both the subject and your logic are proving rather elusive."

She bit her lip and he had the distinct sensation she was engaged in a serious debate within herself. "It's just that . . . oh, good heavens. It's just occurred to me that . . ." She began to laugh, almost wildly, it seemed to him. Should he be alarmed?

"Anne? Anne!"

It was only much, much later that he realized he'd called her by her given name. Or more precisely, that it emerged with a spontaneous ease that startled him each time he thought of it. It was as if he'd done so every day of his life . . .

"I am not a dimwit. Truly! Though I understand why you might think so. But we've been married for . . . what? Almost two full days. And here I am—here *we* are—and I haven't the vaguest notion where we're going." She tipped her head to the side. "Where the devil *are* we going?"

"To my home." If he sounded annoyed, he couldn't help it.

"Yes, yes. You stated your home is the country. But *where* in the country? Where are we going? North, if I should hazard a guess."

"Yorkshire," he supplied. "On the border of the moors."

"I've never been to the moors," was all she said.

She didn't seem displeased, which in turn pleased *him*, though he wasn't quite sure why.

"And your home? Does it have a name?"

Something twisted in his heart. "Rosewood Manor."

"Rosewood Manor," she repeated. A smile curved her lips. "It sounds lovely," she said.

As he thought of his home, the emotions twisting in his gut were suddenly maddening. There was a part of him that was immensely relieved he was on his way home. He'd hated nearly every moment he was away. Despite everything, it was impossible to entertain the notion of living elsewhere.

Ah, yes, he loved Rosewood. The peace and quiet and tranquillity. But there were times he hated it. Not the land. But the rain. The storms.

It wasn't always so, chided a voice in his mind. There had once been a time when he'd treasured everything. Relished even the wildness of lightning streaking across the sky, the thunder that crashed across the earth. He leaned his head back against the cushion, away from the stirring of memories. Once—and one time only—Aunt Leticia had gently said that perhaps he should consider selling Rosewood.

He couldn't.

Everything inside him counseled that it was wrong. He would never sell Rosewood. He had grown to manhood there. It was there that he had wed . . . He loved it too much to ever leave. In truth, he could not imagine living elsewhere.

Yet hatred burned just as strongly for this place he'd always called home.

For Rosewood was both his comfort and his curse. His peace . . .

And his punishment.

Late in the afternoon on their fourth day of travel, Anne removed her bonnet. The air was warm both within the coach and without, though not nearly as hot as it had been in London.

As she did, the sunlight caught the gold band on her finger. The ring was shiny and new, engraved with her initials and Simon's, as well as the date of their marriage.

It felt heavy. Foreign, for she had yet to grow accustomed to the feel of it on her finger.

And she also felt the weight of Simon's gaze. Her cheeks grew hot, and it had naught to do with the weather. Her fingers busied themselves with arranging her skirts, lest he glean her reaction.

"How long before we are there?" It was not boredom, but curiosity that prompted the question.

"An hour," he said. "No more."

Anne straightened and looked out. There had been a subtle transformation in the landscape that had escaped her notice until now. All around were rolling hills. Amid patchworks of farmland, men toiled in the fields. They passed cattle and fat, woolly sheep, and clattered through villages tucked into the valley floor, where children played in front of red-roofed cottages. One little girl waved, her face pink-cheeked and round and wreathed in a smile. Anne waved back, wistfully reminded of Izzie.

On the outskirts, they clattered past an old Norman church, then began a steep climb. The road crept along the crest of a hill, curving sharply.

To the east lay deeply etched valleys. To the west and north, ridge upon ridge of undulating heather stretched as far as the eye could see. Very soon it would be in full bloom, a vista of lush purple carpet.

So very like Gleneden, she couldn't help but make a tiny exclamation.

Simon had been watching her closely. "What do you think, my lady? A world apart from London, both in distance and appearance. Outsiders usually consider it most forbidding."

"Forbidding?"

Clearly he didn't expect her soft tinkle of laughter. He hiked a brow. "You think not?"

"Never," she said simply. "I see magnificence. I see tranquillity. A harmony of earth and all within it."

"You've not yet seen the many moods of the moors," he said quietly. "You may well change your mind."

There was no chance to respond. The carriage left the road and turned down a narrow, winding lane flanked by trees and a low stone wall.

And then the journey was over. Despite her enjoyment of the countryside, she had somehow envisioned Simon Blackwell's home as lonely and grim, much like the man himself.

But before her was a lovely stone manor house, with wide, leaded windows that ran the entire length of the house, and wisteria-clad walls on the far wing.

The carriage door swung open. Duffy appeared, looking rather pleased, Anne decided. Simon leaped down before the old man could lower the steps—a task he did himself—then extended a hand.

"Welcome to Rosewood Manor, my lady."

There was no assemblage of servants to greet their master and his new wife upon their arrival. Standing in the entrance hall where a beautiful English oak stairway led above stairs, Anne glanced around, aware of Simon speaking to Duffy in low tones near the doorway.

It was Duffy who showed her to her second story bedchamber. Anne found it a bit odd that no other servants appeared to greet them, but reminded herself it was rare that the McBride household observed such formality at Gleneden.

As for her, what the deuce was she thinking?

She uttered a silent rebuke. Gleneden was no longer her home. Rosewood Manor was her home. Nor was her name McBride.

And perhaps—oh, but it was both a stout resolve and a fervent prayer!—it would not prove such a hardship to live here after all.

Her room was of modest size. The walls were a mellow gold, the woodwork and door a crisp, clean white. There was the smell of fresh paint—how sweet of Simon to have gone to such trouble. The bed hangings and draperies were made of crimson velvet, the counterpane a silky red and gold patterned damask. All were distinctly feminine, an observation that immediately sent her gaze swinging to the door on the wall opposite the wide four-poster.

Her heart picked up its rhythm. Simon's room? she wondered.

Putting it from her thoughts, she turned away to examine the room further. A seat had been built into the window, covered with plump, inviting cushions. Next to it, a set of French doors beckoned. Anne stepped outside onto a balcony that stretched the length of the house.

She couldn't help but exclaim her pleasure aloud. A far-ranging view encompassed deep green valleys, the endless stretch of heath and heather. She had no trouble envisioning a silver moon etched high in a midnight sky. She could imagine no more perfect place to wish upon stars—

How silly she was. She was too old to wish upon stars any longer. She was married now, and such things were for children, anyway.

Suppressing a sigh, she turned to go back inside. It was then she noticed another set of doors scant steps away from hers.

Her heart stood still. She could see directly into the chamber. She was right, she realized. Her room adjoined Simon's. She recognized the valise atop the huge four-poster; indeed all the furnishings were on a massive scale compared to hers. The ornately carved armoire, the writing desk directly alongside the doors.

The urge to step inside was almost overwhelming. Indeed, she took a step forward, one hand reaching for the brass handle. Yet all at once she found herself pricked by the notion that she was intruding where she had no right to intrude.

Stepping aside, she quickly turned back to her room.

The journey had been a tiring one. After they left London, each successive day had begun very early and ended late each evening. Anne lay down to nap, but it was impossible. It was really rather amazing how tired one could become while doing absolutely nothing the entire day! There was too much . . . well, she wasn't sure what it was, but it was such that she could not sleep! She began to pace, to and fro.

When a knock sounded on the door, she sincerely welcomed it. Duffy stood in the hall. He offered a wide smile.

"Supper awaits, my lady," he announced cheerfully.

On the way downstairs, Anne ran her finger along the fine layer of dust upon the molding in the hallway.

"Duffy," she asked, "who is the housekeeper?" More to the point, she should have asked *where* was the housekeeper.

He stopped short. "Well, mum, there is none. There is only Mrs. Wilder, the cook," he explained, "Noah, the houseboy, and me. Oh, and Leif, the groom. It's been that way since—" He broke off. "A long while," he finished. "It's a bit much for Mrs. Wilder, I'm afraid."

He was uncomfortable; there was no denying it. And while Anne was rather puzzled, she had no wish to prolong his unease.

She flashed a smile. "Thank you, Duffy. I appreciate your candor."

"Any time, mum. And may I say that it's good to have you here at Rosewood."

His welcome was heartening; it remained with her long after he opened the dining room.

Simon acknowledged her presence with an incline of his head. He held a chair for her, directly to his right. Anne wondered that he'd not put her at the far end. From what she'd seen of the state of the house, Anne was rather pleasantly surprised at the meal. It was hearty, simple fare—and just what she needed.

Afterward, Simon showed her into the drawing room. Perched on the edge of a small settee, Anne gazed around. She eyed the side table beside her. The room was lovingly furnished, Anne thought, but definitely dusty. It was, she decided, something she would attend to tomorrow.

Simon had gone to a table near the window. "A glass of port?" he asked.

Anne nodded. Port, claret, whisky, whatever, she would welcome it if it lessened her sudden nervousness. There was something on his mind. She sensed it. As for her, well, there was little point in denying what leaped to the fore in hers.

The marriage had yet to be consummated. She had been surprised—grateful at the time— that he'd chosen to postpone her initiation until they had arrived at his home. It was only natural to be apprehensive about the night to come.

He poured, one for her, another for himself. She caught herself watching his hands, his fingers long and lean. And she wondered how they would feel, those warm, masculine fingertips sweeping over her body. Her heart climbed high. Her cheeks stung with heat.

Four days ago her world had been rent asunder. She wouldn't fight what could not be altered. But all at once, she longed for this day and night to be over and done with.

She was willing to try to make their marriage work. Once this night was past, it would be easier. It would be *better*, she told herself.

She accepted the glass he offered. He took the chair adjacent.

"I trust you're satisfied with your room?"

She smiled. "The view is incomparable. But I expect you know that."

"I'm glad. I fear it was rather hastily done. If there is anything you wish to change—"

"No, no, it's quite lovely."

He set his glass aside. "There's something we must discuss," he said quietly.

"Yes?" She sipped her port.

"This marriage."

This marriage. Not . . . *our* marriage.

It was his choice of words, not so much the underlying quiet of his tone, that set off alarms ringing in her head. She had thought she knew what was coming. Now she wasn't so sure. Still, he had been pleasant thus far. Gracious, and surprisingly so. Somehow that lent her the courage she needed.

"If you please, I—I have no need for explanations. Therefore, there's no need to discuss—"

"There is every need."

He sounded irritated. Rising, he prowled the room as restlessly as she had paced hers earlier. Finally he stopped before the fireplace.

His expression was hardly reassuring. "Why are you angry?" she asked softly.

He pressed his fingertips briefly against his temples, as if in frustration. "I am not angry," he said.

"Aren't you?"

"I am not. Forgive me for appearing otherwise." His tone was abrupt. His hands dropped to his sides. He raised his head. "Let us be frank, Anne. Truly, I am not angry. And you need not be anxious. You need not dread this night."

"Thank you," she said earnestly. Her cheeks heated anew. "I admit, I *am* anxious. It's not that I wish to—to avoid this night. It's just that I . . . I've never—"

"I would be surprised," he interrupted curtly, "if it were otherwise."

By now her face was scalding. Dear God, was she really sitting here discussing her virgin state with the man who was about to render it no more?

"Yes, well, as such, I would simply like you to know that—"

"Anne."

"—that I am well aware of what to expect. And I shall not—"

"Anne!"

She didn't want to look at him. When she finally did, she discovered he was frowning rather severely. Why was she not surprised? she wondered with a spate of sarcasm.

But no. This was growing out of hand. "It seems to me," she said rather briskly, "that we are making quite an unnecessary fuss about something that occurs in every marriage."

There was an iron grimness to his features. "I assure you, Anne, this is quite necessary."

"How so?"

"I don't think you understand what I'm saying."

"What then, precisely, *are* you saying?"

"I will not touch you. Not tonight. Not tomorrow. Not ever."

He was right. She had not understood. She *did* not understand. These nights of their journey, she had thought that perhaps he was waiting until their arrival here at Rosewood. In deference to her virginity. Why, what else could it be?

"What?" she said faintly.

"You needn't be afraid, Anne. I'm sure you've undoubtedly been brought up to believe that a wife must oblige her husband in their bed. I simply want you to know that I will not require that particular duty of you."

Well, he had warned her he would be frank. Still, she hadn't expected such bluntness—or such an announcement in the first place!

She looked at him, bemused.

Judging from his expression, he didn't appear disposed to repeat his statement.

She took a steadying breath. If he had no qualms about such frank discussion, then neither should she. Still, the thought proved much easier than the deed. "Are you saying you expect me to stay here, to live with you here . . . like brother and sister?"

He did not like the term. "Not precisely."

"How then—precisely?" Anger began to gather in her breast, sharp and ripe. Anger—and the image of his mouth on hers, the night he'd kissed her on the terrace.

"We won't live together as husband and wife."

Anne swallowed, her eyes fixed wide on his face. "Are you"—Lord, but was there any way to put this delicately?—"unable?"

His look of chilling reprisal left her in no doubt he was not.

She stared at him numbly. The workings of her mind seemed sluggish. "What then?"

His jaw clenched. "This is not easy for me, Anne!"

"And it is for me?" She was on her feet, as if someone had suddenly dug a knife into her back. Her lips compressed. Her eyes were sizzling. "Why, Simon? I believe I am due a proper explanation. *Why* won't we live as husband and wife?"

"I cannot be a proper husband." His tone was gritty. "Rest assured, Anne. It's not you. It's me. I—I cannot be a proper husband to anyone."

Rest assured, he said. Anne was anything but assured. Why, she was outraged. Bewildered. Hurt. She felt herself flooded by a dozen different emotions.

But most of all, she was humiliated. Beyond reason. Beyond comprehension. Beyond anything she'd ever known before.

"So," she said slowly. "We will not share a bed. We will not share a room. We will not be lying together. Is that what you mean?" She formed each word carefully, with slow precision.

He said nothing.

"You did state that it is quite ... *necessary* ... that I understand. So please, I suggest you speak plainly."

Still he did not speak.

"I presume, then, that we won't make love?"

His expression had turned black as night. His mouth was a grim slash in his face.

"Say it, Simon. Since we are being *frank* with each other, say it."

"You are right. We—we won't make love."

Anne thought of her parents. A squeeze of the hand. A shared glance when they thought no one was watching. She was not an innocent, not in that way. She knew what physical love was. She also knew what *real* love was, the kind her parents had experienced. What Caro and John had. The kind of love she had always thought would someday be hers.

Oh, how she felt the fool!

It seemed she was to be denied it. Denied everything. Her heart cried out in angry despair.

And in that moment, she thought of Caro and John. God, it seemed a lifetime ago that Izzie and Jack had bounced on her bed. While she hadn't given the prospect any real thought, she had never doubted that *she* would someday have little ones of her own.

"What if I want children?" she asked levelly.

"I want no children."

A flat denouncement. A cold finality. So. It wasn't enough that she must endure this sham of a marriage. He would deny her what many women cherished above all else.

A painful tightness wedged in her chest. She almost wished she had not asked!

Helplessly she stared at him. Did he see the pain in her heart? Did he even care? She didn't understand it. She didn't understand *him*.

"We'll wait a suitable amount of time," he was saying, "then separate. A year should suffice. Perhaps two. Once we are divorced—"

Anne gasped. "Divorce?" she cried. "I'll never be able to marry after that. I'll be ostracized."

"I'll take the brunt of it. No one will blame you. You can say whatever you like. That I was unfaithful."

Her head was spinning. Was she so thick-headed, then, that she hadn't considered the possibility? Her throat constricted. It was a common enough practice—one she loathed—one she'd certainly never imagined she might have to contend with!

"*Will* you be . . . unfaithful?"

It seemed forever before he answered. "No," he stated very quietly. "I will not be unfaithful."

Bitterness choked her. He asked much of her. Yet he allowed her no choice but to agree.

"Do we understand each other?"

Anne drew a deep breath, steadying herself both inside and out. Inside she was scalded. But she wouldn't let him see it, not even a glimpse. She would not shrink. She would not cringe, she would not cower, and by God, she would not cry. Instead she kept her head high, her shoulders back, unflinching in her regard.

"It seems we do," she said, her voice very low. "You choose not to think of me as a wife. Therefore, I shall strive not to think of you as a husband. But there is something I wish for *you* to understand. Were I to choose to lie in the arms of my husband night after night, I should consider it a privilege—and not a duty."

Eight

Never again had I thought to feel . . . anything.
But perhaps desire most of all.

Simon Blackwell

She would never know what those words cost
him. There was a price to be paid, Simon decided grimly, a very dear price. Not by Anne.

But by him.

I cannot be a proper husband.

He had sensed her confusion. He'd felt the
exact moment it crystallized into something far
different.

A twinge of admiration cut through him.
Though her pride had been wounded, she did
not run, she did not hide, she did not retreat.
Instead she had faced him with courage and

dignity. She had not liked what he'd had to say—no, she'd not liked it at all! But she had stood up to him, her eyes never wavering from his as she delivered those final words.

Simon was well aware she was convinced he was an unfeeling bastard.

It would be easier this way, for both of them. She did not see it now, but perhaps she would in the years to come when he was no more than a memory. An unpleasant one, at that.

Yet now that it was over and done, in its wake came a wealth of regret.

Even now he battled his conscience.

It was best this way, he decided wearily. Best that she thought him an ogre. Best that she expected nothing from him.

It could *only* be this way, he told himself. It would not be fair to her to hope for what he could not give.

Because if she did, he would only fail her.

Welcome to Rosewood, mocked a voice in his mind. Oh, but he could not! Perhaps it was wrong. Perhaps he would end his days in the fiery pits of hell. For the very lovely Anne continued to rouse a feeling long dormant in him. Something that had been absent for five long years . . .

And Simon most surely did not welcome it.

Given the state of affairs, Anne had not thought to sleep a whit. Instead she slept like the dead, not rousing until the morning light peeped through the curtains. Through the draperies, she saw that while yesterday's marvelous sunshine had dimmed, it looked to be a lovely day. She lay unmoving for a few seconds, tempted to stay where she was. But no. *No.* She was neither weak of limb nor faint of heart. Whatever this day would bring, she would face it head-on.

Her trunk had been brought in last evening while they dined. After a quick wash in the basin, she rummaged through the assortment of gowns, tugging out a lightweight muslin with a minimum of fuss and fripperies. There was no hope of lacing up a corset by herself; she donned but one petticoat. Through a goodly time of twisting and reaching and stretching, she managed to struggle into the gown. Standing before the mirror on the dressing table, she piled her hair into a loose knot on her crown and secured it with several pins.

Duffy was in the dining room when she entered.

"Good morning, mum," he greeted cheerily. "May I fetch you a bit of breakfast?"

She flashed a smile. "Thank you, Duffy. That would be lovely."

The "bit of breakfast" turned out to be enough to feed a Scottish regiment, Anne declared as he set several plates before her.

Anne ate her breakfast alone, with the exception of Duffy, who poked his head in the dining room occasionally to see if there was anything she needed. Once again the fare was simple but filling. Anne ate heartily of the plump sausages, potatoes, and bread slathered with rich yellow butter.

When Duffy next appeared, Anne looked up with a smile. "Is my husband about?"

"No, mum. He left early this morning to tend to his business."

"And what is his business, Duffy?"

"Well, mum, he has a good bit of everything. Land, tenants, crops"—Duffy grinned—"and the fattest sheep in the county, I daresay."

Just what he'd said he was. A country gentleman. Anne glanced outside. She was almost disappointed to see that the day was brightening. She'd much rather be out-of-doors than closeted inside. She'd hoped to spend at least part of the day walking or riding. But she was a married woman now, she reminded herself staunchly, with the responsibility of taking care of a daily household. Regardless of her role in Simon's bed—or lack of it, she thought with a touch of derision—it was a task that must be dealt with. It might as well begin today.

And there was no denying there was a good deal of work to be done.

Her first task was to meet the cook, Mrs. Wilder. She was a ruddy-cheeked woman with a manner as hearty as the food she prepared, and Anne liked her immediately. Anne's compliments were genuine; Mrs. Wilder beamed.

She spent the rest of the morning and afternoon inspecting each room, paper and pencil in hand, Duffy serving as her guide. She was rather shocked by the condition of the house, though she kept her opinion to herself. With the exception of the kitchen, which was positively spotless, the dining room, and the master suite, dreadful was the only way she could think to describe the rest of the house. It was not the patina of age that made it so, or a shabby state of disrepair. It was simply that all was in need of a thoroughly vigorous cleaning.

"Duffy," she asked as they proceeded down the last long hall, "has there ever been a full staff employed at Rosewood?"

"Oh, yes, mum. But not . . ." He paused. "Not for a long while," he finished.

A long while.

He'd said it again, yet Anne harbored the distinct sensation he'd been about to say something else. Her curiosity was more than a little piqued, but she decided it wouldn't be wise to press further. Duffy was clearly loyal to Simon, and it would not be fair to him. She certainly didn't want him to feel he was telling tales on his master.

They had halted midway along the main corridor of the house in front of a massive pair of oak doors. Anne looked them up and down. "What is this room?"

"It's the library, mum."

Anne smiled. "How delightful."

Duffy, however, appeared rather discomfited. "I don't think you'll wish to go in there, mum."

"Whyever not?"

"I just . . . I just don't think you will, mum."

Anne closed her fingers around the door handle.

His eyes widened. "Mum—"

"Oh, it's quite all right," she said calmly. "I'll be freshening up for dinner after this, so there's no need to accompany me any longer."

"Of course, mum." There was no doubt he was unhappy.

"Oh, and Duffy?"

"Yes, mum?"

"Thank you for your assistance today."

His smile was wide and genuine.

Anne waited until he'd disappeared around the corner, then entered the library.

Her nose wrinkled. The air was stale. It was so dark she could scarcely see. There was no question the room had not been in use for weeks. Months. Perhaps even years, she thought in irritation.

She marched forward. Her footsteps echoed on the dark mahogany floor. She headed toward the bank of windows, tripping several times as she made her way. Finally she thrust her hand through the draperies, which had been closed tight as well. Feeling for the latch, she finally found it.

Rats! It was stuck. She mustered her strength. There! A vigorous push and the window opened. With both hands she shoved the draperies wide, only to grope for her handkerchief and press it to her mouth in the next instant, coughing at the sudden whirlwind of dust. But it was worth it, she thought, as light flooded inside.

Stepping back, she dusted off her hands in satisfaction and turned.

The sheer immensity of the room stole her breath, yet in a vastly different way than the dust had robbed her of breath, which, of course, mired everything. A matter of course by now, she thought wryly, gazing around.

And indeed, everything in the room seemed to match that immensity. It was circular. Towering shelves scaled high, clear to the ceiling. A balcony encircled, granting access to the highest shelves.

Once, this room had surely been incredible. It didn't matter that there were no grand Corinthian columns reaching to a domed, handpainted ceiling. It would have been out of place here anyway, she thought absently. Instead, bookshelves of English oak climbed aloft, stately and tall, meeting the wood-paneled ceiling.

A desktop globe perched atop the ebony table in the corner. Beyond the massive desk in the center of the room, a pair of Georgian library chairs flanked the fireplace. She could only imagine curling up in one of those chairs on a rainy day, a fire burning warmly in the grate, the gilt and bronze mantel clock ticking away the hours.

But it was not the grime of disuse that shocked her. That stunned her to the breadth of her soul . . . and that held her rooted to the spot.

Many of the shelves were bare. Literally dozens of books lay scattered across the floor, in every direction. They were not stacked neatly, waiting their turn to be shelved. No, it was more as if they'd been caught in a tempest, a tempest that had spun through the room and spent its anger.

There was a faint scent of mustiness. Anne trailed a finger down the back of the leather chair behind the desk; the leather was worn smooth. Someone had once spent a great deal of time here. Yet now the dictionary stand stood empty, the shelves naked. How sad. How tragic that something so marvelous had been abandoned, left to molder.

It was as if time had suddenly ceased, like a door left ajar, never to be opened again.

Who had done this? Why? And why had it been left in this state? She suspected she knew the answer to the first; she had yet to discover the others.

But it could be easily set to rights. Oh, she

could see it already, the shelves waxed and shining, the wood richly agleam. And with the sun aslant, pouring through the bank of mullioned windows, what a heavenly retreat it would be!

One by one, she began to gather up the books—poetry, the classics, volumes of histories, travel journals—it was an extensive library. When her arms were full, she piled the books on the long, trestled worktable, sorting them by size. She would sort them again later. Eventually her arms and back wearied. She stood up, stretching.

There were various nooks and crannies built into the shelves where one might read or study. Her eyes lit on one such place. This one, however, had once housed a large display case.

No more. Shattered pieces of glass littered the floor. It was then she noted the manuscript pages, which had suffered the same fate as so many of the books. She guessed that they had been locked away in the case. Some of the pages lay under the glass, some over, spread across the floor like a deck of cards left to the mercy of the wind.

She moved closer, easing down on her knees and bending low. With utmost care she picked up the nearest one. As she suspected, it was vellum. Reverently she fingered it; it was fragile and worn.

The text was Latin. In the center of this particular page was a drawing of three men atop donkeys. They traversed a path that led to a church, while angels hovered overhead. It was beautifully embellished, the edges gilded. It was easy to envision a scribe, hunched over a table lit by candlelight, poring over his task for weeks, perhaps even months.

Anne had seen such manuscripts before, but only in museums. It was surely hundreds of years old, she thought in awe. Again the question surfaced. Why had it been left like this? What possible reason could there—

"What are you doing?"

The voice came from directly behind her. Unalerted as she was, Anne pushed herself upright. The heel of her hand bore the weight of her entire body. But she'd forgotten the broken glass. She felt a sharp pain as a hundred tiny slivers bit deeply through the skin.

Anne ignored it. She jerked upright, spinning around to face her husband.

His brows were drawn together fiercely, his tone no less than icy. His gaze went from the vellum to her face—and did not stray. She could have sworn she heard his jaw lock.

"You're just the person I wished to see," she said brightly. "Your library is quite lovely, but atrociously maintained, I fear. Which brings me to ask . . . may I have your leave to hire a

housekeeper? Forgive my directness, but Rosewood Manor is sorely in need of one, and perhaps several housemaids as well. And I do
believe their first task should be this library."
Anne's cough was not entirely exaggerated. "My
word, it's enough to send a body into fits!"

"No," he said.

Anne blinked. "I beg your pardon?"

"No." This time it was quite deliberately
stressed. "I want no one snooping in this room."

I don't want you snooping in this room.

That was what he really meant. He left her in
no doubt!

But while he made no pretense at manners,
Anne accorded hers most generously, she was
certain. Her mother would surely be proud.

"This is the most glorious room in the house,"
she said pleasantly. "I'm hardly a scholar"—she
waved the page in her hand—"but these pages
may possibly be quite rare. Indeed, they may
be quite valuable. Perhaps you should consider
having an expert in to—"

"I know exactly what they are. And I repeat,
this room is never to be used."

Anne's smile froze. Her iciness matched his.
"If it's never to be used," she pointed out, "then
perhaps it should be locked."

"I live here alone," he said curtly. "There's
been no need."

Anne stood as rigidly erect as he, her injured palm hidden behind her back. His control was maddening. And, damn it all! her hand was beginning to throb. And she could tell it was bleeding. She twined it into her skirts. Blast it, she could only hope it wasn't dripping onto those precious pages of vellum!

"You are free to employ a housekeeper," he went on, "and whatever maids you wish. Do whatever you like in the rest of the house, but this room is not to be touched."

"Ah," she said snidely. "Are we to come to another understanding?"

Their eyes locked. Each tested the resolve reflected in the other's eyes.

"Call it what you will," he said finally.

"I do believe I've married a madman," Anne remarked. "What I cannot believe is that I ever allowed you to kiss me."

He appreciated neither the cut of her words themselves nor the slice of her tone. In fact, she had the feeling he was gnashing his teeth.

All at once his eyes narrowed. "What are you hiding?" he asked sharply.

"I . . . nothing."

He pulled the vellum from her hand and laid it aside, then reached for the other, turning it palm up.

"For pity's sake, why didn't you say you were hurt?"

"I-it's just a piece of glass." She made the

mistake of glancing at her hand. Blood smeared the lower half, pooling thick and crimson.

She gasped. Her knees began to wobble. Giddiness flooded her. No, she thought in horror. Oh, no! If she pitched forward, she would surely die of humiliation. She'd always considered herself brave, but not when it came to the sight of blood. Then she was a willy-nilly fool.

Despite her most stringent self-admonitions, she felt herself swaying. She was queasy. She couldn't see Simon. Black dots whirled in her vision, misty swirls of gray. She could hear him though. His voice was buzzing so that she couldn't understand a single thing he was saying. How odd he sounded.

The next thing she knew, his hands were on her. She was caught and held close against his side. Dizzy, light-headed, she would have collapsed if not for him. One long, booted leg came out. He dragged a chair close and eased her into it.

"I'm sorry." Her voice wasn't as shaky as she feared. She even managed a tremulous smile. "This is ridiculous, I know. It's just that—"

"Hush. It's all right. Don't fret. Don't *look*." His voice was almost soothing. "Close your eyes, Anne. Breathe deep, that's the way. Don't think about it. Just breathe."

Long moments later, she opened her eyes. He was watching her. He'd wrapped his handkerchief around the base of her hand. His fingers curled warmly around the other, oddly reassuring.

"Better?" he asked quietly.

She gave a jerky nod.

"Good. Let's see if we can't get this patched up. Don't go wandering off," he said. "I'll be back shortly."

There was a slight, reassuring squeeze of her fingertips. Those hard lips curled up in a faint, unexpected smile. Her gaze followed him up. Stupidly, she wanted to cling to him. A huge lump lodged in her chest. God, she thought, what was happening?

She leaned her head back against the cushions of the chair and closed her eyes.

It wasn't long before he reappeared.

The handkerchief he'd wrapped around her hand was already soaked through.

He'd brought a glass of whisky back with him. "Is that for you or for me?" she asked.

He gave a rusty laugh. Rusty, but a laugh nonetheless.

"Drink up," he advised.

She took a healthy swallow and grimaced.

"All of it, if you please."

She complied. The whisky burned all the way down her throat and into her stomach. "That's quite ghastly," she complained.

"An acquired taste." Long fingers extracted

the glass, brushing against hers. Again that rusty chuckle. Anne was thoroughly amazed.

She winced when he applied pressure to the cuts. He spoke in low tones, telling her he was waiting until the bleeding had stopped. Or perhaps it was the whisky that began to take effect, she realized later.

She turned her head away when he reached for a bottle of antiseptic and dashed some on her hand. It burned mightily. She jerked. Her fingers curled hard around his.

"Easy," he said a bit gruffly. "You've a good bit of glass in there, I fear. I'll try not to hurt you."

She looked away. Yet before long, her eyes slid back. The sunlight glinted off the small knife poised above her hand. She gasped. Her stomach lurched anew.

An admonishing black brow arose. "No," he commanded sternly. "Don't look."

Once again her gaze veered away. She felt herself unconsciously shrinking back, instinctively trying to avoid the hurt—and the way he held her gently in place. The knife probed deeper. Inhaling sharply, she focused instead on the feeling of her hand cradled in his. The vision remained in her mind long after her gaze flitted away. He had lean, wonderfully strong hands; hers appeared dwarfed within his. His skin was warm and faintly rough. It declared him a working man, just as she'd thought. His fingers were dark against hers. She was only too aware of his strength. It should have been discomfiting.

Instead it was comforting. And it was that realization which in turn roused the expected twinge of dismay.

Why the devil did he always manage to make her feel so contrary?

He sat very near, so close one of his knees wedged between hers. Anne's heart was suddenly pounding. His head angled low. There was a faint crease on his forehead. His lips pressed together ever so slightly, so intent on his task was he.

Memory invaded, swift and unrelenting. Her breath wavered unevenly. Awareness stirred. She recalled with an almost painful acuity the smooth heat of his lips upon hers. She'd liked it. Even now, the remembrance made her heart clamor anew. Did he know she wouldn't have refused if he kissed her again?

Merciful heavens, it appeared *she* was the one going mad. It was the whisky, she thought shakily. What else could it be?

She watched as he set the knife side and wrapped several strips of clean white linen around the wound.

"There." His tone was rather brusque. "It's done."

Anne looked up into his face. Outwardly she was composed, but her insides were a mass of quivering jelly. "I . . . Thank you." She could manage no more.

Storm-gray eyes moved over her features. Anne had the unsettling feeling that the very same awareness had claimed him too.

"You're still pale," he observed. "I'll take you to your room so you can rest."

She was shaking her head, speaking almost before she was aware of it. "You need not accompany me. Really!"

A dark brow rose.

Anne flushed. "I'm fine. Truly." Praying that he would not glean her embarrassment, her gaze slid away.

It didn't help that he'd not yet released her hand. She started to tug it back. His grip tightened.

Anne looked up sharply.

His expression was unreadable. "May I trust that you will heed my wishes with regard to this room?" He spoke very quietly.

A part of her longed to argue. A part of her was ready to lash out. A part of her wanted almost desperately to be angry. Somehow she couldn't.

"Please."

His tone was very low, even gritty. Yet this time the words were more plea than directive— and how much more effective!

She gave a jerky nod.

He walked with her to the stairway. Anne quickly climbed the stairs. Yet she had the uneasy feeling his eyes followed her form long after she'd turned down the hallway to her room.

And all the while, her mind circled and churned, as if through a maze.

He was a man of secrets. A man of sorrow. She'd never been more certain of anything in her life.

And suddenly she wanted very much to know why.

Nine

Loss has a way of changing a man. Loss has a
way of changing everything.

Simon Blackwell

Simon would have dearly loved to ignore his
alluring new bride. Anne, however, made it impossible.

Within a matter of days, she made her existence known. A change began to take shape
within Rosewood Manor. Buckets of water and
soap were hauled inside. Carpets were beaten
and cleaned. Newly waxed panels of oak shone
throughout the house. When before dark and
dreariness pervaded all, light and warmth and
coziness began to emerge.

Simon was both impressed and angry. Who

was she to take charge of his home? It was, he grudgingly admitted, far more habitable. Still, at times he felt he'd been given the role of spectator. She had invaded his life, disrupted his home. Yet he could not protest, for he'd granted her license to do as she pleased. He had no choice but to watch grimly as everything around him was changed.

And Anne strolled through the halls as if she'd done so every day of her life. In her wake was the lingering scent of roses . . .

It drove him half wild.

He'd been furious the day he discovered her in the library. For one searing moment, an almost savage rage had blackened his vision. She intruded where she had no right. She invaded his sanctum, and he was almost beyond conscience.

He had not set foot within that room for many a year—shortly after Ellie and the boys had been laid to rest. That day with Anne carried him back . . . back to the night when vile rage erupted . . . the night he'd torn apart the treasures that had once meant so much to him.

He'd wanted to burn it, burn everything. Burn it the way *they* had burned.

For this room above all others called forth the memories. Memories of the three of them, laid to rest in the garden, the garden that Ellie so adored. The garden where his boys had always loved to play . . .

He'd failed them, all of them. He could not protect them, any of them. He could not *save* them.

Simon had no wish to remember. He'd thought the years had dulled the pain, but he was wrong. How much better to be empty and numb! How much better to be alone!

But with Anne in his house, he was no longer allowed the solitude he craved.

If he was bitter, he could not help it. He had done what needed to be done. He'd wed her. He'd brought her to his home. And now she invaded that most private sanctum of all—his mind! Would she allow him no measure of peace? He resented her. Her presence here in his home. His life. She was there wherever he looked. It was almost a violation of all the happiness that had once filled his heart.

But she was no intruder. No invader. No coquette.

She was his wife.

And perhaps it was that which he resented most of all.

Anne had never been one to keep her head down. Once she'd made up her mind, there was no swaying it. Simon might have been satisfied with his dismal surroundings, but she was not. She threw herself headlong into the task of setting Rosewood Manor to rights.

Two days after her arrival, she hired a

housekeeper, Mrs. Gaines. Within the week, a staff of housemaids had been secured. By the end of a week, sunlight streamed through the arch of windows newly cleaned. The floors of the entire first floor were scrubbed and shining.

There was still a good deal of work to be done, but Anne was pleased at the progress that was being made. Simon's reaction—or lack of it—stung. She wished that he would have made some acknowledgment of her effort. He did not disapprove. He did not debate. He turned a blind eye to everything. Just as he turned a blind eye to her.

But at least her days were filled with activity. She rose early and tumbled into bed exhausted. But mealtimes, when it was just the two of them, were particularly trying.

They were, in sum, no less than an ordeal. There was no dispelling the strain in the air. The meal began and ended with the requisite greeting and farewell. In between there was little sound but the clinking of china and cutlery. Anne was reduced to admiring the newly polished silver she'd found stowed away in a cupboard.

She hated it. Throughout her life, mealtimes were conducted with talk and laughter and sharing. With Simon, she was growing to despise those hours, but she certainly wasn't going to hide away with a tray in her room because her husband chose to be a boor.

And it appeared this particular morning was no exception.

Simon was already seated at the table.

Anne strode briskly to the lovely Pembroke table that served as a sideboard. An assortment of dishes had been laid out. "Good morning," she said pleasantly.

"Good morning." One long finger was curled about his cup. He didn't bother to look up.

Choosing a croissant, she moved to the dining table. As usual, Simon's morning sustenance consisted of coffee, strong and black. Her nose wrinkled distastefully. She reached for the teapot, glancing at him from beneath her lashes. And in that instant, she vowed this meal would not pass in strained silence. With that in mind, she wiped her fingers on her napkin and addressed her husband.

"Have you already breakfasted?"

He sipped his coffee, his gaze trained on his newspaper. "No."

Obviously he found the question superfluous. Anne dug in, determined to stay the course. "It's a long time till luncheon. And Mrs. Wilder prepares a lovely coddled egg."

"Perhaps you should tell her so."

"Actually I have." Anne studied him openly. Certainly there was no need to worry that he would notice. She might have been a lump of clay for all the awareness he took of her. Rising, she returned to the sideboard and filled her plate with various hot dishes. Scooting her chair into place, she sat once more.

She speared a bite of sausage and chewed thoughtfully. It wasn't that they were at odds, she mused, slathering her toast with marmalade. He was not outwardly hostile; it was more as if he chose to look through her. She wiped her fingers on her napkin. Reaching for her fork once more, she dropped her knife onto the carpet.

She reached for it—certainly Simon didn't notice. Her head connected with the edge of the table while she was retrieving it. When she straightened, a pair of icy gray eyes held her in rebuke. Of course it was when she least required his attention!

"Must you clatter about so? I find it difficult to read."

Anne did not particularly care for his tone. She stabbed another bite of sausage and popped it in her mouth. "I fear," she said with mock sweetness, "that your manners have gone awry, sir. Perhaps it's different for Yorkshire folk, but I was taught that it was rude to read at table."

Simon paused, his cup suspended halfway to his mouth. He lowered it slowly to the saucer, then sat back and regarded her, a faint smile—if it could be called that—curling his lips. "Indeed?"

"Indeed." Anne savored both the word and the moment.

And it appeared she'd finally managed to

maintain his attention. His smile grew tight. "Being of hearty Yorkshire stock, I'm not entirely certain how most London folk were raised, but I was taught that it was rude to talk when one's mouth is full."

Anne finished chewing, then swallowed. She wasn't about to concede victory. "Scots," she said at length. "I own that I am half English, but I've spent far more time in Scotland. My father was Scots. Therefore I prefer to think of myself as—"

"Let me guess," he drawled. "Scots."

"Aye," she said with relish.

His eyes had narrowed. What, did he expect her to leave? The servants might quake and quiver, but by Jove, she wouldn't. And she didn't. She'd grown up with two older brothers; she'd learned early on how to stand up for herself. Neither Alec nor Aidan had ever bullied her—not that they hadn't tried—and neither would he.

"Perhaps," she suggested, "your foul mood might be much improved if you were to eat something. Mrs. Wilder would surely be pleased."

His eyes glinted. "My mood, as you call it, is not foul."

"Is it not? I daresay you make an earnest endeavor to make it exactly so."

His mouth was drawn in a straight line. The

newspaper rattled. "Precisely what are you suggesting?"

"I suggest nothing. I merely make the observation that perhaps you are not a particularly brilliant conversationalist."

"You criticize my manners. You criticize my moods. Is there anything else you wish to criticize?"

Anne smiled sweetly. "Not at present," she said mildly.

"Ah. And do I have leave to grant similar observations in turn?"

"I should imagine," she demurred. "After all, you are the master of the house."

"You are given to say what's on your mind, aren't you?"

"If I do not, who will?"

"A pragmatic approach," he observed. "You've a temper too, I see."

"Not I."

"And you pride yourself on your outspokenness."

"I merely consider myself forthright."

"Forthright. Is that what you call it?"

"What would *you* call it?"

"If I were asked, I might say that you are the most obstinate woman I have ever known."

"I am neither," she returned pleasantly. Did he think he could insult her? She was made of sterner stuff than that.

"A poor choice of words. You are not obstinate, but stubborn."

"Certainly not! Though I will own to being a trifle independent."

"Ah." He looked her straight in the eye. "A family trait, is it?"

"I fear so," she said lightly.

"Is there anything else you wish to say, Anne?"

Anne opened her mouth. "Not—" she began.

"At present," he finished.

It was victory at its most glorious. The following morning, there was no newspaper at the table.

He also partook of a substantial breakfast.

And he actually deigned to inquire how she'd slept!

Several days later, Anne chanced to pass by one of the maids, who had just received the post. Since Simon was elsewhere, Anne smiled and took the packet from the girl.

"Thank you, Mary. I'll see that it's delivered."

Simon's study was located in the east wing. Anne had glanced in briefly that very first day with Duffy. Like the library, she considered it Simon's domain, which seemed to suit him quite well, she thought with a touch of the acerbic. And indeed, the location fit him quite well too—it was at the far end of the hall.

Stepping inside, she glanced around. The room was large, done up in the same English oak as the stairway. Just beneath the windows was a lovely chaise, upholstered in burgundy velvet and gold.

A path of sunlight led the way to the desk. Anne dropped the post in the center of his desk, then paused and looked up.

A large cobweb stretched from ceiling to wall in the corner. She shuddered, started to leave, considered—then retraced her steps. She fixed the offending cobweb with a glare. There was no help for it—it simply had to go.

There was a maid's closet just down the hall. Retrieving a broom, she returned to the study and climbed atop the lovely velvet chaise in the corner.

"What the blazes are you about?"

The sound of her husband's voice nearly made her lose her balance. He did not mince words, she thought stubbornly, and neither would she.

From the corner of her eye, she saw that he'd stationed himself behind his desk.

"What the blazes does it look like?" The retort was accompanied by a vigorous swipe of the broom.

It missed by a good foot. "Damn," she muttered.

Simon's head came up. She glanced over her shoulder.

One dark brow climbed high.

"My brothers talk much worse," she defended herself.

"I should prefer it if my wife does not."

Oh, bother. Who was he to chide her so? Ignoring him, Anne took a breath and balanced herself on tiptoe. Her mouth pursed determinedly, she set her target in sight once more. It was an even more valiant effort than before, only this time she nearly fell from her perch.

"For pity's sake, let me do it." The growl sounded from directly behind her. "If you break your neck, I won't have it on my conscience."

Strong hands closed around her waist. The world swirled briefly before she was set on her feet. She watched while he dispatched the cobweb with ease—and without benefit of the chair.

Anne glowered as he took a seat behind his desk. Their eyes met briefly. What, she thought, did he wish to be left alone? Her lips compressed. He could ask then. After all, she had been here first.

Deliberately she presented him with her back. She busied herself, righting a stack of books on the table in the corner.

She was unaware of Simon's eyes narrowing as she flitted to the other corner and back again.

"My God—are you never still?"

It was less a question than an accusation. Anne froze.

He tapped his fingers together. "Have you finished here?"

"A thousand pardons," she said stiffly. "I gather you wish to be left undisturbed?"

"If it's not too much to ask."

He was faultlessly polite. Anne was not so gracious. She sent him a fulminating glare as she withdrew, unaware of the regret that had already seized hold of Simon's conscience.

A scant quarter hour later, she descended the stairs in her riding habit. Simon was in the entrance hall with Duffy when she came down the stairs.

He fixed her with a silent query.

"I thought I would go out riding." Her tone was coolly defensive.

He glanced at the grandfather clock that had just tolled the hour. "It's almost time for luncheon."

"Please don't hold it on my account. I may be quite late." It should please him to be left alone.

Her steps would have skirted him—if he hadn't caught hold of her elbow.

Anne's gaze narrowed on the clasp of his fingers. His fingers released her . . . his eyes did not.

His expression bore a faint consternation. "Anne, of course the stable is at your disposal. But this is not a good time."

Her brows shot high. "Why not?"

His gaze slid beyond her shoulder to the high windows at her back. "Look there." With his chin he indicated the sky. Anne saw that a low bank of clouds gathered on the horizon. Even as she glanced behind her, the sunlight began to dim. "We are in for bad weather."

"Ah, but you forget," she said lightly, "I've lived most of my life in Scotland. A trifle of rain is scarcely of note. And I do believe I shall molder if I remain indoors another minute."

"You do not know the terrain here." A faint edge entered in his tone.

Anne's smile receded. "How else shall I get to know it?"

His eyes caught hers. "Heed me in this, Anne. The storms here are unlike anything you're used to. You are not to go out during one, do you hear me?"

"It's quite impossible not to," she said through her teeth. It was on the tip of her tongue to argue further. But just then, there was a thunderous *boom*. He looked at her with a tiny little smile—as if to say, *Ha! You see, I told you so!*

His smile rankled. Anne cast him a withering look. "If you wish to find me, sir"—oh, and there was a novel idea indeed!—"I shall be in the library. Reading perhaps. Or perhaps *cleaning* it."

She did not wait for his reaction, but spun around and marched away, determined to put some distance between them. Her temper—the temper she'd avowed she did not possess—was unraveling.

An hour in the library did little to calm it. Another hour in her room, and she was still restive. After so many days indoors, she hadn't realized just how much she missed the time spent outside. She needed a little time away from the household; more to the point, time away from *him*. A ride would clear her head. Chafing, she stepped to the window.

The clouds had scuttled onward. What few remained were high and distant.

Her good humor restored, she released a peal of laughter and headed downstairs.

The stables were just a short walk from the manor house. A ruddy-faced youth named Leif emerged when she called a cheery "Hello."

Very soon she left the stables atop a glossy black filly named Lady Jane. She reveled in the sudden feeling of freedom. The air was fresh and invigorating, exactly the release she needed. It felt good to be in the saddle again. She hadn't realized how much she'd missed it. She relaxed, lifting her face to the sky. Not far from the house was a square of lawn, choked with weeds and sadly in need of manicure. She made mental note of it. She guided Lady Jane down the lane that led to the main road, past hedgerows abounding with ferns and foxglove.

The air was pungent with the scent of nature gone wild. The surrounding countryside was both raw and lovely, an ever-changing vista of hills and valley. She could learn to love it here. The thought crept in, taking hold with tenacious vigor. Ah, she thought wistfully, but it wouldn't be wise to grow attached. She reminded herself that her time here was limited. Odd, but she felt almost sad . . .

She rode long and hard. To the north, the moorland lay vast and wild. A lush carpet of heather softened the rocky contours of the land. Captive to the land, to its beauty, she rode on, heedless of all but her pleasure in the day.

At length she reined Lady Jane to a halt atop a grassy hillock. She'd left the house when the air was warm. It was now laden with a damp, heavy stillness. She peered out from beneath the brim of her hat toward the sun.

But there was no sun. The boundary between earth and sky had blurred. Anne twisted around in the saddle. The world had gone eerily still. Then all at once, as if summoned by some unseen mighty hand from far away, the wind stirred, gaining force as it raced across the land. The temperature plunged, in naught but seconds. The sky overhead turned ink-black and eerie. As if they were a living thing, the clouds began to seethe and churn, oozing closer.

Anne's gloved hands tightened on the reins. Simon had warned her. Too caught up in her enjoyment, she hadn't realized how quickly the weather would change.

Thunder rumbled. The darkness and clouds seemed to close in simultaneously. Lady Jane sidestepped nervously. Anne laid a hand on her neck. The filly quieted. She took a fortifying breath. There was no discerning north from south, east from west. But she'd been facing north. Wheeling Lady Jane around, she urged her into a gallop.

She hadn't realized she'd gone so far. Was she going in the right direction? Staving off panic, she uttered a fervent prayer. She pushed Lady Jane onward, but the filly was skittish. A fierce gust ripped her hat from its jaunty perch atop her head. Rain suddenly poured from the sky. And this was no dull gray drizzle. Mother Earth released her rage with a vengeance.

Rain stung her skin like hail, stealing her breath. Her lungs began to burn. It was like riding into a wall of rain. Wind blasted from all directions. She struggled to see.

Then all at once the hairs on the back of her neck rose eerily. A peculiar sensation shot through her, from her fingertips to her hair. Lightning forked across the sky. She was literally blinded, yet instinctively she threw an arm over her eyes. Lady Jane gave a frightened scream and ground to a halt. Anne very nearly vaulted over her head. Leaping down, she braced herself against the buffeting wind, grabbed the reins and struggled forward.

She gasped at the chill. Mud sucked at her dainty kidskin boots. She skidded and slipped. If not for her hold on the reins, she'd have fallen flat on her face. At last she spied the gates, the lane that wound between.

There was a ramshackle building just inside the gates. She'd caught a glimpse of it earlier and had wondered at its dilapidated state. Fighting the buffeting wind, she ducked beneath the eaves, tugging Lady Jane beneath as well.

There was a pile of charred, blackened timbers heaped in the opposite corner. Water gushed through a gaping hole in the roof. Its shelter was questionable, but it was better than braving the open sky.

A nagging little voice in the back of her mind refused to be quieted. Simon had been right. And she'd been gone longer than she anticipated.

It was, she supposed, too much to hope he hadn't noticed.

Ten

God, how I hate the rain!

Simon Blackwell

Shadows stretched across the floor when Simon rose to stretch his legs. He rubbed the crease in his forehead, grimacing a little as he rolled his right shoulder forward and back. It was stiff and ached abominably, a far more accurate prediction of inclement weather than he might have wished for.

The air had turned heavy, cold, and damp. He glanced outside, then wondered why he even bothered. Mist shifted around the treetops, shrouding the distant hills. A steady, leaden rain fell from the sky.

In the entrance hall, a maid was lighting the lamps set into the walls. "You there." He waved a finger. Her name escaped him. He wasn't even sure he'd learned it to begin with, now that there were so many.

She bobbed a curtsy. "Sir?"

"Is your mistress about?"

The girl shook her head. "I've not seen Her Ladyship since early this morning, sir."

Simon wasn't sure he liked the sound of that. He contemplated briefly, then swung around and advanced toward the library.

At some point she—or someone—had been there. The glass had been swept from the floor; the books had been cleared as well. Whether it was today, or some other day, he couldn't tell. He prickled a little, but that was all.

He poked his head inside the drawing room. No sign of her there either. He vaulted up the stairs two at a time, only to grind to a halt outside her room. The urge to throw open the door was strong. It was, after all, his house. Checking the impulse, he knocked.

There was no answer.

He rapped again.

Still no response.

"Anne!" he called loudly.

This time Simon didn't hesitate. He opened the door and glanced inside. The room was empty, but the gown she'd worn earlier lay rumpled on the bed.

A wide-eyed maid hovered on the threshold. He whirled, clutching the gown in his hand.

"Where is Lady Anne?"

"I've not seen her since she left for her ride, sir. Has she not returned?"

Ice ran through his veins. He went very still, but only for an instant. He bolted past her. Just as he reached the foot of the stairs, Duffy appeared.

"I'm going out," Simon said tersely.

"What! In this weather?" Duffy was incredulous.

A sizzle of lightning lit the hall, followed by a violent crack of thunder.

"Anne's out there." The words were ground out.

Duffy went as pale as his master. He alone understood the frantic fear in his master's eyes. He alone understood his master's hatred of rain—and storms. "Oh, no."

"Oh, yes." Simon flung open the door and ran outside.

It was strange the way it happened. He heard a voice calling . . . *her* voice. He saw the horse, trotting through the mists—and then he saw *her*. A bedraggled little figure atop Lady Jane. And for one horrifying instant, he was terrified she wasn't real. That he'd conjured her up from the depths of his mind.

And perhaps he went a little crazy. He couldn't be sane. Not about this.

In the far distant depths of his mind he noticed the rain had stopped. And Anne was laughing. *Laughing.*

"Hello! It appears you were right—"

His control snapped. He was suddenly raging. If he'd had to wed, why couldn't his bride have been a docile, meek-mannered miss who appeared only when he wished. Independent, Anne called herself. God above, it was true! She would challenge him at every turn, try his temper, and test his patience to the limit.

He plucked her from the saddle. "You goddamned little fool."

Anne gaped. She'd been prepared for his censure, prepared for a little needling that he was right after all. It was typical of men in general to adopt such airs of superiority.

But she hadn't expected this particular outburst. Two things struck her. One, this was the first time she'd heard him curse. Two, he wasn't just angry.

He was livid.

She clenched her jaw. "I'll have you know I'm an accomplished horsewoman."

His tone was as blistering as the look he turned on her. "It's not your horsemanship I question, it's your sanity."

Anne flung her head up.

"Your family said you had a talent for landing yourself in trouble. Must you be such a fool?"

Perhaps she hadn't shown the best judgment.

But she'd never admit it in light of his imperious behavior.

"I am not," she stressed, "a fool. And you, sir, can go to bloody hell!"

His eyes narrowed. "A lady," he said dangerously, "does not speak like that."

"Well, this lady does."

With that she stalked inside and made for the stairs. Behind her, Simon was barking out orders. He caught up with her halfway, curling his fingers around her elbow.

Anne tried to yank it back. "I am not in need of your assistance."

"Nonetheless, I shall lend it."

Not until they'd reached her room did he relinquish his hold on her arm.

Simon opened the door. Her chin angled high, Anne marched past him.

It never occurred to her that he would follow. When she turned, it gave her a start to discover he was directly behind her.

Her head tossed. By heaven, she wouldn't retreat. "I don't recall inviting you inside," she stated coolly.

"I don't require an invitation." His gaze flickered over her, his countenance thin-lipped and stony. "Get out of those wet clothes."

Anne felt her jaw drop. "I will not," she gasped.

"You're soaked to the skin."

That, she thought shakily, was not the point

in question. "I'm certainly not disrobing in front of you!"

His smile was rather tight. "Aren't you forgetting I'm your husband?"

Aren't you forgetting I'm your wife? The retort trembled on the tip of her tongue. It was, she decided mutinously, a contentious point.

Audrey, the girl she'd hired as her maid, had come in and pulled out the tub. Not wanting to argue in front of the servants, Anne maintained her silence while the tub was filled and the coal lit in the fireplace.

Simon had crossed to the washstand. Grabbing a towel, he wiped the rain from his face.

Anne remained where she was. What the devil? He displayed no sign of allowing her privacy. She eyed him uncertainly, all at once overwhelmingly conscious that she'd stationed herself near the side of the bed.

The towel was flung aside. "For God's sake," he said irritably, "get into the tub while it's hot. You'll be sick if you don't."

Anne didn't move. She couldn't.

Hiking a brow, he took a single step forward.

"All right! But I can manage on my own, if you please."

"Then please do."

Anne's hands flew to her jacket. She rallied her wits. Turning aside, she fumbled with the silver buttons of her riding jacket.

A valiant effort, but her teeth had begun to

chatter. For the first time she was conscious of a bone-deep chill. Her fingers had gone numb. She struggled to make them comply—she willed them most fervently!

Alas, in vain. She was shaking too badly.

Her fingers were brushed aside. Simon's form blotted out the last wavering light of the day. In shock she felt her jacket peeled from her. She heard it slap wetly to the floor. It was, she noted distantly, quite ruined.

Her frilly white blouse was next. In deference to the heat of the day, she had shunned both corset and camisole. But now the fabric clung wetly to every hill and valley—and in such a way that it was rendered utterly transparent. Aghast, Anne discovered her nipples stood high and taut and clearly visible. Her hands lifted. She sought to tug it away from her skin.

But Simon had already started to work on the buttons, nimble and sure-fingered.

"I can do it," she said breathlessly.

In shock she felt the heel of his hand drag over the very tip of her breast. Anne bit hard into her lip. Her one consolation was that he wasn't looking when it happened. His expression was dark, utterly intense.

The rest of her attire was dispatched with the same impersonal efficiency. A blanket was settled over her shoulders. It was all done in a minimum of time, his manner a trifle brusque, his hands coolly efficient.

But the harm had already been done. Anne was mortified. Simon had seen her naked. *Why do you care?* mocked a voice inside. He had no awareness of her as a woman, despite the searing kiss they'd shared in London.

She couldn't have been more wrong.

She stood there quaking from the cold, waiting for the maid to return with the last bucket of water . . . waiting for *him*. Her eyes were huge, a clear blue ringed with sapphire; eyes that had given him no peace since that day they'd met in Hyde Park.

She couldn't know the icy fear he'd felt when he realized she was gone. She thought it was anger. Ha! he thought bitterly. Then when he saw her . . . Christ! She made him lose his head. And now he was losing his mind.

It had been so long. *Too* long. His blood was pounding, fire burning fitfully in his belly.

He looked down at his hands, clenched so tight his knuckles showed white. It was the only way he could keep from reaching out. He wondered what it would feel like, the press of warm, female flesh against his length . . . what *she* would feel like. A tremor of heat shot through him—no, more than that. A torrent. A torrent that raced along his nerve endings, heightening his awareness until it throbbed in every pore of his body.

Desire raked his insides. Ah, what he wouldn't

give for the chance to undress her once more!—
to reveal that which he had only glimpsed—but
this time with slow, deliberate leisure, that he
might look his fill. He longed to pull her tight
within the cradle of his thighs, that she might
feel what she did to him, the burning rise of desire, taut and full and aching.

He tormented himself. And he tormented
her.

Why did he stay? he asked himself. Would
she stop him? Yes. No. At least she wouldn't
have, he recalled dimly, the night they'd arrived
back at Rosewood. No, not then. But now . . .

Her eyes evaded his. Her gaze settled on his
chin. It almost amused him that she would allow her eyes to stray no higher. He sensed her
uncertainty, glimpsed the shadows that crept
into her eyes, the way she swallowed hard. The
way she clutched that damned blanket like a
shield of iron.

Good God, did she really think he would
ravish her?

"Your bath is growing cold."

He heard the ragged breath she drew. "Turn
your back."

Simon's jaw clamped shut. Their eyes tangled.
Hers were wide and desperate and pleading.

Turning on his heel, he left her to bathe alone.
In the corridor, he heard the splash of water.
Smiling tightly, he made his way downstairs.

A half hour passed before he returned. Perhaps a little more. She'd finished her bath and sat on a low stool before the fire, running a silver-edged brush through her hair. She was barefoot, clad in a white wrapper tied at the waist. A glimpse of lace peeped from beneath as she turned slightly. She stilled, the brush motionless in her hand. Her regard conveyed both surprise and dismay when she saw him. He proceeded as if he hadn't seen it, shutting the door with the heel of his boot and advancing without pause.

Wordlessly he slid the tray he carried onto the round lacquered table beside her. He saw the deep breath she drew; flushing, she set aside the brush. Simon's eyes flickered over her. This was the first time he'd seen her with her hair loose, he realized. It was incredibly long, pouring over her shoulders, swirling past her hips, like sunlight drizzled through honey, amber and topaz and whisky all mingled together.

God, she was sweet. So goddamned beautiful, she made him ache inside.

Wordlessly he pulled a chair adjacent to her stool. A stab of dark humor shot through him. He couldn't decide if she was unnerved or displeased.

Either way, her recovery was admirable. She sat there as if they'd done so every day of their lives. Ah, but if she knew the wild rush of longing that crowded his mind and stirred his blood, would she have been so calm? He had the feeling she'd have bolted from the room, clear from the house.

And this really wasn't wise at all, advised a voice within Simon's head. Why the devil had he returned? He could have sent a servant with the tray. He shouldn't be anywhere near her. Not now. He should have maintained his distance, in heart and body and mind.

And he was still angry about her carelessness, he reminded himself.

None of that seemed to matter just now.

Stretching out his legs, he filled two snifters with brandy, offering one to her. "Drink," he said quietly.

Their fingers did not touch when she took it. Did she intentionally avoid him? he wondered. He found himself abruptly irritated at the thought.

Anne made a face as the brew slid down her throat.

"More," he said.

She coughed, pressing the back of her hand to her mouth. "I do believe you're trying to poison me. First whisky. Now brandy."

Simon forced himself to remain still. A questing restlessness simmered in his veins, though he gave no outward sign of it. He recognized it for what it was—desire. Almost hungrily his eyes fastened on the graceful length of her throat. When she drank, her head tipped high and back, calling attention to the fragile length of her neck. He imagined sliding his fingers beneath the fall of her hair, caressing her nape. The image captivated him. Captured him as surely as the walls of a prison.

And perhaps this prison was meant to be, he thought broodingly. Perhaps it was a prison of his own making . . .

He knew how she would feel. He knew *exactly* how she would feel. Her flesh would be warm, as soft as a babe's, the texture of her hair like spun silk sifting over his knuckles. He imagined pressing his mouth into the hollow of her throat, laying his tongue there at the place where her pulse beat so strongly.

His regard drifted to her mouth. Her lips were ruby-red, hued with the brandy—and damp with it as well.

Every pore in his body tightened with awareness. A slow pulsing seeped throughout his being, like a fist clenching and unclenching in his belly.

He gripped the glass, his fingers fairly burning with the need to reach out. To *touch*.

Simon did not deny the smoldering hunger that seeped along his veins. He did not savor it. He most certainly could not assuage it. Perhaps, he thought dimly, this was his penance, his price—to want her with a searing, blatant need that ripped into his very soul.

Anne proceeded to tuck her bare feet beneath

the hem of her wrapper. A faint smile rimmed his lips, a smile she did not see. There was nothing overtly provocative in either her bearing or her attire. Both nightgown and wrapper were modest. There was certainly nothing to warrant the sharpness of his need . . .

Save the fact that he'd seen her naked. And every womanly curve was burned into his consciousness like a brand.

Anne appeared to have forgotten her earlier unease. Her pose was prim, so at odds with the bent of his thoughts that he almost gave a shout of black laughter. Indeed, she appeared wholly oblivious to the twist of yearning in his gut. Yet why should he expect otherwise? goaded a mocking voice in his brain. He'd made it quite clear he would not assert his husbandly rights.

Yet his body betrayed him. And somehow his acknowledgment only increased tenfold the surge of heat that swelled—and settled—between his thighs. Simon decided it was a good thing he was sitting, else he'd have surely embarrassed them both.

He turned his attention to the tray that sat between them. There was cheese, thick slices of crusty bread and freshly churned butter, and meat pie covered with gravy. Simon filled a plate for her, and one for himself.

Anne nibbled on the bread, partaking rather liberally of her brandy. After a while, Simon noticed her regard had settled on him. She scrutinized him rather closely, her head tipped to the side. She had a habit of that, he'd noticed, when she was considering this possibility and that. It was almost as if he could see the thoughts circling in her mind, one after the other.

"Is there something you wish to say?" he inquired.

"Actually, there is," she declared. "It's quite ridiculous, you know."

"What?" He tasted the meat pie. Delicious.

"The way you avoid me."

The words were a distinct challenge. Simon arched a brow. "Am I avoiding you now?"

"You know you are not." She cast him a frown—or was it a glower? Simon was still debating when she spoke again.

"I would, however, like to ask you something."

"Please do." Simon smothered a smile. He eyed her glass, which was nearly empty. The brandy, he suspected, had nourished her courage and loosened her tongue.

"Very well then. I should like to know if you are always so difficult."

Why, the chit! "I wasn't aware," he said rather stiffly, "that I was."

"Well, you are," she announced. "I think you go to great lengths to avoid me. I think you want me to think you difficult. Indeed, I think you *want* me to dislike you."

Simon said nothing. Perhaps he did. Perhaps she would.

"You're wrong," he said shortly.

"Am I?"

"Yes, go—" *Goddamn it.* He clamped off the word just in time.

He began anew. "I don't avoid you," he lied. "I certainly don't dislike you." That, at least, was the truth. "If such were the case, I wouldn't have been so concerned when I discovered you'd gone out in the storm." *Against my wishes*, he almost reminded her, then thought better of it.

"Well, you needn't have been," came her hearty rejoinder.

Simon watched as she took another healthy swallow of brandy. He was sorely tempted to pluck the glass from her grasp. Ah, but no doubt she'd have called him difficult.

"I was frantic, Anne." His voice was very quiet.

"Rubbish!" She vehemently declared her opinion.

"Oh, but I was." His tone relayed the gravity of the statement. "Promise me you won't do such a foolish thing again."

He'd startled her, he realized. She blinked, as if perplexed. She gave a little shake of her head.

"Simon"—she spoke his name—"I was fine. You needn't have worried. Truly. I took shelter throughout most of the storm."

He frowned. "Where?"

"The building just inside the gates. I waited there until the worst of the storm was over."

He sucked in a breath. "The carriage house?" he asked sharply.

"Is that what it is? I'm not sure. But there was once a fire there, I think." Her eyes fixed earnestly on his.

For the space of a heartbeat, Simon couldn't breathe. He couldn't think. He certainly couldn't speak. Everything inside him rushed into a dark void.

"Good Lord," he said sharply. "Do you how dangerous it is? Surely you saw that the roof has caved in."

"Yes, yes, I saw that. But if it's dangerous, why don't you have it razed? Or rebuilt? If someone could get hurt, would it not be best to—"

Some strange, raw emotion seized hold of him. He could stand no more. He could *listen* no more.

He laid down his fork. He folded his napkin into a neat, precise square—it was the only way he could steady his hands.

Anne had broken off and was staring at him.

Pushing his chair back, he got to his feet. Bemused, she looked at him.

"Simon? Is something wrong?"

He heard the confusion in her tone. He sensed her dismay. But he couldn't answer her. He couldn't even look at her! Damn him for being a coward. Damn him for being a cur. But everything inside had suddenly twisted into a stranglehold.

"I must beg your pardon." He gave her a stiff bow. "I fear I've lost my appetite."

Without a backward glance, he strode from the room.

Eleven

It's foolish, I suppose, to continue this journal.
Yet I know I will.

Simon Blackwell

It was late when Anne awoke the next morning, bleary-eyed and as tired as when she'd crawled into bed last night. Her temples were pounding—the brandy she'd consumed last night? Or her husband? No doubt, she decided, a little of both.

A glance through the window did little to improve her frame of mind. The day was dismal and gray. Ominous clouds huddled on the horizon, foretelling the possibility that yesterday's downpour might reappear.

Sleep had proved elusive last night. She knew

that Simon hadn't slept well either. It was near dawn when she'd heard the creak of his door, the echo of footsteps in the room that adjoined hers. Not that it was so unusual. Since her arrival at Rosewood Manor, nearly every night she'd heard the floorboards creaking in his room, long after midnight.

Not for the first time, she wondered what kept him from his rest. A mistress perhaps? No. She didn't know how she knew it, but she did.

He'd left the house early this morning. Anne heard the whinny of a horse shortly after dawn. Rising, she went to the window and peered outside just as Simon set his heel to his mount and galloped away.

It was nearly ten when she made her way downstairs. She wasn't surprised that Simon didn't join her, given the lateness of the hour. But when he didn't appear at luncheon, she glared her displeasure at the empty head of the table where he should have sat.

Hearing a rustle at the doorway, she glanced up sharply. But it was only Duffy.

"Good afternoon, mum."

"Good afternoon, Duffy." She offered a warm smile. "I've not yet seen Simon today. I was just thinking that perhaps I should have Mrs. Wilder wait luncheon."

Duffy's answering smile vanished. A faint consternation replaced it.

"The master had business with his tenants

this morning. It appears he's been delayed."

Despite the hastiness of his response, Anne had the distinct sensation he hadn't known what to say.

She inclined her head. "Yes," she said pleasantly, "so it does."

"Shall I tell him you wish to see him, my lady?"

"No, thank you, Duffy. There's no need."

"Good day then, mum."

Anne took a breath. "Good day, Duffy."

She didn't blame him for his master's faults. But it wasn't right that he should have to offer excuses for his master. Far better to take it up with Simon.

It gave her a jolt to realize she'd been twisting her wedding ring in her lap, over and over. All at once it felt oppressively heavy.

It was probably a good thing he was absent, Anne reflected crossly. If he had been present, she would surely have strangled him. The man could starve, she decided rebelliously, for all she cared. In fact, given the foulness of her mood today, she rather hoped he would.

She was reading in the drawing room when she heard footsteps in the entrance hall. It was he—she recognized the rhythm of his gait. The footsteps stopped. She heard his deep baritone and a feminine voice that belonged to the housekeeper. She couldn't make out the words. Raising her head, she glanced toward the doorway, holding her breath expectantly.

Oh, but a foolish notion that was! The sound of his steps dwindled away. He was either in his study or in his chamber. What a fool she was to think he would seek her out!

His neglect—no, his utter disregard for her— cut to the bone. Bitterly she told herself she need not trouble herself with him, just as he refused to trouble himself with her.

She was on her feet in a heartbeat. She needed air. She needed *out*. God, if she stayed indoors another instant, she would surely smother. Throwing open the terrace doors, she stepped outside.

As if on cue, the drizzle of rain ceased. A watery sunshine began to shine through the clouds. Anne strolled the length of the house, her footsteps taking no particular direction.

There was a garden just off the south flank of the house, enclosed on three sides by a low stone wall. She found herself following the footpath. A bird flew out of a thicket, startling her from her reverie.

Anne glanced around. The crickets renewed their cheery chirp. A butterfly weaved and fluttered high and away. A bee whizzed by her ear. A smile curved her lips, the first genuine smile of the day. Raindrops glistened and sparkled like jewels. The air was heavy and moist, laden thick with the smell of damp, pungent earth and a fragrant richness. Moss and ferns grew beneath the shade of the north wall, still wet with the recent shower of rain.

On the opposite end was a zigzag row of rose bushes.

Anne had never been particularly fond of formal, exquisitely manicured gardens. There was something to be admired about the order of nature, the swirling fall of leaves from the trees, the nurturing sleep of winter, and fresh shoots bursting through the soil in spring.

But this was Mother Earth gone somewhat awry, a shame really, for this was a garden that could be quite lovely, a peaceful haven in which to bask. She fixed an eye on the roses. In the center were three bushes of pale, creamy white blossoms. Lovely as they were, they looked rather lonely sitting behind the rest. As for the others, the branches twisted and twined and vied with one another, as if doing battle.

Anne placed a finger on the center of her chin and considered. How much more attractive, she mused, if those three lonely white bushes were brought forward and set between the vibrant blush of the red.

A gardener really should be employed, she thought. Why was she not surprised?

It took but a moment's consideration. Why wait for a gardener? Indeed, why wait at all?

Hurrying inside, she borrowed an apron and

gloves from a maid in the kitchen. On her way back, she stopped at the gardener's shed just behind the wall and retrieved a small spade and pail, then set out briskly for the garden once more.

Duffy encountered his new lady just as she emerged from the kitchens.

"My lady!" He had to stop himself from gaping in astonishment. An apron tied loosely over her gown, her bonnet askew, she looked so young and vivacious, his heart nearly stopped. And judging from her gay smile, her temperament was much improved since luncheon.

"Oh, hello, Duffy!"

"My lady, the master has returned. Shall I tell him you wish to see him?"

She wrinkled her nose. "I think not," she said.

He stared. "My lady?"

"There's no need, Duffy. I shall be engaged elsewhere for a while. However, if he wishes to know where I am, I shall be in the garden."

"The garden?"

"Yes," she returned gaily. "Have you been there of late? It's dreadfully in need of tending, you know."

Duffy gulped. "My lady, perhaps you should—"

"I know what you're thinking, Duffy, and it's quite generous of you. But I don't need any help. Truly. I'm quite capable of moving a few rose bushes on my own. The earth is quite soft, particularly after this rain." She laughed breezily. "Carry on, if you please, and so shall I!"

Duffy's eyes widened as she sailed outside. *No*, he thought. *Oh, no . . .*

With heavy heart, he made his way to the master's study. He rapped lightly on the door, then stepped inside.

"Sir?"

The master looked up from his desk. "Yes?"

Duffy hesitated. He disliked being the bearer of tales. He particularly disliked telling tales on the new mistress of Rosewood. He liked her— nay, he'd grown to love her, for already she had brought light and warmth to a place that had seen only shadows and darkness for far too long . . .

If only his master could see it. If only he would allow himself to see *her*!

But it was not his place to judge. And oh! but he had no choice to do what he was about to do.

"Her Ladyship, sir. She is . . ."

"She's what? Speak up, man."

"She's in the garden, sir." He gulped. "There." He pointed to the windows.

The master's eyes followed his finger, where a figure had just breezed down the footpath.

"She . . . she   said . . . something   about . . . moving the roses, sir."

The master was already on his feet and

wheeling about the corner of his desk. A blistering curse seared the air.

Duffy's shoulders sagged. Fiercely he berated himself. He was a traitor. And he could only hope his new lady would forgive him—

And that she would understand.

"What the devil are you doing?"

Anne jumped at the voice booming above her. It resounded in every pore of her body, much like the thunder that had roared across the earth yesterday.

Hauling in a steady, calming breath, she blew aside a wisp of hair that had fallen across her brow and regarded her husband.

What the devil was *he* doing? she thought irritably. He looked a madman, every bit as ominous as yesterday's storm. Dropping the pruning shears next to the largest of the three ivory rose bushes, she sat back on her heels. She would not lose her temper. She would *not*.

"I should think it would be obvious," she stated coolly. "I'm clearing the garden." She dusted off her hands. "I do believe that rose belongs over there." She pointed. "The white would look so much prettier against the red. Besides, just look at it—why, it's so atrociously overgrown it looks perfectly horrid—"

"Do not cut it. Do not move it. Do not touch it."

Strong hands caught her beneath the elbows and dragged her upright.

Anne yanked away. "What!" she cried, incensed. "Leave me be, Simon! I'm tired of your rules. I'm tired of your moods. Do not go here. Do not go there. I'm tired of being told where I can and cannot go. I *won't* be told what I can and cannot do."

His eyes fairly sizzled. "Hear me, Anne. You will not cut it. You will not move it. You will not touch it."

His speech heated her temper, like flame to tinder. "And why not?" she cried. "Why can't I move it? Why can't I touch it? Or any other one I please?"

The look he turned on her was utterly fierce. "Because my wife is buried there. My wife— and my boys."

 *Twelve*

If only I'd never lit the candle.

Simon Blackwell

A splinter of shock tore through her. Scalded inside, stricken, Anne nearly stumbled back beneath the onslaught of his gaze.

His statement stopped her cold. The ground seemed to cave away beneath her feet. Fraught with confusion, doubt swelled, then receded like the ebbing of the tide. No, she thought. She was mistaken. She couldn't possibly have heard him right.

The moment of weakness passed. She flung up her chin, fixing him with a blistering stare.

"I do believe you've taken leave of your senses. I am your wife, Simon. *I* am your wife.

However much you dislike it. However much you did not wish it . . ."

Her voice trailed away, for he didn't say anything. He just stood there, his features closed and taut. The very air between them seemed to thunder and pulse.

Then his eyes flickered. Something sped across his face. Something that made her face go bloodless. Her brain scrambled, as if to take hold of what he'd just said. Her mind still rebelled, but her heart . . .

Her gaze climbed high, colliding with his. She stared at him, stared until her eyes were glazed and tear-bright, her insides twisted into a sick knot.

"My God," she said, her voice half stifled. She pressed tremulous fingers against her mouth. "My God! Do you mean to say that you—"

"Yes. *Yes.*"

Her mind balked. It was beyond comprehension. She couldn't move, she couldn't even breathe. Scalded by his harshness, she struggled for composure.

"Damn you," she said unevenly. "Damn you!"

Hot, burning shame washed over her; in its wake surged a biting fury. She reacted without thought or care. Her hand shot out. She slapped him. She slapped him as hard as she could, relishing the sting of her palm across his cheek, the white mark on his skin.

His lips thinned, but he said nothing.

"Does Alec know?"

"Yes." His tone was curt.

"You told my brother and not me?" Incredulous, she longed to slap him again!

It was as if a shade had been drawn over his eyes. His eyes revealed nothing of his thoughts. "I told him I would handle it. I felt it was something you should learn from me."

"Did you now! And when—exactly—did you plan on telling me?"

A dull red flush crept up his neck.

Anne was sick, sick to every corner of her heart, clear to the depths of her soul. "Is this why you shut me out? Is this why you hate me?"

"Don't be absurd."

An almost hysterical laughter bubbled up inside her. "You bastard!" she burst out. "When did they die?"

Silence lapsed, a silence that was never-ending. "Five years ago," he said finally.

"How?" She shook her head. "Were they sick? Ill?"

A muscle jumped in his cheek. "No."

"How then?"

"I will answer your questions, Anne. But not here. Not now."

She sensed the darkness in his mood, the darkness in his heart. She didn't care. Anger vanquished all caution.

"No!" she said wildly. "I deserve to know. It's my right to know—"

"What must I do, Anne? Beg? Plead?" He spread wide his hands. "I will. Indeed, it seems I must. I beg of you, not now!" He didn't wait for an answer but swung away.

Her mind recorded the square set of his shoulders, the rigid lines of his back. By now he'd reached the edge of the garden.

Anne had gone rigid. Helpless fury burned inside her. Damn him, she thought raggedly. Damn him to hell!

"Simon!" she almost screamed. "Simon!"

If he heard, he gave no sign of it. The lines of his back were rigidly immobile. He did what he was so adept at doing.

He walked away.

Anne didn't go down to dinner. Audrey, her maid, brought her a supper tray. Anne refused it. The thought of food made her physically ill.

A knock sounded a short time later. She pretended she didn't hear.

The door swung wide. Simon stepped inside.

Anne huddled on the window seat, her knees drawn tight to her chest. Outside a heavy gray drizzle had begun to fall.

When she saw who her visitor was, her lips thinned into a straight line. Deliberately she averted her face.

"Go away," she said coldly.

He didn't. She could hear his soft footfalls on the carpet.

She looked at him, her eyes ablaze. "Didn't you hear? I don't want you here. I don't want to see you. Surely you understand when someone says they wish to be alone!" She took a certain relish in hurling his own words back at him. Ah, but it was bravado, sheer and simple. Inside, Anne's composure dangled by a thread.

He stopped before her.

"Very well then," she announced. "It appears I shall have to go elsewhere." She tugged at her skirts, swinging her legs to the floor.

Simon studied her. "Anne, I know that you—"

"No!" she burst out. "You don't know. You don't know anything! You know nothing of me! What I think, what I want, what I feel! What my favorite color is, whether I prefer coffee or tea—"

"Tea. Two lumps of sugar, an ample dollop of cream."

She was so outraged, so indignant, her color was as high as the angle of her chin. And somehow, Simon just couldn't help it. He simply could not.

One side of his mouth curled up in a glimmer of a smile.

"Och, don't you dare laugh at me!"

"Your Scots is showing, Anne."

She shot up from the cushions. But Simon was there before her, strong hands curling around her shoulders.

She tried to push her way past him. He wouldn't let her. She was ever moving. Ever changing. So passionate. So full of life. Like the color of her eyes, he thought, changing with the light, with her moods. So damned expressive. *Too* damned expressive.

She wasn't one to hide what was in her mind, her heart. Her anguish lay nakedly vivid, her eyes shadowed and dark and shimmering with tears.

"Anne," he said softly. "*Anne.*"

She burst into great, wrenching sobs.

Her desolation caught at his insides. His conscience stabbed at him. Some nameless emotion surged in his breast. He couldn't have turned his back on her if the world had stopped spinning this very moment. And he didn't. His arms crept around her, bringing her close. He held her shaking body tight against his form, her head notched beneath his chin, aware of her tears seeping into the hollow of his throat.

What was he to say? How could he explain? He deserved her wrath, not her understanding. He deserved her rage, not her compassion. The words had slipped out unthinkingly, before he could catch them, before he could stop them.

She should never have learned about Ellie and the boys in such a manner. The blame was solely his. Lord, but he was a fool!

His mouth rested on the baby-soft skin of her temple. Her hands lay coiled against his chest. She was leaning against him. He wondered fleetingly if she was even aware of it.

"Forgive me, Anne. I should never have said what I did."

He drew back, his eyes roving her face. Tears glistened on the ends of her lashes.

Framing her face in his hands, he skimmed the dampness from her cheeks, running his thumb across the fullness of her lower lip.

He pulled her tight against him once more. "Christ, I've been an ass," he muttered.

"An astute observation." Her tone was muffled against the front of his shirt. Simon knew the exact moment she recaptured her control. He felt the deep, jagged breath she drew. Soft, plump breasts brushed against his chest as she inhaled, then exhaled. His belly tightened. He put it from his mind, for that was dangerous territory where neither his mind—nor his hands!—dared trespass.

Slowly, she drew back. Her eyes caught his.

"Simon," she said, a slight quaver in her tone, "I swear I do not mean to make you hurt. But there's so much I don't understand. So much I don't know. So much I *need* to know." She hesitated, then laid a tentative hand on his forearm. "Your wife, Simon." She gave a tiny little shake of her head. "I—I don't even know her name."

Simon went utterly still inside. Her eyes sought his, wide and liquid, her regard unwavering. He recognized it for what it was, an entreaty.

His gaze shifted to the small, white hand curled beseechingly on his sleeve, then slid back to her face. A vague sense of unreality slipped over him, a weary bleakness. Very gently, he disengaged himself, moving to stand before the window, where he stared out into the thin curtain of mist.

He did not turn. "Eleanor," he said finally. "I called her Ellie."

He sensed Anne's nearness, even before he saw her from the corner of his eye. She stood to his left, hovering less than a step away.

"And your sons? There were two?"

The pitch of his voice was very low. "Joshua was the elder. He was four."

"And the younger?"

Emotion tightened his entire body. He fought a halfhearted battle against it, only to give in, for what was the use?

His hand lifted to the window. Slowly his fingers splayed wide against the foggy pane.

A sad, aching remnant of a smile touched his lips.

"Jack," he said softly. "His name was Jack."

Anne stared at him. A half-formed suspicion spun through her mind. She sucked in a startled breath. Oh, but it was all beginning to make sense. To fall into place . . .

Anne had no conscious recollection of moving. One moment she was behind him, the next beside him. She longed to touch him, but somehow she didn't quite dare.

"Tell me what happened," she said quietly.

Silence drifted. For the longest time, he said nothing. His eyes grazed hers, then slid away.

"The day of your arrival," he said. "Do you recall the manuscript pages you found in the library?"

As if she could ever forget! "You're a collector?"

"I was," he corrected. "From a very young age my parents instilled in me a love of all things written. When I was seven, my father gave me my first journal. I wrote in it daily. Quite faithfully, especially for one so young. My father had a small collection—I began my own a year later, when my mother gave me a diary penned by a general in the war against the Colonies. By the time I was in my twenties, my collection was rather extensive. Prose, poetry, books in Latin, Greek, Anglo-Saxon. It was quite varied, actually—correspondence, a vicar's sermons, personal memoirs, even a book of magical spells. I was quite passionate about it. To me they were implements of history, the chance to learn about the characters and attitude of our predecessors and the world in which they lived.

It was a love I hoped to pass on to my children."

There was a faraway look in his eyes. It was almost as if she could see him slipping back through the pages of time.

"It was clear that Joshua would ever be the more studious of the boys. On his bureau was a book of rhymes. Every night when he climbed into bed, he insisted that Ellie or I read to him. He would not sleep until we did."

Ellie. There was no question he'd loved her deeply. There was a resonance, a tenderness in the way he said her name.

"Joshua recited each and every rhyme by heart. He'd even begun to read a little—and he had only just turned four."

"And Jack? What was he like?"

There was a heartbeat of silence. Something painfully acute sped across his features, something that made her throat constrict.

"Jack was a year younger than Joshua," Simon said slowly. "He was . . . oh, I don't mean to sound trite! but Jack was the happiest child in the world. He rarely cried, even as an infant. And Ellie always used to say that he did not smile, he beamed. I swear, it was true! He was always moving, always exploring." He paused, then said quietly, "They were beautiful little boys."

"I can only imagine," Anne murmured. Vivid in her mind was a family bound by love and laughter and life, much like her own. And she couldn't help but think of Caro and John, Jack and Izzie.

"You mentioned your collection," she said.

He nodded. "I'd just purchased the last, final pages from an illuminated manuscript, a fourteenth-century Gospel. I'd been trying to track it down for several years. I even made the trip to Ireland, to the monastery where it was completed. The workmanship was unlike anything else in my collection. We'd gone to the village to fetch it—the vicar had collected it for me when he was in London. I remember holding the pages in my hand, basking in my good fortune. The vellum was so fragile, yet the colors were so vibrant. Hundreds of years old, and it was mine, my most valued—and valuable—acquisition to date.

"It was my intent to wait until the next day to fetch it. I couldn't. I was eager to see it, so we left home in the afternoon. We stayed for supper with the vicar, so it was early evening when we set out again for Rosewood. Ellie wanted to take the barouche, for it was the warmest day of spring thus far in the year, and so we did. She was laughing when we left the church. She had the most wonderful laugh, full and pure and sweet. 'I suppose you're feeling rather pleased with yourself,' she said.

"And I was. It was such a glorious day. Life was good. Life was more than good, I thought.

God had granted us two sons thus far, strong, sturdy boys I was certain would grow tall and hale and hearty. I was ecstatic over my find; my precious pages were safely stowed in a satchel tucked under the seat. Joshua and Jack were playing in the back of the barouche. The weather was divine. Oh, there were a few clouds when we left the village. Nothing to be troubled about, I assured myself."

There was a spatter of rain against the window. Simon's eyes were fixed on some far distant point. Anne was aware of the long, deep breath that Simon took.

"We turned onto the road that climbed from the village. Thunderheads began to creep in from the north. I urged the horses onward a little faster. At the top of the hill, Ellie glimpsed my frown. I didn't want to worry her. I assured her we'd be home long before the storm hit."

"But you weren't?" Anne guessed.

"No," he said very quietly. "It approached at an alarming rate. Ellie had gathered the boys around her. She sang to them, so they wouldn't be afraid. The sun"—he shook his head—"it seemed to vanish in a heartbeat. The clouds closed in . . . so very quickly! Ellie and the boys were shivering. A stinging wind had begun to blast. By then we were racing, racing the clouds, racing the wind. The bank of clouds swirled, almost directly overhead. There was a huge flash of lightning. Ellie jumped. Joshua saw it. His eyes were huge. And Jack . . . Though he was younger, he was fearless. He wasn't even frightened."

Listening to him, knowing they were gone, Anne felt her chest began to tighten.

Simon continued. "The storm seemed to come out of nowhere. The sky had turned a queer, sickly color. I'd seen such skies before. I'd seen such storms before, terrible storms. I wanted Ellie and the boys out of harm's way, so we stopped at the carriage house."

A prickle of foreboding shot through her.

"The wind was buffeting the doors so that it was a struggle to even get Ellie and the boys inside. The minute we were, Jack dashed off to hide beneath a wagon. I was vexed. When I caught him, I scolded him quite severely and told him it wasn't a game. He was squirming as we went into the attic upstairs—but that was Jack. Never still, never quiet. The attic was dirty and dusty, but there was a table and chairs where we could sit and wait out the storm.

"I'd grabbed the satchel when we left the barouche. The shutters were closed, so it was rather gloomy. I lit a candle and set it on the table, along with the satchel. Just then there was a tremendous crack of thunder. The floor shook beneath our feet. Joshua began to wail. Ellie tried to soothe him. 'Don't cry, sweeting,' she said. I rumpled his hair and teased him. 'The angels in heaven are having a bit of a ruckus,' I said."

A shadow seemed to slip over Simon then. "I looked over my shoulder. Jack, I saw, had gotten hold of the satchel. He was such a scamp, ever the mischief maker . . . He sat on the floor, busily plucking out gilt-edged manuscript pages, one after the other. I berated him again, but Jack had a mind of his own. He paid no heed. I started toward him and he finally dropped the satchel. More pages spilled out, all around his feet now. I lost patience then. I—I yelled, I think. I remember Ellie looking at me, startled. And then Jack. He climbed to his feet, grasping the edge of the table to pull himself up. And then—"

Anne sucked in a breath.

"The candle toppled to the floor. Jack stared up at me, his eyes wide. I—I yelled at him again. I'm not sure. And then I saw my manuscript— the pages that were still on the floor—catch fire. I snatched up Jack and stomped out the flames. And then the door burst open. It was Duffy. He'd seen us and came to help with the horses. But the storm had spooked them. They'd bolted."

Silence descended.

"I still held Jack," Simon said at last. "Whirling around, I set him in the chair beside Ellie. 'Do not move,' I told him sternly—too sternly, for my mind was on my manuscript pages and I didn't want him touching them again. I didn't want them damaged. There was anger in my eyes . . . my voice . . . 'Do not move until I get back,' I said."

Simon closed his eyes for a moment, as if trying to shut out the past. He stared past Anne's shoulder, his eyes filled with such haunting despair, she nearly cried out.

"I could see the hurt in his little face. His lip was quivering. 'Papa,' he cried, lifting his arms to me. *'Papa.'*

" 'Be still!' I told him. 'Be still and do not move!' I—I was shouting, I think." Simon shoved a hand through his hair. "Jack started to cry. I didn't care. I was too furious with him."

Anne's gaze was riveted to his face. There was an awful tension strung throughout his body. How she longed to touch him, to wrap her arms around him and take away his pain. If only she could!

"Duffy and I gave chase to the top of the hill. Suddenly I stopped. I-I'll never know quite why. But all at once I had the oddest sensation. It was strange the way it happened . . . So many images. So many sounds. The charging of the horses, the rush of my breath pounding in my ears, the thunder . . . I turned and looked at the carriage house. And then I saw it . . ."

A terrible dread crowded Anne's throat. She

could only stare at him. Ice ran through her veins. A horrifying sense of inevitability swept over her. No. No, it could not be—

"Something drifted over the roof. I remember staring at it stupidly. I thought it was fog." His voice had plunged so that she had to strain to hear. "I didn't realize it was smoke until I saw the flames shooting out the windows."

The rigorous hold on his emotions began to crumble.

Anne was being given a glimpse into the window of his past. But it hurt to watch him. It hurt to listen. Her eyes were swimming so that she could barely see.

"I ran . . . ran like a madman, but there was no sign of Ellie and the boys. I'll never forget . . . it was then the rain began. Too little. Too late." His voice grew hoarse. "I couldn't open the door. I tried, but . . . I realized then that Ellie and the boys were trapped. Trapped and helpless . . ."

In the window, Anne could see the reflection of his face. Drawn. Tired. So angry.

So very anguished.

"Oh, that it had been me rather than them!" He slapped a hand against the wall next to the window. "I finally kicked the door open . . . But I couldn't see. There was so much smoke, and then something struck me. Part of the ceiling, I think. It knocked me down, but I got up. I kept shouting. Shouting for Ellie. For Joshua. For

Jack." Facing Anne again, he took a deep, jagged breath. "I swear I could hear them. I swear I could! But—I couldn't reach them. I couldn't save them."

His expression nearly rent her heart in two. His torment lay mired in every word.

"I'll never forgive myself. I failed them. Ellie and Joshua. And Jack. Oh, God, Jack . . . I'll never forget . . . The last time I saw him, he was crying. Holding out his hands to me. Christ, I was so harsh. I made him cry. I made my boy cry. And Jack never cried. He never cried . . ."

There was a heartrending silence. And then he whispered:

"If only I'd never lit the candle . . . *If only I'd never lit the candle.*"

Thirteen

The nights continue to plague me. Now more than ever.

Simon Blackwell

The muscles in her throat had closed so that she could barely speak. Her heart wrenched. Anne didn't stop to think. She didn't pause to consider. She simply did what everything inside compelled her to do. She wound her arms around his waist and clung.

"I'm sorry, Simon. I'm so terribly, terribly sorry."

The words seemed so inadequate! Yet she didn't know what else to say.

She had startled him. She knew it from the

way he suddenly froze. Twisting slightly, he peered down at her.

Something nearly broke inside her at the gentleness of his gaze. She was perilously near tears. She couldn't say any more.

He whispered her name. His arms stole around her, with an almost painstaking slowness.

"I'm all right, Anne."

But he wasn't. That long-ago night still haunted him. Never did it leave him, never for a moment. It lay beneath his skin, a thorn that forever pricked, every hour, every day. A sharp, rending pain pierced her breast. She could not bear it. Yet if she could not, how could he? *How could he?*

But, oh!—that he should seek to comfort her! She could have wept all over again.

For she suddenly understood all that she had not.

The day in Hyde Park when she and Caro had been walking with Izzie and Jack—the day they'd met, the way he'd lashed into her after he snatched up Jack.

His reluctance to hold Jack that very same evening, that splinter of something she'd never quite been able to decipher.

His neglect of Rosewood. The shambles in the library, his dictate that she leave it as is.

His anger yesterday when she'd disregarded

his wishes and ventured out in the storm. The look on his face when he saw her, a look she recognized now as blind, sheer panic.

She hadn't understood any of it. She hadn't understood *him*.

Now she did.

When Ellie, Joshua, and Jack had died, the pages of his life had stopped turning. He had shut himself off, shut himself away to ward off the pain.

Oh, but she had been so wrong about him! He wasn't cold. He wasn't unfeeling. He was simply a man who bore on his shoulders a weight that no one should ever have to carry.

Caro had thought that he was lonely.

But he needn't be alone any longer. He had her . . . whether he knew it or not. Whether he *wanted* her or not.

Even if it was only for a year.

Squeezing her eyes shut, she laid her cheek against the soft linen of his shirt. A huge lump had settled in her throat. She couldn't have gotten a word around it if she'd wanted to. And all at once, his nearness had an unpredictable effect. A tremor tore through her. She wasn't prepared for the stark, sudden yearning that swamped all through her; it swept over her like the raging of a storm, so intense that for one paralyzing moment, she could not breathe. And when she could, her breathing came in a desperate, labored rush.

Her pulse knocked wildly. Did Simon hear? Did he *know*?

If he did, there was no sign of it. He didn't move. He simply held her—a feeling that suddenly wrought as much pain as pleasure.

She swallowed a pang when he finally eased away, for she hated that it should end! A torrent of longing shot through her. She could have stayed like that endlessly, locked in the warm protection of his hold. She wanted desperately for him to reach for her once more. But not in comfort this time. This time with fever and fire, with passion and promise . . .

Oh, but it was futile to wish for things she knew could never be. As futile as wishing on stars.

Fighting to quell the clamoring of her heart, Anne smothered a sigh. It gave her a start to see Simon's regard fixed on her intently. Her mouth went dry, her gaze tangling helplessly with his.

With one hand he skimmed his knuckles over her cheek, a touch so unbearably gentle, it tied her insides in knots.

"Are you all right?"

Anne felt herself nod shakily.

He would have stepped back, but Anne took a deep breath. "Wait," she said.

He looked at her questioningly.

She clasped her hands before her, grateful for the shadows that hid her burning cheeks. She was trembling inside. "The terms of our marriage have been set out," she said, the pitch of her voice very low. "I—I understand that you do not want me in your bed. I understand that you do not want me as—as mother of your children. But we must live together for the next year, Simon. And . . . we need not be enemies."

She hadn't known she was going to say it until she did. Now that she had, well, she didn't regret it.

There was a rush of silence. "It was never my intention to make you feel unwelcome, Anne. But I have, haven't I?"

Now it was Anne who hesitated. She could feel the weight of his gaze.

"Yes," he said slowly. "I see that I have."

"It's been difficult," she admitted.

A ghost of a smile rimmed his lips. "You need not spare me, Anne. *I* have been difficult. Indeed, I've been quite intolerable, haven't I?"

Anne wasn't quite sure what to say.

His smile faded. "I should like it"—he appeared to choose his words very carefully—"if you would forgive me."

Oh, God. *God!* How could she not?

"I . . . of course." She felt suddenly lame.

"I shall endeavor to do better, I promise. But you must make a promise too."

Anne blinked.

"If I am, you must tell me."

She bit her lip. "Simon—"

One dark brow climbed a fraction.

"Very well then." The words tumbled out in a rush. " 'Tis a promise."

"Excellent," he murmured.

He shocked her then, for she expected him to leave.

He didn't. Instead he stepped close, so close she sucked in a breath. Both the movement and his nearness caught her off guard.

His knuckles curled beneath her chin—and with the slightest pressure, he tilted her face to his.

Her eyes locked helplessly on his. Something lurked in his eyes, something that made her heart trip crazily. A tiny little jolt shot through her, an arrow of fire. For one mind-shattering moment, she wondered if he meant to kiss her. At the prospect, a perilous curl of heat gathered in her midsection.

But all he did was sweep his thumb across the fullness of her lip. Was she relieved? Or was she disappointed?

Then it was gone, as suddenly as it appeared.

"Good night, Anne." Leaning forward, he brushed his mouth against her forehead, the merest breath of air. "Sleep well."

The contact was brief, fleeting—and chaste. So very chaste.

Slowly she let out her breath, unaware she'd

been holding it. Long after Simon had gone, she stood frozen to the spot, trying desperately to still the irrational fluttering of her pulse. Perhaps it was madness. Perhaps *she* was mad. Her mind spun, like the wind across the moors. For the chaste kiss he'd delivered was not the sort of kiss that she suddenly longed for!

She wanted more. Much, much more.

But she hadn't conjured up that intense look on Simon's features in that instant when he touched her. She hadn't imagined it. But what *was* it? Fondness? Affection? No. *No.* It was more than that. She could feel it in every corner of her soul.

And in that moment, Anne took heart.

If Simon's mood was unsettled that night, he couldn't help it. He sat in his study, swirling the whisky in his glass. Strangely, there was no shame at all that he'd divulged to Anne. It wasn't that he was relieved. It simply *was*, and there was no more consideration beyond that.

No, it wasn't that which compelled his reach for another glass of whisky. It was his conscience. It besieged him, battered him as never before. It gnawed like a blight upon his soul. A restless stirring quested inside him, like the swirling of winds gaining power and might before the onslaught of a storm.

He disliked knowing he was such a beast. He

disliked knowing what his lovely wife thought of him! He'd changed, he realized darkly. He'd changed far more than he cared to admit!

His mood grew vile. A bitter ache settled over him. And to think he'd once been a man of utmost patience. He was lucky. Lucky that the lovely Anne had deigned to forgive him.

The minutes sped into an hour. Another glass of whisky burned down his throat, downed in a fiery gulp. Yet another.

What was it she possessed? he pondered. Yes, she was a beauty. But Ellie had been just as beautiful. And Anne was fiery, even contentious—at least with him! Not that he could blame her, he allowed. She filled his mind, in a way he did not welcome. In a way he'd thought would never happen. Never again in this life. Never again in this world.

His gaze strayed toward the ceiling, again and again.

Anne's chamber lay directly above his study.

Near dawn, he finally stumbled up the stairs.

Fired by drink, fueled by desire, he halted just outside her door.

He was gripped by a longing he could not control; there was simply no help for it. Conscious thought was lost. Simon did not care. His thoughts roamed unfettered. Did she sleep naked? he wondered. No, not Anne. Anne would be wearing a fine lace night rail. And if she were to rise—if the light of the fire were behind her, perhaps—every sweet, luscious curve of her body would be revealed. As if she *were* naked.

His fingers curled around the polished brass handle. He had to see her. He had to *know*.

Before he could stop himself, he stood above her.

His gaze slid over her. Her hair tumbled across the pillow, a temptation such as he had never known. His jaw bunched hard, but his gaze roved at will, lingering as long as he willed, wher*ever* he willed. He gave a fervent prayer of thanks, for he was not to be dissuaded. He was not to be dismissed.

She lay on her back, the covers rumpled over her breasts. Alas, she wasn't naked. But the wide neckline of her night rail had slipped low, revealing the slope of one bare, silken shoulder.

Her head was angled in such a way that it bared the slim length of her throat, which had always harbored such strange fascination for him. The compulsion to touch her was nigh uncontrollable. Simon battled it, though he longed to trace the slivers of her brows, the contours of her cheeks. But most of all he wanted to twine his fingers in the cloth of her night rail and drag it down—down!—that he might see her breasts, round and pale and perfect as he remembered, when he'd stripped her of her garments after the storm . . . Oh, he'd managed to maintain a shuttered facade. For her sake, he'd told himself. And for his as well! And he'd tried not to look, but by heaven, he couldn't help himself either.

Unaware of his scrutiny, she slumbered like a child. Her cheeks were flushed, her lips parted, her hands flung back on either side of the pillow, her palms up, slender fingers curled ever so little. She twitched, and Simon was sorely tempted to laugh, yet he'd never felt less like laughing in his life!

A cold sweat broke over his brow. Unable to stop himself, he trailed a finger over the delicate line of her jaw, marveling at the texture of her skin. The slightest movement, and he caught a silken skein of hair between his fingers and lifted it to his mouth.

Anne slept on.

Time spun out. Her lips were stained the color of a rose, a deep, vibrant pink. He bent low. His lips hovered above hers, so near he felt the warm wash of her breath upon his mouth. He wanted a long, hot sampling of her mouth. Indeed, he wanted far more . . . What would she do if he woke her? If he stretched out beside her and let happen what would, and the rest be damned!

He didn't dare. She trusted him, implicitly. Simon didn't know how he knew, but he did.

His body clenched. But his heart squeezed. If

only he could dismiss his awareness of the lovely Annabel as lust. He couldn't. Because it wasn't. Yet he couldn't deny the white-hot flare of passion that seized hold of him whenever she was near.

Nor could he submit to it.

Some dark, inexplicable emotion slipped over him, like a veil of mist. Anne did not see his deformity. He hid it. His ugliness. The ugliness without, the ugliness within.

No, he decided, he couldn't give in. He wouldn't, he told himself harshly. He could tolerate much, for he'd done it before, hadn't he?

A year. A year and they would part. It would be easiest that way. It would be *best*.

Stepping back, he expelled a long, ragged breath. But somehow Simon couldn't forget the niggling little voice in the recess of his mind.

We need not be enemies, she had said.

But, oh, how much easier if they were!

Fourteen

She tempts my heart. She sways my judgment.
Never did I think it possible!

Simon Blackwell

A tentative truce had been established that
night.

After that, meals were no tense, rushed affairs that Anne dreaded with all her heart. Indeed, the time spent with her husband was
soon the highlight of Anne's day, particularly
supper. Oftentimes they lingered, Anne with a
book or needlework, Simon with a cigar or glass
of port. Sometimes he told her of his days in the
fields, his visits with his tenants. Anne was secretly pleased. Little by little, he revealed himself. Little by little, he shared himself. He was no

longer subdued and formal. Anne was no longer plagued by awkwardness and uneasiness.

One day just as they finished luncheon, Anne propped her chin on her hand and glanced through the windows. Outside, sunshine poured down from a cloudless, azure sky. "It's such a lovely day," she mused, more to herself than to Simon. "Too lovely to stay indoors, I think. Perhaps I'll go riding this afternoon."

Simon laid his napkin on the table. "I've a bit of business to attend to this afternoon, but it shouldn't take long. Would you like to come with me?"

"I should love to," came her prompt reply. She relished—and welcomed—the opportunity to share his company.

She hurried upstairs to change. By the time she returned downstairs, Lady Jane and Chaucer—such a fitting name for Simon's big gray—were ready and waiting.

Several miles from Rosewood, they turned down a long, curving lane bordered with hedgerows and wild roses. At the end was a small stone house. Simon dismounted, then helped her down.

A stoop-shouldered man had appeared in the doorway. He shuffled toward them, leaning on his cane. "Why, sir! Are ye back so soon then?"

"I am, Mr. MacTavish." Simon held open the whitewashed gate so the old man could pass through.

"Ye've a fetching young lass with ye." Mr. MacTavish gave a nearly toothless grin. "Who is she?"

"This is my wife, Lady Anne. Anne, Mr. Mac-Tavish. Mr. MacTavish was my father's stable master for many a year."

A thrill shot through her. This was the first time Simon had introduced her as his wife.

"Yer wife!" he said. "And a proper lady yet." The old man's fingers, gnarled and spotted with age, gripped the head of his cane, but he shook Anne's hand heartily. "Are ye from London then?"

"My mother is English, actually. But my father was Scots, and I spent most of my childhood in Scotland, and so I"—Anne caught Simon's eye; one corner of his mouth turned up in amusement—"have always called myself Scots as well."

Mr. MacTavish gave another grin. "No finer place on earth than Scotland," he declared cheerily, "lest it be Yorkshire."

Anne chuckled.

Mr. MacTavish turned to Simon. "Wasn't it just yesterday ye were here?"

"It was. And I promised I'd arrange for a mason to repair your chimney." Simon pointed to a spot near the roof where several bricks were cracked and broken. "He'll be here tomorrow, first thing in the morning."

They chatted on for a few more minutes.

Before they left, Simon brought out a small basket from a pouch at the side of his saddle. "Regards from Mrs. Wilder," he told the old man.

Anne was both pleased and impressed by Simon's attentiveness to the old man's needs. Somehow she'd known that inside he was kind, generous, and caring.

From there they trotted across an ancient stone bridge, past treetops thick with the nests of rooks, an amicable silence between them. The house wasn't so very far away, but the afternoon was rather warm; they stopped to rest for a few minutes beneath the cool shade of a stately elm tree.

In the pasture, two brown and white, floppy-eared goats butted their heads up against the fence.

"Oh, look!" Anne cried. "I haven't seen them before. They're adorable! Are they friendly?"

"Ah, yes," Simon said dryly. "Fred and Libby would stay there all day for a good scratching."

Anne poked a hand through the fence and proceeded to do exactly that. Both goats vied for her attention. Anne laughed and gave in, sticking both hands through to scratch both of them until she lost her balance and tumbled onto the ground. Simon hauled her upright while Anne dusted off her bottom, still laughing.

Together they walked back to the horses.

Simon cupped his hands and hoisted her onto Lady Jane's back. He was still standing when Anne leaned forward, her eyes sparkling.

She tightened her gloved fingers on the reins. "I have a proposition for you, sir. Shall we race?"

Simon glanced up. "Race?"

"Yes." She pointed. "Let's race around the oak tree on the slope of the pasture, and back to here. Agreed?"

Simon's eyes narrowed—and then a half smile courted his lips.

"Agreed—"

Anne set her heel to Lady Jane's flank, leaving Simon behind. Only for an instant, however. He hurtled onto Chaucer's back and gave chase, doing his utmost to catch her.

But Anne already had the advantage. Leaning low over the mare's neck, she urged Lady Jane onward, whipped around the oak tree and back toward the elm.

Simon was rather stunned when he finally reined in Chaucer and brought the gray to a halt beside Anne. "Anne! You cheated!"

"No," she said. "I won!"

"Just this once," he parried. "I neglected until now to note that poor Chaucer is favoring his left foreleg."

"So Chaucer is lame, eh? You sound just like Alec and Aidan. Neither would ever admit defeat. Besides," she said loftily, "it is not the horse so much as the horsemanship."

"Oh, yes, I'd forgotten your unsurpassed horsemanship."

Anne's gaze flew to his. A glimmer of laughter lit his eyes.

"But I still say you cheated," he added.

"I do not cheat," she informed him. "I merely compete to the best of my ability—"

"And to the aggravation of your opponents?"

"You forget I grew up with two brothers, older ones at that." She pretended great consideration. "How else was I to ever win? If I had to—"

"Cheat?"

Anne frowned at him good-naturedly. "If it is any comfort, I only cheated with them."

"And now me!"

She had no answer.

It was Simon's turn to relish victory. "Ah, so you admit it then!"

Anne pursed her lips.

Simon raised his eyes heavenward. "Lord, deliver me. I'm wed to a devil in the guise of an angel."

"Sir, you wound me sorely!" Anne feigned great affront.

"I can well imagine your brothers learned rather quickly not to look the other way when you were near," Simon teased. "Remind me never to engage you in a game of cards—at the very least, never to turn my back."

And he laughed once more. Seeing him like this, so carefree and relaxed, she felt her heart turn over.

All in all, it was quite the most enjoyable day she'd spent at Rosewood. And in the days that followed, Anne was more certain than ever that her husband was not the cold, unyielding beast she'd once thought him.

Yet one thing did not change—and it was Anne's most fervent wish that it would!

For Simon did not touch her, other than a kiss on the forehead when she retired—a kiss so light it was scarcely a kiss at all! What would he do, she wondered wildly one night, if she were to raise her head and offer her lips instead?

In this, however, Anne discovered her courage deserted her. She was afraid of what she would see on Simon's face. She was afraid of what she *wouldn't* see! If Simon rejected her—if he spurned her—she would be crushed. Anne knew it instinctively.

And so in the end, she didn't. She wanted nothing to erase the frail peace that had been forged. She didn't want to go back to the way it had been before. It was too hard for both of them.

Trust was building, yet not as quickly as she wished.

Anne was always the first to say good night. She was aware that after she retired, Simon usually went to his study and worked. She felt almost guilty at keeping him from it, but Anne did not lie to herself—she'd have been lonely if he didn't wait.

But one night she woke in the wee hours. She lay for several seconds, her mind still fuzzy with sleep. Rolling to her side, she glanced at the clock on the nightstand. It was then she noticed the door between their rooms stood ajar.

Frowning, she pushed back the covers. Why was it open? She hadn't been in Simon's room—why, she'd *never* been in Simon's room. Had he looked in on her perhaps?

Rising, Anne crossed the room to shut it. But something stopped her. Some unknown force held her bound, her fingers curled around the knob.

She looked inside.

Utter silence steeped the air, utter darkness but for the moonlight that spilled through the windows. The drapes were parted wide. The night was filled with a brilliant cluster of stars.

Anne's eyes adjusted to the dark. His bed was unoccupied, the coverlet undisturbed. Simon, she saw, was sitting in the brass-pegged chair in front of his writing desk.

She froze. Her senses sharpened.

Her gaze ran over him. He was fully clothed, she noted in surprise. Oh, he'd discarded his jacket, but one booted foot rested atop his knee. Upon that knee was one lean hand.

In it was a crystal glass.

He had yet to see her. Anne bit her lip. She wanted desperately to break the silence, to call his name, to ask if something was amiss, that he had yet to seek his bed. Indeed, his name hovered on her lips—she bit it back. Some little understood sense inside warned her not to give away her presence.

The glass lifted. Tipped. She watched as he drank deeply, then resumed his pose, staring out into the night.

And then Anne couldn't have said a word in *any* case.

High in the night, the clouds shifted. The moon emerged, lighting his profile in stark relief.

Seeing him thus, there was a painful tug on her heart. Darkness enveloped him, but this was a darkness of the soul, she realized achingly. His expression tore at everything inside her. There was such bleakness, such weary despair etched on his face that she could have wept.

Creeping back to her bed, she huddled beneath the covers, her mind so muddled, there was no point in even trying to sleep.

A long time later, she heard the door between their chambers click shut.

Anne swallowed. Her mind whirled. Her

heart hammered. Simon had been here. *Here.* Beside her. Above her.

In the nights that followed, Anne knew. She saw him yet again, one night when she woke and saw the door ajar once more. She heard him rustling in the hours before dawn. And every night . . .

He sat in the dark. He sat in silence. He sat alone.

And nearly every morning she woke with the strangest certainty that Simon had stood at her bedside, watching her.

The days remained warm, sometimes hot, for the second week of August approached. Anne's days were full. Most mornings she tended to matters of the household. Afternoons were hers; often she walked or rode.

She also took on another task—or more precisely, two. Simon was predictable. He left early in the morning, then returned for luncheon. Afterward he left the house once more; he didn't return until early evening, when he spent an hour or so in his study before supper. And that predictability granted her an opportunity that Anne simply could not ignore.

She'd never felt quite right about the chaos in the library—or the overgrown tangle of the garden. It wasn't just her woman's nature asserting itself, though Anne had been brought up to value neatness and tidiness. And perhaps she interfered where she ought not, but she took it upon herself to begin the task of cleaning up the clutter in the library. She dusted and swept, stacked and sorted and shelved. In the garden, she dug and potted and pruned—and carefully tended the three ivory rose bushes at the far end. She worked alone, without any of the servants' assistance.

If Simon was aware of her endeavors, he said nothing.

Anne rather thought he did not know. She rather thought he had not returned to either place.

But she also rather thought that someday he might change his mind. That perhaps someday he might remember Ellie and his boys with some measure of peace, with tenderness and laughter—and without such anguish and heartache.

She hoped that she was right. She prayed that she was right.

For Anne could not bear the thought that it would be otherwise. Ellie and the boys lived on in heaven; Anne was certain of it.

But she could not bear to think that Simon would continue to live such a hellish existence as he had these past years.

On one particularly warm day, Simon stood in the entrance hall talking with Duffy. Anne was just coming down the stairs.

Duffy had disappeared down the hall. Simon turned. "Good afternoon," he greeted.

"Good afternoon to you, sir."

Her tone was light, but her pulse was suddenly fluttering. His sleeves were rolled clear to his biceps. His forearms were long and banded with muscle. He'd undone the top few buttons of his shirt against the heat, baring a wedge of masculine, hair-roughened chest. Anne's throat went dry. It was difficult not to stare!

He offered an arm. "I do believe Mrs. Wilder is the best cook in Yorkshire. Something smells wonderful, doesn't it?"

Anne was quite certain she didn't know. She stayed where she was, crossing her arms over her breasts.

"Simon Blackwell, where the devil do you think you're going?"

He blinked. "Why, luncheon."

"Simon Blackwell," she said, "take yourself back outside this instant."

"What?"

Anne tapped one slippered foot. "Can you not see this floor is spotless? Mrs. Gaines and the maids were here just this morning!"

Obviously Simon neglected to see her point. "And?"

"And you, sir, are not!" She looked him up and down.

"I beg your pardon?"

Her mouth pursed. "Perhaps you'd care to tell me where you've spent the morning."

Suddenly he broke off. His gaze had fastened on the wall next to the doors.

"Where is the painting that was there?"

A rush of heat climbed up her neck, clear to her cheeks. It seemed she'd been well and truly caught. As it happened, a little sooner than she anticipated. She hadn't been trying to hide it from him—as if she could! But she hadn't known she would be present when he noticed the painting was gone—and more aptly, its replacement . . . In truth, that was her real concern. Which was why she'd planned to tell him at supper, before he saw it . . .

"I moved it to the drawing room," she said brightly. "There was a wall there that simply cried out for a painting of a quaint old bridge . . ."

In its place was a tapestry map of Yorkshire, with Rosewood Manor at its center. She'd found it in the library, hung in a dark corner. Now she moved to the tapestry and tugged on one corner.

"I'm afraid I couldn't resist. I thought the colors of the carpet in this room would bring out the red and gold in the threads." Anne held her breath.

Simon had yet to remove his gaze from the tapestry she'd hung a scant half hour ago. Anne's nerves were screaming. She'd been quite rash, she realized suddenly. Perhaps foolish as

He blinked again. "Why, out in the pasture

"Yes, I thought so." Her nose wrinkled i distaste. "Next time, sir, I'll thank you to lea\ the sheep in the pasture!"

She pointed at his boots. Simon's eyes fo lowed both her finger and the direction of he gaze.

A crooked smile crept over his lips—the gave way to a husky laugh.

And Anne couldn't help but laugh along wit him. By Jove, she couldn't. It was disarming that smile. Wholly charming, that laugh. Fo both were so rare, so very precious, that he heart surely stopped.

Later that afternoon she glided into his study Simon was just lowering himself into his chaii

"Oh! I didn't realize you were here!"

"I've only just returned. And my boots, m\ lady Anne, are immaculate."

Was that a twinkle in his eye? It surely was She smothered a smile. "Ah. I shall have to thanl Duffy then, won't I?"

Simon chuckled, then leaned back in his chair, eyeing her curiously. "Was there some-thing you needed?"

Anne held up the cloth in her hand. "I was go-ing to dust off your desk while you were out."

"I won't be long." He pulled out a ledger from one of the drawers. "I've several entries to make here and then—"

well! How she wished he would say something. Anything!

"Of course, if you don't like it—" Her lips felt stiff from struggling to maintain her smile. "I'll have it removed straightaway—"

"No," he said thoughtfully. "It does look as if it belongs here, doesn't it?" His eyes skidded back to her. "Thank you," he told her softly.

She was about to step away when he stopped her. "Wait," he said. He sifted through the post he'd dropped on the corner of his desk. "There's a letter for you. From your cousin, I think." He held it high.

Nearly an hour later Simon saw her sitting on the bench beneath the bank of windows behind the staircase. Her legs were drawn up to her chest, her chin resting atop her knees. Between the fingers of one hand, she clutched the letter.

He frowned. "Anne? What's wrong?"

Her head came sharply around. He'd startled her, he realized.

He nodded at the letter. He knew it was from her cousin. "Is all well?"

"Yes. Yes, of course."

She was trying overly hard to convince him, he decided. "It would seem not," Simon said grimly, taking a place alongside her. "You're upset."

"I'm not," she denied quickly. Too quickly, Simon decided.

She tried to duck her head before he could see, but Simon had already glimpsed her distress. Reaching out, he snared her chin between thumb and forefinger. His gaze captured hers. "You are," he said quietly.

Anne opened her mouth. She considered arguing, then discarded the idea just as quickly.

"Tell me," he said.

"I know it's silly—" She gestured vaguely, hoping she didn't sound as lame as she felt, but fearing that she did. "It's just that I—I miss everyone so much. I miss them all quite dreadfully, I fear. My mother and Alec. Caro and the children. Aidan, though I confess I've gotten used to him being away."

Regret pierced his chest. Regret, and more than a smidgen. High in Simon's mind was the way Anne had looked when they'd departed London for Rosewood. Hardly surprising, considering the circumstances of their wedding had been tenuous at best. *Tenuous?* mocked a scathing voice in his head. Oh, but that was laughable.

"It's certainly not dreadful," he said. "And it's not silly. They're your family. Of course you miss them. I've seen you all together, you know. I would be shocked if you claimed otherwise."

He watched as Anne smoothed the letter with both fingertips, the gesture as eloquent as anything she might have said.

She sighed, the sound wistful, her smile rather

misty. "Caro said that Alec's decided to stay in Town with Mama until Christmas," she found herself confiding. "I expect I'll have a letter from Mama shortly. Caro said she's been writing volumes. She and John are nearly ready to move back to their town house. She and Mama have been busy shopping for the nursery—she and John are expecting again, you know. Izzie has decided she is not to be called Izzie, but Isabella Cecelia—it's her second name, you see. Oh, and they bought Jack his first pony." Her laugh was breathless. "Quite the sight, I gather! Caro said Jack's squeal must have surely been heard across the Thames—"

All at once, she halted. Her gaze veered to his face. Uncertainty flickered over her features.

And Simon knew why.

He shook his head. "It's all right, Anne. You can say it." Bracing himself inwardly, he tucked a stray hair behind her ear, marveling at its softness, even as he offered the only assurance he could. "You can say Jack's name."

Her eyes searched his—searched endlessly, it seemed. She shocked him by laying her palm against the plane of his jaw.

"Thank you for sitting here with me." Her tone was very grave, but the merest hint of a smile curled her lips. "Thank you for understanding."

What she did next shocked him even more.

Leaning up, she kissed his mouth.

The contact was brief, even fleeting—but so achingly sweet, it made his heart catch.

For Simon felt it, that kiss, felt it in every pore of his body . . .

It burned through him like a flame.

And with a bone-shattering awareness that seared his very soul.

Fifteen

A man does not know his greatest fear until he comes face-to-face with it.

Simon Blackwell

Oh, yes, Simon knew precisely what Anne's family meant to her. How close they were.

Riding back to Rosewood, he couldn't get yesterday's scene out of his mind.

Regret lay heavy in his heart. He'd never really considered how Anne must feel, being torn from them as she'd been. How hard it must be for her.

Not until Caro's letter had arrived.

It bothered him. It bothered him mightily. A part of him almost wished she'd never confided in him. How much easier it would be!

But now he couldn't distance himself from it. He couldn't distance himself from *her.*

Should he send her back to London? Back to her family? A visit, perhaps, he reasoned. Damn! but he couldn't accompany her. It would soon be harvest, and he couldn't afford to be away from Rosewood for so long. Yet if Anne returned to London so soon after the wedding— and without him, yet—there might be talk.

And perhaps among her family.

No, he would not put her in that position. He *refused* to put her in that position.

Or was it that his reasons were purely selfish?

It was that which struck a note of truth in his consciousness.

It pleased him, the way Anne took pride in his home. Simon couldn't deny it. Beyond that first week when maids darted every which way—and in truth, he couldn't blame her, for the house had been atrocious!—the changes were now more subtle. A vase tucked here and there, the scent of flowers in the hall . . . He liked it. He liked the little things that Anne had done.

He also liked the way she saw to his needs. He recalled the day in the dining room when she'd dared to tell him it was rude to read his paper . . . He laughed to think that he'd been so opposed, so very stubborn! But Anne was more than a match for him—it hadn't taken long to discover she was just as stubborn! She was tart and outspoken, ever determined, never defeated.

His smile withered.

Yet still his conscience needled him.

If he could not be wholly honest with her, he should at least be honest with himself!

He didn't *want* to send her away.

Still another thought crept in, unbidden. And once it took hold, it refused to leave.

What if she left . . . and never came back?

Throughout the long hours of the day, Simon was never able to put aside the tumult in his mind . . . the maelstrom in his heart.

For these were perilous waters that he trod. Oh, he'd told himself it was better to turn away from his beautiful young wife.

Anne made it impossible.

Every time he looked at her—every time she drew near—desire mounted, a relentless invader. Twice as powerful. Twice as dangerous. Each and every time. Without question.

Without fail.

And Simon was powerless against it.

That was the most jarring truth of all.

His mind thus engaged, he never even saw the speedy little hare that darted across the field in front of him.

His horse reared. The next thing he knew, he pitched from the saddle. He flung out his arm to break his fall. There was a sickening thud as he landed. His lungs searing, he gasped for air.

He wasn't sure which was worse—the horrifying sensation of being unable to breathe, or
the white-hot pain that stabbed at his right
shoulder.

Swearing hotly, he caught the reins and
dragged himself into the saddle.

Inside the house, Anne hummed a merry tune,
passing through the entrance hall on her way
to the dining room.

Suddenly the front door crashed open. Anne
stopped short. Her eyes widened.

It was Simon, his left arm flung around
Duffy. He was disheveled, his shirt dirty, his
gait rather crooked. For the space of an instant,
she thought he was foxed.

One look at his face and she knew he was
not.

"What happened?"

"I was thrown."

"He's injured his shoulder, mum!" Duffy
cried.

Simon shot him a fulminating look. "My
good man, I'm still able to speak for myself!"

Anne pressed her lips together. It appeared
her husband was back to his usual disagreeable
self. The dolt! Duffy was wholly devoted to
him. Didn't he know it?

He was pale, though, almost deathly so.

"There's a doctor in the village, isn't there,
Duffy?"

"I don't need a damned doctor!"

Duffy had already nodded. Worried blue eyes met hers. Duffy was struggling a little at his weight. Sending the old man a tiny, reassuring smile, Anne eased her shoulder beneath Simon's to replace him. To her husband, she sent a ripe glare.

"It wasn't you I was speaking to, sir!" she said through her teeth. "It was Duffy!"

By the time they entered his room, Simon was almost staggering. His breath scraped in her ear. He stumbled to the bed, sagging onto the mattress.

Anne's fingers were already on his shirt, plucking buttons from their berth. He brushed them aside.

"Duffy can help me."

"*I* can help you."

Anne didn't mean to snap. But when stormy gray eyes tangled with hers, she no longer cared.

His jaw closed hard.

"I shall be fine. I just need to sit. Now send Duffy back in."

Anne was blistering. "I am your wife, Simon. I won't be banished!"

His insistence only crystallized her own. As if in defiance, she tugged his shirt from his trousers, dragging the edges wide. She wasn't prepared for the way her throat went dry. The bottom dropped out of her belly. A mat of dark, curly hair covered his chest and belly. This was the first time she'd seen his naked torso.

And it was glorious. *He* was glorious.

Swallowing the dryness in her throat, she sat beside him.

It was then she saw it . . .

The horrible scarring across the upper quadrant of his back . . . The skin looked thick and leathery and dark, drawn tight as a drum across muscle and bone. Anne had never seen such scars before. But she knew where they came from . . . All at once she knew why she'd seen him occasionally rubbing his shoulder.

Something struck me. Part of the ceiling, I think. It knocked me down, but I got up. I kept shouting. Shouting for Ellie. For Joshua. For Jack.

Anne's heart squeezed.

I swear I could hear them. I swear I could! But—I couldn't reach them. I couldn't save them.

She knew he'd gone in after them. Tried to rescue Ellie and his sons. What a fool she was! She hadn't realized that he'd been burned . . .

A sharp, ragged breath broke from her throat. She'd yearned to understand him—to know why he was so distant, so aloof! And now, knowing what she did, could she blame him? He wasn't cold. He wasn't made of stone. He certainly wasn't heartless. But the scars he carried were on the inside as well—and those were the hardest scars of all to heal, she thought achingly.

How could any man withstand such loss? Such pain. She made a faint, choked sound, for it hurt just to think of it.

Simon's head jerked up, his expression utterly fierce.

Slowly, tentatively, her touch whisper-light, she laid her fingers on his back, the place on his shoulder where those horrible scars began.

Simon recoiled. Visibly. Physically. Pulling inside himself where Anne couldn't see. It was keenly evident in the proud, rigid angle of his head.

In the flinch of his muscles beneath her fingers.

"Don't," he said tautly. He stared straight ahead. "I'm sure it turns your stomach."

It didn't. What hurt was seeing his withdrawal. *Feeling* it.

What hurt was knowing the agony he had surely endured.

"Actually it doesn't," she said evenly. Even as she spoke, her gaze shifted—along with her hand. But she didn't pull away. Her fingers drifted over the front of his shoulder. Mottled, purple bruises had already begun to darken and swell. She shook her head worriedly. "This doesn't feel right, Simon. It's different than the other side. I hope it's not broken."

He dismissed it curtly. "It will be fine by morning."

Anne's chin climbed. If he chose to be difficult,

then so would she. "It won't," she said shortly.

There was a knock on the door. Duffy peered inside. "Mum? The doctor should be on his way."

"Thank you, Duffy. Please see that he's sent up as soon as he arrives."

Simon was sizzling, she saw. Was it because Duffy addressed her and not him? Oh, bother, she thought. Why was it that men were so convinced they were indestructible? That they dare not display any hint of weakness? She recalled once when Aidan was ill with fever, shortly before he'd left for India. He wouldn't admit it. No one knew until he collapsed on the stairs one day, frightening her mother half to death. No one could be strong all the time. Not Aidan. Not Alec. Not Simon or any other man. How ridiculous!

He didn't seem to want her near him. Fine, she thought coolly, rising. Her eyes lit on the wing chair in front of the fireplace. She tugged it around and angled it toward the bed, then installed herself on the seat, squirming a little until she was comfortable.

Simon glared.

Anne savored her satisfaction.

By the time the doctor arrived, Simon was leaning back on the pillows, holding his arm across his stomach. His eyes were closed, his lashes long, feathery crescents against his skin.

Anne hurried to the door. "Hello," said the man who stood beside Duffy. "I'm Dr. Gardner."

A big, robust man, Dr. Gardner whisked off his hat. His manner was capable and reassuring, his hands gentle despite his size. Anne stood near while he gently probed Simon's shoulder.

Finally he drew back. "Well," he said cheerfully, "it's not broken. But it needs to be pushed back into place." He lifted Simon's right arm, extending it fully. "I warn you, this is going to hurt like the dickens."

Anne scarcely had time to draw breath, and it was over. She heard a popping sound, and Simon went rigid. His eyes glazed with pain, and his face went pasty white.

It was mercifully quick, however. Still, his breathing was heavy as Dr. Gardner eased his shoulder into a sling. "Leave it in place for a few days," he instructed. "A little rest and you'll be right as rain," he told Simon.

Anne accompanied the doctor into the hall.

"It's not serious," Dr. Gardner said. "I'd advise wearing the sling for several days. Hot compresses if he needs them." He paused. "A pity this happened to the same shoulder. I should imagine he still has a fair amount of discomfort . . ." He glanced at her inquiringly.

"Simon is . . . not one to complain." Anne felt lame. She didn't quite know what to say.

They were on the landing now. "I'll never forget that night," Dr. Gardner was saying. "His recovery took so long . . . I saw the beam that struck him"—he shook his head—"it's a miracle his shoulder wasn't crushed. And those burns . . . I'm just a country doctor. I wasn't even sure how to treat them." The doctor shook his head. "He was fortunate, I always told him. So very fortunate."

At the bottom of the stairs, he paused. "We've heard about you in the village," he said. "It's a pleasure to finally meet you."

Anne shook his hand. "Thank you, Doctor. I appreciate you coming so quickly."

Slowly she closed the door, her mind still whirling.

When she turned, Duffy stood behind her, his expression anxious.

"He'll be fine, Duffy. Truly." She sighed. "I'm sorry he was so surly earlier. He's rather trying sometimes, isn't he?"

"It's all right, mum."

Anne bit her lip. "May I ask you something?"

"Of course, mum."

"The night that Ellie and the boys died . . . Simon said you were there."

"I—I was, mum."

"He went in after them, didn't he? And you went in—after him."

Duffy nodded slowly. "He was barely inside

when the roof collapsed. I'll never forget what
he said when he woke . . . He said I should have
left him there. That I"—tears stood high and
bright in the old man's eyes—"that I should
have let him die, too."

A hot ache filled her throat. She reached for
his hand. "He's lucky to have you, Duffy."

The old man swallowed. "I was about to say
the same to you, mum." She gave his fingers a
little squeeze, then retraced her steps to Simon's
room.

He was tugging on the heel of his right boot
and swearing rather heatedly.

"Oh, that should help immensely," Anne observed from the doorway. "Would you like some
assistance?"

Scowling, he expelled an impatient breath. "I
should think it would be obvious. I need help
with my boots."

Anne didn't move. "As Caro and I have occasionally told Izzie and Jack," she said lightly,
"it's quite rude to make petulant demands. Besides the fact that they rarely yield results, I
find that a little courtesy—"

"Please," he said brusquely.

Anne arched a brow. "Please . . . ?"

"May I please have your assistance in remov-
ing my boots?"

Anne smiled sweetly. "Sir, you had only to
ask."

She very nearly landed on her bum while

tugging at each boot, but at last they were off. Dropping them near the end of the bed, she straightened.

Simon was on his feet, fumbling clumsily with the buttons on his trousers.

Anne rolled her eyes. "Lord, but you're stubborn! Here, let me."

She stepped up. Her gaze slid down, her hands came up to the level of his hips . . .

And all at once, Anne wasn't feeling quite so lofty or so brisk.

She'd already twisted her fingers around the first button. It popped free. Her knuckles skimmed down, down across warm, hair-roughened flesh.

Her heart was suddenly pounding. She nearly snatched her hand away. *Now you've done it, Anne!* came a voice in her head. She'd gone quite mad, she realized. What the devil had she been thinking? She hadn't, of course.

The first button was undone. The second as well. Readying her nerve, steadying her resolve, she attacked the third.

It held fast.

She concentrated harder, ignoring a swell of panic. *Stop being so maidenly, Anne! You can do this. Just don't look.*

She twisted harder, the knuckle of her index finger digging into the knotted grid of spare, taut muscle between the crease of his hips. In her earnestness, she didn't even think to try to avoid his—

Heaven above, she didn't.

She looked down. She couldn't *not* look. She felt it then, the heat rising from his body. She felt *him* rising.

Directly beneath her hand.

Simon's head flung up. Mortified, Anne's heart nearly choked her. His entire body clenched, his breath hissed in.

"Oh, dear," she said faintly.

Simon was dragging at her fingers. "I've got it," he said with an odd catch in his voice. "I've got it."

It lasted but an instant.

Oh, Lord, it lasted forever.

Swinging around, Anne turned her back. She could hear the rustle of the sheets as he climbed into bed.

At length, she turned around. A jolt ran through her. He was naked, she thought shakily. The sheet lay draped across his lap; he had turned slightly to the left. She saw the shape of one round, spare buttock.

Her heart lurched. Even though he was adequately covered, his naked chest seemed to leap out at her. Disconcerting though it was, Anne was utterly curious—and utterly fascinated.

Stretched out on the mattress, his powerful frame seemed bigger than ever. Some might have called him daunting, yet in all honesty, Anne couldn't. And she didn't. No, she discovered herself musing, it wasn't that he was intimidating. It was more that he was . . . overwhelming.

Air seeped slowly from her lungs. Both the sheet and the sling were very white against the dark pelt on his chest. She swallowed as her gaze strayed lower. No power on earth could have stopped her from staring—and none did. Her eyes trailed the curling hairs on his chest down across the plane of his belly, curling and crisp, clear to where it disappeared beneath the hem of the sheet. An odd little shiver tore through her.

She thought of the sleek, silent grace with which he moved. The breadth of his chest, the width of his shoulders, the sinewy length of his arms. She didn't need to see him naked to know how hard he was. She didn't need to touch him. But she wanted to—oh, how she longed to! She ached with the need to reach out, to thread her fingers through the dense mat of hair on his chest and splay her hands wide. She yearned to know what it was like to *feel* a man. To feel *him*.

Was it curiosity that moved her so? That compelled the clamor of her heart? A little, perhaps. Yet Anne was instinctively aware it was more. So much more.

Fascination. Desire. A fervent churning of

the blood. A cresting of something that sent a tremor all through her.

The lamplight wavered, casting the blade of his nose into prominent relief, the proud arch of his brow, the captivating beauty of his mouth. He moved his head on the pillow, and she saw his eyes, pale and silver.

His legs moved restlessly. Anne's heart leaped. Had he noticed her immodest regard?

Again he shifted. This time the sheet caught beneath his hip, drawing taut over iron-hard thighs. And for one sheer, mind-splitting instant, her gaze strayed yet again where it should not.

This time there was no refuting it. She saw the outline of his sex against his belly.

Anne couldn't breathe. Her cheeks were scalding. She certainly couldn't summon the nerve to look at him. Flustered, her pulse clamoring riotously, she finally stammered, "I-I'll check on you shortly."

Safely in her room, she flattened her palms against the door, gulping in a stinging lungful of air. Not until Audrey stepped in did Anne raise her head. The girl helped her out of her clothing. By the time she pulled a gauzy white nightgown into place, she was calmer.

Audrey had brought a light meal with her. A silver hairbrush in hand, Anne glanced toward Simon's bedroom. No doubt he was hungry.

He'd been gone most of the day, and she didn't think he'd eaten since breakfast. And while it wasn't dread that clogged her throat at the thought of facing him again, how could she look at him without—

In Simon's room, something clattered to the floor.

Anne flung open the door. A wooden cigar box lay upended on the floor; cigars lay scattered like twigs across the rug.

Simon was trying to get out of bed.

Anne rushed forward. "What are you doing!?"

The look he turned on her was almost ferocious. His tone certainly was. "I am not helpless, Anne. I am not a child."

"Then pray don't act like one," she said evenly. "You roar at Duffy. You snap at me. You're angry at your clumsiness. You are unhappy, and so it appears everyone around you must be too."

His jaw was bunched. "I want a drink," he growled.

"You drink too much," she challenged.

"I do," he agreed stiffly. "But that won't change my mind."

Anne's eyes narrowed. "Are we having a row?" she asked pleasantly.

"We are not," he said brusquely. "And if you think to dissuade me, Anne, be advised you will not. I want my whisky. I will have my whisky.

And I have no objection about fetching it myself, however it may offend your sensibilities."

Oh, the irascible brute! When he thrust out one long, lean leg toward the floor, it was shockingly apparent he meant every word. Exactly what she would have done if she hadn't glimpsed the creases of pain etched beside his mouth, she wasn't quite sure.

"Oh, for pity's sake! Stay where you are. I'll get it for you."

This time it was Anne who glared—and Simon savored his satisfaction.

She marched to his desk where the bottle sat. Her lovely mouth pinched into a straight line, she handed the tumbler to him without a word.

Simon took a long, satisfying draught. Their eyes caught; Anne's flashed mutinously.

Yet the very next instant his smile was wiped clean.

She wore no dressing gown. Her nightgown was a simple gown. A plain gown. And most *un*provocative, the neckline wide and unadorned, the fine batiste loose and billowing.

But it was just as he suspected. The light was behind her. And he could see every inch of her—those long, slim legs, the rounded flare of her hips—every sweet line of her body. As if she *were* naked.

His eyes tracked her every move as she bent to pick up the cigar box and its contents, granting him an unrestrained view of a very lovely little bottom. Simon paused, the tumbler suspended halfway to his lips.

It seemed she was in no hurry. All the while she swayed ever so slightly, to and fro as she gathered up the cigars. Through narrowed eyes, Simon tracked her form as she straightened, pushing back a gleaming skein of chestnut gold hair and revealing the graceful line of her neck and shoulder.

"I'm quite well, Anne. You needn't hover."

"I'm not hovering. I'm merely tidying up."

Leaning over, she plumped the pillows behind him.

The neckline gaped wide. Her breasts were clearly visible, ivory and soft, full and trembling with her every move.

Simon choked—and very nearly dropped his tumbler.

Anne looked at him sharply. "What? What is it? Did I hurt you?"

Simon didn't spare her. He could see all the way to the concave of her belly, the shadowy triangle beneath, but it was those delectable breasts that held him bound. If he wasn't mistaken, he noted vaguely, her nipples were the same lush pink as her lips.

It was damned disconcerting, that's what it was!

"Is it possible," he said succinctly, "that you could cover yourself?"

She blinked. For one precious second, she didn't move. Simon could feel himself growing hard once more. He wondered if Anne would have remained thus if she knew precisely what havoc she wreaked on his body. It crossed his mind to show her exactly what effect her display—and her proximity—had on him. But even if she saw, she wouldn't know what it meant . . . or would she?

Confusion flitted across her face. She looked down at herself. "Oh," she gasped, and then again: "Oh!"

She jerked upright, her cheeks flushed with color. And then she looked at him as if it were his fault!

Stepping back, she straightened her shoulders. "Is there anything else that you require?"

Her calm was admirable, her tone carefully neutral. Simon took a breath. "My journal. It's in the top drawer of my desk."

Her gaze flitted to the sling. She frowned. "But you can't wr—"

Something about his expression must have brought her up short. She retrieved the leatherbound journal, placing it on the bedside table.

Simon took another breath. "Thank you."

"I'll say good night then," she said softly. She seemed to hesitate. "Simon . . ."

He did roar then. "Good night, Anne!"

Her chin came up. "Call me if you need anything."

"Thank you. I will."

They both knew he wouldn't.

At the doorway, she stopped and glanced back at him. Simon felt the touch of her eyes like a brand.

The door clicked shut. The rumble of a dozen fiery curses left his chest.

He tossed down the whisky, then sagged down on the pillows.

It was no use. His body betrayed him. Betrayed him most thoroughly and most traitorously.

Over and over Anne's image flitted through his mind. The throbbing in his shoulder was nothing compared to that in his loins until at last there was no help for it.

He set the glass aside. Odd, how he'd felt not the slightest twinge of desire until Anne came into his life.

He was disgusted with himself, with his craving for her, but there was no help for it. He was hard as stone. He rolled to one side.

His hand stole beneath the sheet. His hand clamped tight . . . Gritting his teeth, he squeezed his eyes shut, as if to close out the image of her face. Oh, God help him, it was no use. He couldn't help it. He couldn't fight it. Anne, no doubt, would say it was rude. Crude. But by God, he was still a man. With a man's urges. His body reminded him of that most assuredly.

Anne, he thought. *My lovely Anne. What are you doing to me? It's you who makes me come undone. It's you who runs me to ground. It's you who sends me fleeing to the shadows, like a fox flushed into the bushes.*

The motion of his hand quickened. His body went taut. He felt himself straining. Then he was shuddering. Gasping, craving, desperate for release.

And when at last it came, sprawling facedown, Simon laughed blackly. There would be no true release, he thought. Not tonight, or any other night.

Not without Anne.

Sixteen

My heart lies in peril. I know it . . . yet I cannot stop it.

Simon Blackwell

Early the next morning, Anne peered cautiously into Simon's room. Usually he was awake long before she was; sometimes she heard him stirring, the creak of floorboards, the click of the door.

He was still asleep, lying on his uninjured side, the sling tucked carefully against his stomach. Quietly she entered, her steps carrying her to his bedside.

What would he say if he knew she watched him so? Her throat tightened oddly. Seeing him thus, his guard laid low, brought a stark wave of emotion, so intense she went weak inside. She'd been granted the opportunity to study him at leisure, a rare opportunity, at that! she thought with a faint catch in her heart. There was no need to hold back. No need to wonder or worry about what was—or was not!—in his mind. There was no tension, no awkwardness, no strain or doubt or resistance.

With the tip of a finger, she traced the square of his sideburns, lightly scratching a nail up and down, loving the slightly bristled texture.

Loving *him*.

Her breath caught. Unbeknownst to her, a fist crept up, coming to rest directly above her heart.

She loved him. She *loved* Simon.

She shook her head in mingled wonder and confusion. She could never say precisely when it happened. In truth she didn't know!

For it was just as Caro had told her the night before the wedding.

Sometimes it's just there and one can't explain where or how or why or even when *it happened. It's just there.*

Her smile slipped away. Their marriage could be so much more, she thought with a pang, if only Simon was not so set against it. His *life* could be so much more. He could be happy again, she was certain of it, at least in some measure! But he held his guilt drawn tight about his shoulders, a weight no man should bear! And Anne had no idea how to ease his burden.

Or even if she could.

If Simon had his way, when the year had waxed and waned, forever would they part. Never would she forget him.

Forever would she love him.

Yet how could she ever tell him? When it might only hurt him more?

He'd suffered so much already.

But perhaps it needn't be like this.

Perhaps there was another way . . .

By mid-morning Simon was up and about. Anne was on her way inside with a basket full of flowers when she caught sight of him with Duffy. One large hand lay clasped on Duffy's shoulder as they made their way down the hall. Anne stopped. She had no wish to eavesdrop on their conversation, but saw that Duffy was nodding. Simon's features were earnest, but not grave. And when the old man lifted his head toward Simon, he was smiling broadly—

When Anne entered the house, her step was as light as her heart.

Her heart would be her guide. She loved this man, and she wasn't going to let him go without a struggle; if Simon didn't quite see things her way just yet, well . . . he would. A sudden bubble of laughter resounded in the hall. One of the maids glanced at her, startled. Anne slanted her a grin, then continued on her way, her basket swinging high.

Her stubbornness would serve her in good stead, she decided. For Anne was determined. She would do whatever she must, whatever it took. She would cosset and cajole. Persuade and persist. She had nearly a year, she reminded herself, a year in which to convince him they belonged together.

She had only to be patient.

Her heart would not be swayed. She knew what she wanted.

And what she wanted was her husband.

But first—ah, first!—she had to make him want her as well.

From the beginning, she could not look at him without feeling a sizzle of awareness . . . a tremor-in-the-heart sort of feeling. Even when she hadn't known what it was, it was there. In every look, in every heartbeat. Did Simon feel the same? Even harder, how could she *make* him feel the same?

Anne pondered her approach long and hard over the next few days.

Something inside warned that where Simon was concerned, brazenness would gain her little. Besides, it had never been her way to tease and flirt. Oh, how she wished that Caro were here to advise her! She must be subtle, she decided, but also bold. Yet how did one be bold and provocative without appearing to be so?

As usual, Anne retired before Simon. But it wasn't long before she heard him in his room. Grasping for courage, she paused in front of the connecting door. A wife had every right to enter her husband's room, she told herself. It wasn't wrong. It certainly wasn't odd.

Nonetheless, it took almost more daring than she possessed to raise her hand and knock— still more to open it wide and sally forth as if she'd done so countless times before!

Simon sat before his desk, writing in his journal. At her entrance, he half turned, the quill in his hand.

Anne's heart seemed to stumble—thank goodness she didn't. His shirt was partially undone, revealing a darkly masculine wedge of chest that nearly sent her fleeing back across the threshold.

"I fear I must trouble you for your assistance. I'm having a dreadful time with the clasp of this necklace. If you don't mind . . ." Thank heavens her voice wasn't nearly as shaky as she feared. She even managed a laugh as she swung around and presented her back.

Behind her, she heard the scraping of the chair. She knew the precise instant he drew near. Her every sense clamored in awareness.

"Of course it's no trouble, Anne."

She'd halted in front of his shaving table. Twisting her head ever so slightly, she managed a peek in the mirror. He was staring down at her, faint consternation on his features.

"I'm so glad you weren't in bed..." The words dangled, along with her breath. It seemed an eternity passed while she waited, before his hands finally lifted.

"How is your shoulder?"

"Right as rain. Hold still, will you? The chain is all tangled up in your hair."

His tone was rather gruff. Ah, but laden beneath it was something that made her tremble in reaction. Anne couldn't have moved if she wanted to. Shivers were dancing up and down her spine—the most delicious shivers she'd ever felt.

With Simon so intent on his task, Anne dared another peek. His eyes were hidden, but there was something in his expression that made her stomach go suddenly weightless.

And no wonder.

Simon grappled for composure. He battled for strength. Everything inside him was running wild, yet he felt trapped. Imprisoned by her nearness, held captive to her heat.

Her head was bowed low, baring her nape. His gaze fixed long and hard and avid on the tender sweep of her neck. He wanted to plant his open mouth against that fragile, vulnerable spot, run his tongue across curling wisps of sun-drizzled hair. Her scent made his nostrils flare, that uniquely delicate scent of roses that always managed to drive him half wild.

He tried to confine his attention to the soft, downy fuzz on her nape. He sawed in a breath, then set his teeth. Blast it, it was no use.

"There it is."

Lifting a hand, she opened her palm. He dropped the necklace into it.

Anne didn't move. "As long as I'm here, you may as well undo my gown."

Her tone was quite prim, her profile etched in marble.

Simon took a searing breath. "Where is Aggie?"

"Audrey," she corrected. "She's gone home for the night."

His jaw set hard, Simon obliged, tugging the row of tiny buttons free, one by one. And all the while, unable to tear his eyes away. Little by little the gown gaped, from her nape to the small of her back, revealing smooth, creamy flesh. Simon tried not to touch—he tried not to look—but there was no help for it. His knuckles skimmed the valley of her spine. He must see what he was doing.

Oh, Lord, he fooled no one, least of all himself. It had been so long . . . Too long. And Anne was so warm, her skin like alabaster, milky white and finely textured, almost translucent. He was nearly shaking with the urge to plunge his hands inside the fabric and tear it wide.

Drag it down, all the way down. And drag *her* down too, atop him. Between him, against him, her buttocks caught hard against the swelling of his sex.

"My stays too, if you please."

Oh, God, how could she be so matter-of-fact?

Yet when it was done, she held herself immobile, as if to allow him the chance to look his fill. In some distant realm of his mind, he noticed her hair had loosened from its topknot. Silky strands curled on her nape. A tug, and it would slip from its berth, down over his hands.

Bloody hell, he thought suddenly. If Anne didn't care, then why should he?

His gaze roamed hotly down her flesh, down between her loosened stays, the slender valley of her back, clear to the dimples above her buttocks.

It was all he could do not to turn her around and snatch her up against him. Conflict warred in his breast, a conflict such as he'd never known.

Just when he thought he could stand it no longer, she turned.

It was as if he'd been kicked in the stomach. Every nerve in his body went taut.

Oh, but he could almost believe his sweet, lovely bride knew precisely what effect she was having on him. He knew she was innocent. He knew she was a virgin. There was never a doubt in his mind—indeed, he'd dared not dwell on it at all! Yet it spun through his mind that this was a ploy, a plot. A game, perhaps?

No. Anne didn't play such games. Anne *wouldn't* play such games.

But suddenly he knew, with heart-stopping awareness, that Anne was ripe for the taking— *his* for the taking. He could do whatever he wanted . . .

She wouldn't reject him.

She wouldn't stop him.

It was unnerving, that certainty. It tempted him to the pit of his soul. Other men might surely envy him, for Anne was a beauty. To some, the fact that he had yet to consummate their marriage might have been unfathomable. The fact that she shared his home and his name—but not his bed—must have been ab- surd. To some, the fact that he had denied himself—deliberately checked his desire be- neath tightly leashed restraint—was no doubt laughable.

Oh, but she tempted him. She tested him. By God, she *tortured* him.

His jaw clenched hard. His fingers curled— and uncurled. He tried to pull back, to swallow his desire and turn it inward. He couldn't with- hold the twist of longing clawing through his gut. It was lust, he told himself flatly. It had to be, for anything else . . . it simply could not be. He simply would not allow it.

He broke out into a cold sweat. How foolish

he was! How arrogant to think that he could deny it or hide it.

He burned for her.

She laid her fingertips in the center of his chest. "You looked very handsome tonight at dinner."

His gaze roved her face. "So did you," he said solemnly.

Anne laughed softly. "Why, thank you. I don't believe anyone has ever called me hand-some before."

A faint smile grazed his mouth.

All at once the air was close and thick. The breath that seared his lungs was scalding. And now his blood was pounding almost violently, on fire with longing.

His smile was no more. One lean hand came up behind her head. Then the other. Plying his way across her scalp, threading into her hair, slowly he pulled her head back.

The look on her face shattered his insides. She didn't hide. She didn't retreat. She didn't waver. Her expression was soft, her eyes luminous.

His grip tightened, ever so little. A bone-jarring rhythm thudded in his chest. His head began to buzz. A sample, he told himself rag-gedly. Just one taste. Just one touch. Just one kiss.

His mouth closed over hers.

He tasted wine. He tasted pleasure. He tast-ed *her*.

And he kissed her as he'd never kissed her before. He kissed her the way she'd never been kissed. He kissed her the way *he* had never kissed her before.

Her mouth was warm. Wet. Clinging. Her hair tumbled down, down over his hands, thick and rich. He crushed it in one fist; the fingers of his other hand spread wide across her hip. Pitched into a shattering realm of sheer, sensual awareness, he bent her frame to his.

And Anne reveled in it. Relished it as nothing before. It was no chaste kiss that she wanted. No chaste kiss that he gave.

It blazed through every part of her. His palm closed around one breast, stroking her nipple through the cloth. She felt it like a white-hot jolt of fire. She wondered what it would be like to feel it again, with nothing between them. Not her clothing, not his.

She wanted more. So much more. They were wedded together from breast to belly. Anne was starkly—shatteringly—aware of his thighs against hers. With one hand, he trapped her against him, her hips clamped tight against his.

Her heart ceased to beat. She knew what that swelling ridge of taut male flesh signified. Even through the layers of her gown, she could feel him, thick and rigid.

Simon wanted her. He might hide it. Deny it. His body could not.

It didn't shock her, or frighten her. She knew what it meant. She was new to this thing called passion, to the feelings that clamored all through her. She was new to this, the reaction of man to woman. But she knew what it meant, this stirring heat of arousal.

A wild exhilaration poured through her. She felt reckless. Triumphant. Elated. Twining her arms around his neck, she clung, shamelessly and without reservation.

Then all at once, Simon froze. He broke away, lifting his head.

Anne's eyes snapped open. Their gazes collided, each heart-shatteringly aware of their nearness. They were both breathing fast and hard.

Abruptly he released her.

"Christ," he said raggedly. Something fierce leaped in his eyes, speeding across his features, something she didn't fully comprehend. Confusion? Regret? Perhaps a little of both . . .

He ran his fingers through his hair, then turned his back. Placing his hands flat on the top of his desk, he lowered his head. When he finally turned back, his features were shuttered.

"I'm sorry, Anne." His voice was low and taut. "Please forgive me."

An almost regal tilt to her chin, she stared him straight in the eye. "Don't be sorry," she said clearly. "Because I'm not."

* * *

How she ever made it back to her room was surely a miracle, Anne decided fuzzily. It was surely a miracle that she could walk at all! Still half dazed, she sagged back against the door, else she would surely have fallen.

Her knees were still weak, the world spinning dizzily. Unable to stop herself, she touched her fingers to the tips of her breasts, drawing in a sizzling breath. They were still prickled and achy and taut. Those same trembling fingers stole up to her lips, still throbbing from the brand of his kiss.

Anne had sensed the hunger in him. She'd tasted it in the utter fierceness of his mouth upon hers. By heaven, she'd *felt* it in the shocking surge of heat and hardness, taut against her belly. Through the cloth of his trousers—through the layers of her gown.

A man couldn't kiss like that and feel nothing.

She wished it could have gone on forever and ever, that kiss. So full of emotion, so full of him! She wanted to be held, in tenderness and passion. She could swear he'd been shaking as much as she! She yearned to be possessed—by him. By Simon. In all the ways—in every way!—a man could possess a woman.

Her heart still thumping madly, she made her way to the bed.

Anne had learned much tonight—much about him.

He was not as indifferent to her as she had thought. And she had the feeling that Simon too had discovered he was not so indifferent. He was battling his attraction to her with everything inside him. Oh, but it was heady and sweet, that mounting certainty!

Fast in her heart beat the strength of her resolve, the determination to forge ahead.

For Anne would not be forsaken. She would not be forgotten. She would not let him *go*.

And if he would not come to her, then she must go to him.

Seventeen

She plagues me in the night. She tempts me in the day.

Simon Blackwell

They did not speak of that night in his room. Nor was there any need. Simon couldn't forget. And he had the oddest sensation Anne didn't want to!

Unless he was losing his mind, his wife was flirting with him.

Precisely when the awareness set in, Simon was never sure. Indeed, he had trouble believing it. He was astonished. Amazed. Even a little aghast.

She found every excuse to touch him. The merest brush of her fingers as he filled her wineglass. The curl of her hand inside his elbow when he delivered her to her room each night. A certain lingering, lovely smile when they chanced to meet in the hall.

A dozen other things gave her away as well.

Each night when she appeared for dinner, she was freshly bathed, coiffed, and perfumed, each gown more exquisite than the last—her décolletage more plunging than the last. Three nights in succession, her napkin—accidentally, of course—fluttered from her lap to the floor between them. Naturally, being a gentleman, Simon leaned over to retrieve it. Also, three nights in succession, she leaned in just as he raised his head—

Affording him a view of lush, exquisitely remarkable breasts. And then she laughed, sending them all atremble.

Simon's reaction was immediate and intense. Hunger flashed throughout his body. An elemental heat fired along his veins, a heat that had been smoldering for days now. And that was precisely how Simon felt in that instant. Primitive and raw and wild.

And all at once he remembered what she'd said the night of their arrival at Rosewood . . .

Were I to choose to lie in the arms of my husband night after night, I should consider it a privilege—and not a duty.

They seared through his brain, those words. Branding him. Burning him inside and out.

Three nights in succession, Simon didn't trust himself to speak. It took every ounce of will-power he possessed not to drag her onto his lap, tear open his trousers, and let desire rule then and there.

Anne was a vibrant, sensual woman. And he was not made of stone.

She was trying to seduce him. The signs were unmistakable. How could he ignore them? How could he ignore her? How could he *resist* her?

The day began innocently enough, he sup-posed. Or *not* so innocently, depending on one's point of view.

Over breakfast, Simon mentioned his plans for the day. A trip to the next town to look over a stallion he thought would make an outstand-ing addition to his stable. It wasn't long before he realized he was the one doing most of the talking.

It gave him a jolt to see that she was studying him, her regard unwavering—her head tilting first one way and then the other—no bones about it!

A rare flush seeped into his neck. He took a sip of coffee to cover his unease. Damn it, he might as well be direct.

He looked at her. "Is something wrong, Anne? Do I have egg on my chin? Soap in my hair?"

"No," came her ready reply.

"Is something else amiss then?"

"Not in the slightest."

"Is there something you wish to say then?"

"Nothing in particular."

She propped her chin on her hand, her elbow on the table, her manner quite leisurely.

"Anne, you are staring at me."

"Oh, do forgive me! Am I?"

"You are," he said severely. "Obviously there is something on your mind."

Her forehead puckered. "It isn't so much that there is something on my mind—"

"Anne!"

"It's more of a question, actually. I suddenly find myself quite curious about something—"

"Out with it, Anne!" He could stand no more.

She looked at him doubtfully. "Are you quite certain?"

"I am! Say whatever you wish. Ask whatever you wish!" Leaning back in his chair, he reached for his cup.

"Very well then . . . Do you pleasure yourself?"

Simon nearly choked. "I beg your pardon?"

Her mouth pursed. "I believe you heard me quite clearly."

"I don't believe I did!"

"Then I shall ask again, sir. Do you satisfy yourself?"

"That is not a question you should be asking."

She looked at him calmly. "It's a logical one,

I think. You had a wife. Two children. I'm sure you did not beget those children out of thin air. Obviously you did not have a chaste relationship with Ellie. And since then, you must have had a need for . . . companionship. A need for"—only then did she stumble—"for physical gratification."

"You want to know if I've been celibate since Ellie died."

Her tone was surprisingly level. "Have you?"

"That's none of your affair," he said sharply.

"I think it is." Her chin rose a notch. "Particularly when I am your wife. Particularly if you have a mistress."

"I do not," he said through his teeth. "And this discussion is concluded." He was already on his feet.

Anne's eyes flashed. "Well," she muttered, "you did say I should ask whatever I wanted."

That exchange was to remain in both their minds. Simon couldn't believe her audacity on a subject so intimate.

And Anne marveled that she had been so bold.

It didn't matter that he didn't answer her question. His silence was all the answer she needed. Simon had not lain with a woman for five long years. How desperately he had loved Ellie! How desperately he *still* loved her.

And how desperately he missed her.

The breath Anne drew was bittersweet and painful. A hollow emptiness welled in her breast. Was it guilt that held him back? Anne did not begrudge his love for Ellie; she truly did not! Yet she was suddenly terrified that his heart was forever taken. And Anne's lent her no peace. If Ellie had loved Simon the way that Simon loved her—and somehow she knew that Ellie had!—would she want him to forever mourn?

She had to believe that Ellie would not. She must cling to that hope. She mustn't forget how Simon had kissed her—Anne—with fire and passion and yearning. She hadn't imagined it, she was sure of it! Yet why did he pull away? Why did he *push* her away?

A sharp, knifelike pain tore through her breast. To want for the two of them to share a bed, to share their lives . . . it wasn't wrong. She wanted this marriage. She wanted *him*. And Anne was coming to know what drove this man she had wed. His vulnerability—for he was so very, very vulnerable!—and his strength.

But it was that very strength that stabbed at her soul and ripped her to shreds—that tremendous strength of will.

He needed to heal. He needed *her*.

How long would he keep her at arm's length? How long would he keep her at bay? How could she penetrate such iron restraint? What would it take to reach him?

Little wonder that her mind was fraught with a mad jumble of hope and uncertainty. She lay awake long into the night, tossing and turning restlessly. Finally she donned her wrapper. Perhaps a little warmed milk would help.

The house was dark and filled with shadows as she made her way downstairs. Her bare feet made no sound as she glided down the hallway. She started to pass Simon's study, then saw that one of the doors stood ajar. She veered across the hall to close it.

And then she saw him.

He sat behind his desk, but his chair was turned toward the window. Her gaze flickered over him. He'd discarded his jacket, but he wore the same clothing he'd worn at dinner. Clearly he hadn't been to bed yet. His long legs stretched out before him, he stared through the windows, his profile arresting, etched by moonlight. He looked so tired, so heartbreakingly lonely, that everything inside her went out to him.

Uncertain, Anne paused, her fingers still curled about the door handle. She didn't want to see him like this. She didn't want to *leave* him like this. She was half afraid to speak, yet something inside compelled her.

"Simon," she said quietly.

He glanced up.

Anne was a trifle nervous. Rallying herself, she moved just inside the doorway.

His pale eyes followed her, but he said nothing. He never even moved.

Seeing him like this wrought a poignant wave of yearning. "Are you all right?"

"Of course. I'm fine. Why wouldn't I be?" Wearily he rubbed the back of his neck.

Anne bit her lip. "Were you working?"

"No."

She persisted. "Why are you here at this hour then?"

"I don't sleep well," he said briefly.

"Is that why you come to bed so late?"

The moment lay wrapped in utter silence.

Nervously she wet her lips. "I've seen you before, you know." It slipped out before she was even aware of it. "Sitting in your room. Sitting in the dark . . ."

Through the shadows, a glimmer of a smile danced across his lips. "Spying on me, Annie?"

Annie. It was the first time he'd called her that. Hearing it, an odd little pain clamped tight about her heart. Silly, foolish tears pricked her eyelids. Furiously she blinked them back.

"You—you left the door open."

And so he had. Simon's smile withered. Too long and too well he'd guarded what was inside his heart. It was easier to conceal his feelings in the deepest reaches of his soul, where she couldn't see. Where he need not think of them.

Anne made it impossible.

For five long years, midnight had been his refuge, if not his solace.

No more. Not with Anne here. Not since that moment they'd met, he thought with brittle candor. He'd had no peace since then, not a single minute.

And now she was here again, tearing him apart.

"Anne," he said softly. "Go back to bed."

The breath she drew was deep and ragged. "Not unless you come with me."

Simon's heart stumbled. Dear God, was she asking—

"Come with me, Simon. Come with me now."

A dozen runaway emotions scrambled in his chest. God help him, he felt trapped. Battered. Besieged by the storm in his heart, a tempest of need and longing and fear.

One by one, she was tearing down the barriers he'd erected between them. Simon didn't know how to stop it. Or even if he could.

It was madness to want her. Madness even to think of it! He could never take her and be done with it. It wasn't his way. He couldn't make love to her without emotion, without heart.

It was why he hadn't lain with any woman since the day Ellie had died.

No, he could never make love to Anne and turn his back on her. His feelings were too engaged. He couldn't allow himself to touch her. To care for her. He couldn't allow himself to *love* her. He'd told himself to take the easy way. The only way. To keep his distance.

But Anne would not make it easy.

She was moving toward him now. Rounding the corner of his desk . . .

She knelt between his booted feet.

His heart was slamming. He trod a precarious balance between desire and despair. He'd told himself he couldn't allow her close. That he couldn't let her near. He couldn't give her what she wanted. What she deserved. A man with hopes and dreams as far-reaching as her own.

There was too much at stake. Too much at risk.

Everything at risk.

He couldn't love her . . .

And he certainly couldn't *use* her.

But now she was before him . . . on her knees. And Simon wanted to scream aloud his rage and his fury. Love and loss had made him bitter. He didn't deny it. He couldn't.

Yet he was terrified—absolutely terrified— that he could never have one without the other.

For so long now, he'd been detached from the world, detached from life. It was better to be alone than risk such devastation and loss again . . . Was that so selfish? Was it so wrong?

It had been too long . . . and perhaps it was too late.

But there was only so much a man could take. Only so much that *he* could take.

And he was a hairbreadth from going over the edge.

Yet if he took her to his bed, he would never forgive himself. And he had the awful sensation that Anne might never forgive *him.*

He took a breath, steadying his voice. Steadying his will.

Steadying his heart.

"Anne," he said, his voice very low, "we agreed this wouldn't happen."

No, Anne thought vaguely. There had been no agreement.

"Don't you see? It *can't* happen. I . . . it would change everything."

"How?" she asked tremulously. "How would it change things?"

The taut, hollow silence that followed nearly bled her of all strength. Her mouth quivering, she laid her hands on his thighs. Her heart quavered, along with her voice.

"Simon," she whispered achingly, "why don't you want me?"

Beneath her fingers, his muscles tightened, rock-hard and rigid. Something flitted across his face, a look of such agony, she felt herself cringe, both inside and out. Was she so wrong then? Was she truly so blind?

Just when she thought she would break apart, she heard him.

"I want you too much," he whispered, a whisper at once both feeble and fierce.

Her heart contracted. That ragged tone rendered her weak all over.

"Then show me, Simon. Show me tonight. Show me *now.*"

He caught her face between his hands. "Anne," he said helplessly. Hopelessly.

Reaching up, her eyes never wavering from his, she laid trembling fingers against the plane of his cheek . . .

And kissed him.

Her dignity swayed him. Her courage defeated him.

Her tenderness melted him.

Just that quickly, in the span of a heartbeat, the dam in his heart broke free. The skirmish that raged in his chest was no more.

Oh, Anne, he thought raggedly. *Make me hard. Make me feel. Make me forget.*

His chest thundering, he dragged her up . . . up and into his arms.

She buried her face against him, a gesture of such trust, he came wholly undone.

Conscious thought was obliterated. The tumult in his soul was forgotten; in its stead was a passion unlike anything he'd ever felt before.

His blood pumped. His temples pounded. Ellie was but a memory. But a moment in the vast breadth of time. But the woman in his arms was flesh and blood. And *his*.

Without a word, he carried her up the stairs and into her room. Once there, he lowered her to the floor. But he didn't want to let her go. Not yet. She possessed an allure no man in his right mind could ignore—an allure he could not ignore!

Not anymore. Not since he'd tasted her unbridled longing, the yielding of her body molded tight against his own. She was ripe for the taking, ripe for *him*. The knowledge that she wanted him as desperately as he wanted her was heady and sweet—and stirred him to a state of arousal that was almost past bearing.

The curtains at the window were open. Silvery spears of moonlight flooded the room— while desire flooded *him*. She beguiled him. Bewitched him. Beneath the gauzy silk of her gown, her breasts stood high, enticingly full. Her nipples were clearly visible, her areolas standing taut against the fabric, a sight he found incredibly erotic. His mouth grew dry. Somehow he knew they would be the same rosy pink as her mouth.

Her nearness—her scent—drove him half wild. Desire crowded his chest. A part of him wanted to snatch her close. A part of him longed to plant his stance wide, tangle her legs around his waist, and drive himself home, hard and fast and furious.

But another part of him—the rational part, thank heaven—wanted to savor every moment, burn every sweet, lingering caress into his mind and make it last all night.

But her eyes were trained to his, her eyes so clear and pure and blue, they made his breath catch and his heart turn over. Slipping a hand beneath the tumbled masses of her hair, he caressed the softness of her nape. His eyes captured hers, probing, as if to unearth every emotion held deep in her soul.

She stepped closer, directly between his booted feet. "Simon," she said softly. "Kiss me. Touch me. *Love* me."

Her tremulous little smile turned him inside out. His eyes darkened. Gripped by an irrepressible need, his hands went to the tie of her robe.

Slowly he tugged it loose, then peeled her robe from her shoulders. It slid to the floor. A flick of his fingers, and she was naked before him.

That tremulous little smile never wavered.

His gaze trickled low.

Anne's climbed higher.

His eyes were riveted on the very tips of her breasts—and hers on his mouth.

Her hands lifted. She laid her fingertips on

his shoulders. "Simon," she said, his name but a wisp of sound. "Simon, please . . ."

Once again he was lost.

His arms engulfed her. In one swift move he laid her on the counterpane. His boots hit the floor with a thud. He dragged at his shirt, the buttons of his trousers. Impatiently he kicked them aside.

Anne had levered herself up on her elbow. He saw the way her gaze skipped down his chest, venturing lower . . . Her innocuous astonishment wrung a groan from him. Her eyes widened.

Her lips parted. "Oh, dear," she said faintly.

Simon couldn't hide his desire. He couldn't hide his craving, not now. He didn't want to. Tumbling her back, he trapped the sound in the back of his throat . . . her mouth beneath his.

He couldn't help but recall the other night in his room. One taste, he had vowed. One touch . . . It was laughable, the very notion inconceivable.

He almost crushed her against him. The clinging of her arms—her mouth—flung him headlong into a storm. His body was burning, his blood afire. He wanted to be slow and easy and careful. He prayed that he could!

Never had he felt a passion so exquisite, so keenly intense as that which gripped him now.

His pulse was pounding. His mouth opened over hers. Bare, slender arms crept up around his neck. Blindly she clung. Blindly she gave, her lips parting with no hesitation. He ran his tongue over the ridge of her teeth, winding around hers. His kiss was hot and fervent and rampant. One bare, shapely leg wrapped around his, bringing her mound against his sex. He'd been in a perpetual state of arousal, half erection for days now. Willpower alone kept him from spilling himself in that instant.

She was so willing. So warm. So giving. The way she gave herself over so completely tugged at his heart. Desire rushed at him, like the rush of the wind. With his hand he touched her. With his eyes he saw her. With his mouth he explored her.

His kiss was raw and needy. Perhaps even greedy, for when he kissed her, the world slipped away, like sand beneath his feet.

She was warm. Vital. *Alive.* His mouth slid with hot, agonizing heat down the length of her throat. Deliberately he placed his mouth on the base of her throat, feeling her blood pulse beneath his tongue, her heart quicken. And with each heartbeat, he felt himself grow hard. Harder. Harder than he'd ever been in his life.

Raising his head, he sent a scorching appraisal the length of her body, a devouring gaze that thrilled her to the tips of her toes.

Within her breast beat the clamor of her heart. She felt his scrutiny as surely as if he touched her. Her cheeks blushed scarlet, but Anne didn't care. She longed for him to want her. She *needed* him to want her. She needed to see it. Feel it. Hear it.

And Lord above, she did. Her reward came in the flickering heat in his eyes that made her heart soar giddily and her pulse clamor wildly.

It seemed like forever that she'd waited for this night. Waited for *him*. It felt so right. She knew it now more than ever. This was what she needed. What he needed.

"You're as beautiful as I remember. So lovely, Anne. So unbearably lovely."

His low, husky whisper made her head spin, her heart stop. She felt it in the marrow of her bones. In every fiber of her being.

Unable to tear her eyes away, she watched as one lean, strong hand swooped low, settling full upon the ivory swell of one breast. She stared in utter fascination at the pale ivory of her flesh. Her nipples stood high and tight, seeming to strain and swell. The tips of his fingers painted circles around both rouged, straining centers, warmly tormenting, again and again until she was half mad with want at his tauntingly elusive caress. She strained high, arching against him, a wordless entreaty.

She nearly cried out when at last he caught one pouting pink nipple in his mouth, his tongue employing the same evocative play as his fingers. Needles of sensation centered there, at the very point of each breast. Heat gathered warm and damp between her thighs. Dazed, she could only look on as his tongue circled the ruched peak, laving it with the wet wash of his tongue, drawing her full into his mouth and sucking hard. Her breath rushed from her lungs. For one paralyzing instant, she could not breathe, for never had she felt sensation so painfully intense.

Hearing it, Simon raised his head. Something raced across his features, something that made her limbs turn to water.

His gaze impaled her. His jaw was tense, so very tense.

"You make me burn."

His jaw was taut, his tone fierce. There was a touch of ragged harshness in his voice. Yet hearing it thrilled her to the core.

Laying a finger in the center of his lower lip, she loved the feel of him, mesmerized by his smoldering expression. She gave not a thought that her heart lay in her eyes.

"No more than you make me burn." Her confession spilled out before she could stop it.

His eyes caught the light like the flame of a candle. "Truly?"

Her throat clogged tight, all that Anne could manage was a nod. Heaven help her, it was true. He kissed her again, a searing, sizzling kiss that left her utterly weak—and utterly aware of the way his lean, dark hand coasted down her belly.

Her breath was a ragged pant. Eliciting fire wherever he touched, brazen fingertips tangled in the tight curls at the apex of her thighs, ending in a soul-shattering quest—or perhaps it only began. A lone finger stole within damp, sleek flesh—grazing, stroking her furrows, skimming her outer folds, then dipping within soft, pink folds once again. And this time he found the center of her desire, a tiny flange of flesh hidden high in her cleft.

It was shockingly intimate, that caress. Shockingly bald, shockingly bold. Anne felt scorched inside—no, she was melting, there where his fingers circled unendingly. She was slick and wet, drenching his fingers with liquid heat. Should she be embarrassed? She wasn't. She couldn't be. Not with Simon.

"I want to please you, Anne." His look was searing, his touch blistering. He worked with unerring precision. "I want to pleasure you."

Anne's throat was clogged tight. Her tongue was all twisted in her mouth. "You will," she said unsteadily. "You do."

But she hadn't known precisely what he meant . . . until all at once, she felt herself writhing . . . tightening on his finger. Around it. Pure sensation shot through her.

She clutched at him, feeling herself whimpering, crying out his name. He caught the sound of her release in his mouth. His eyes burned like embers, shearing directly into hers.

Dragging his mouth away, he stared down at her. She ran her hands over the knotted contours of his arms. His skin was sleek and smooth. For days now she'd wondered what it would be like to lie in Simon's arms. Lying naked against him, no barriers between them, nothing but need.

Above her, his shoulders blotted out the moonlight. He was the beautiful one, Anne thought in awe. Mesmerizing, his image was branded forever in her mind

Her heart was pounding so hard it hurt. "Simon—" His name was a faint, choked sound. A sound of need, an unspoken question he caught in his mouth.

"Anne," he said. *"Annie."*

His expression nearly made her cry out. She sensed his fierceness, saw it build and race across his face. But it didn't frighten her. She didn't fear it. He looked . . . hungry. There was no other way to put it.

And it turned her inside out, that look.

Their eyes cleaved. Within his sparked a flame; it flared higher with every beat of her heart. Anne could feel the tension in him, feel his restraint in the rigidity of his body above hers, the agony etched on his features. Above her—against her—he was boiling hot. She couldn't look away as he raised himself above her. Sensing his desire—seeing it thick and swollen—the bottom dropped out of her belly. A quiver shot through her.

She was entranced. He was inflamed.

"Part your legs."

His searing whisper demanded compliance. "Wider . . . *wider.*"

His thighs straddled hers.

His features were etched with strain. His head bowed low. His forehead touched hers; hot breath rushed past her cheek.

Their fingertips grazed. Touched, one by one. Their fingers weaved . . . clamped together— his between hers, hers between his—borne down alongside her head.

"I won't hurt you," he said grittily. "I won't."

His whisper was raw. He felt raw.

Her heart caught, along with her breath. "I know," she cried. "I know!"

The radiant tenderness in her eyes sent him hurtling over the edge.

It was just as he'd said. She scalded him. She set him afire. She stormed him, and Simon could not fight it. He could not fight *her.*

Their bellies pressed. The round, swollen head of his shaft prodded deep—plowing through dense, damp curls. Sweat popped out on his brow. The urge to thrust hard and deep was intense. Immense.

His entry met with the frail membrane of her virginity.

It spun through his mind that he'd been remiss. He should have readied her further. Primed her for his possession. He rallied, rallied hard, bringing his desire in check—bringing himself in check, reminding himself of her innocence.

A muffled sound rent the air, part frustration, part surrender.

Her voice was muffled against the side of his neck. "You can't stop," she cried. "You can't stop now."

And dear God, he couldn't.

With a groan of defeat—a twist of the hips— he claimed her.

He hadn't known surrender could be such bliss.

Slowly he raised his head. He stared down, down to where they joined. Down where coarse dark hair met fleecy chestnut curls. Down where hot, silken flesh clamped tight around his member. Swallowing his flesh. Swallowing him until he didn't know where his body ended and hers began.

A tremulous little smile graced her lips. "I knew it would be like this. I knew it!"

But Simon hadn't known. Or perhaps he hadn't admitted it.

Awash in an agony of pleasure, his eyes

squeezed shut. Fever shot through him. He was steaming inside. The air was suddenly sweltering—and so was he. He could not leave her. He could not stop. He couldn't hold back. He couldn't go slow. Not now. Not with her twisting beneath him. It had been too long.

He wanted her too much.

And she was far, far too lovely.

His hands gripped hers. He kissed her nose, her eyes, her lips. Abrim with dark, sweet pleasure, he plunged deep, a driving possession that tumbled them headlong into the storm.

His mind was a red-hot haze. His body had a will of its own. All he could do was *feel* . . . and all he could feel was her. Again and again, in mindless ecstasy, in mounting frenzy. The clinging of her body around his turgid flesh was unbearably erotic. His heart aflame, his mouth sought hers; she offered hers with a breathless, sobbing moan.

Shivers raked his spine. A shudder wracked his form. Burning his veins was the scalding rush of his climax. He gritted his teeth, but he couldn't stop it. Couldn't stave it off. Couldn't hold back. It thundered through him, his seed erupting, flooding her with heat, spurting hot and thick and blistering.

The most intense, powerful orgasm of his life.

Little by little, the strength seeped from his body. Barely able to breathe, he fell on his side and wrapped her close. One single thought resounded in his mind.

It was like coming home from a long, arduous journey . . .

Eighteen

I had thought my heart forever taken ... Yet now I am not so sure.

Simon Blackwell

All in all, Simon decided, it was quite a miserable day.

Not an hour passed that he didn't think of what had passed between them last night. Burn for her, yearn for her. And last night . . .

He remembered how she melted against him—how she melted *him*. How her lips tasted like cherries in the summer. How clinging and tight she'd been. How *good* it felt to be embedded tight in her body. It only crystallized what he already knew.

Over breakfast she smiled so prettily. Throughout the day, he saw her flitting this way and that, twisting her hips just so . . . He could almost believe she dared him to snatch her up, carry her up the stairs, and make love to her the entire day . . . hell, the entire month.

Which was ridiculous, of course.

He couldn't forget. He couldn't ignore her. He certainly couldn't pretend he'd never made love to her.

His conscience lashed him. His weakness stabbed at him. He'd vowed to keep her distant, far from the boundaries of his heart. But he was afraid now, terrified he'd made a grave mistake. He should never have allowed her close! He couldn't *let* her close.

Nor, he discovered, could he lie to himself.

His feelings for Anne frightened him. *She* frightened him. If he was weak, she would slip inside—to his very soul.

The very thought sent him into sheer, stark panic.

He was caught in a tempest, and for the life of him, he didn't know where to turn! It even crossed his mind to send her back to London, to her family. But he had a sneaking suspicion his lovely bride would resist that tack. Besides, her brother Alec would be breathing down his neck in a heartbeat.

In all honesty, Simon knew he wouldn't. He

couldn't. Anne would be humiliated. Embarrassed. He didn't want to hurt her. Not Anne, not sweet, brave Anne.

Christ, who did he fool? Truth be told, he didn't want her to leave!

He liked the feelings she put in him. He'd been lost for so long. But now his life had purpose again.

She made him want to hope. To dream. To dare.

But Simon was a man who was afraid to believe in new beginnings, afraid to believe in hope. A man for whom all belief in hope had been extinguished the night he'd lost his family.

Far greater was his fear. Indeed, he'd never known such fear.

Anne would never understand. Simon wasn't certain *he* understood.

All he knew was this . . . He didn't dare love her. For if he should love her, only to lose her . . .

He couldn't do it. He couldn't *stand* it. Not again. Not ever again.

Eleven o'clock that night found Simon climbing the stairs to his chamber from his study. In the corridor, his footsteps were straight and unfaltering. He strode straight to his room with nary a glance at the door of Anne's room.

He was, he realized, feeling rather proud of himself—and quite determined not to give his lovely wife another thought until breakfast.

He did, however, note that she had yet to retire. Which was, he also realized, rather unusual.

Particularly since she had fluttered into his study shortly after nine, yawned hugely, and declared her intent to retire. Naturally, he bid her a polite good night. She then proceeded to flutter over—there was really no other way to describe it—and brush her mouth against his cheek.

Anne was smiling benignly as she strolled from his study.

Simon, however, was not.

His cheek still burned from that sweet caress. Climbing the stairs to his room, he had vowed this would be no different than any other night.

Eventually, the clock downstairs chimed midnight. Hearing it, Simon leaned back from his desk, scowling at the square of light that slanted onto the carpet. His journal still lay open, the entry for the day unwritten. Indeed, jabbed a sneering voice in his brain, what was he to say? That he lusted for his wife, who even now waited for him to bed her? Who ever beckoned, ever lured . . . Who, to all accounts, was set on her course to oh-so-charmingly seduce him!

And succeeding quite admirably, damn it all!

Flinging down the quill, Simon squared his jaw and set *his* resolve. One night, he reiterated. One night he'd let down his guard and allowed her trespass. He wouldn't be so careless again. He wouldn't be so weak.

Every so often over the next hour, he saw the undulating flicker of her shadow as she passed the door in the next room. Finally the light in her room sputtered out. He swore to himself, long and fluently, suddenly furious with himself.

Was this what he was resigned to? A game of cat and mouse that stretched long into the wee hours of each night?

He wouldn't. He couldn't. And so he sought harbor in the only way he knew how—the only way that let him cope.

The whisky he gulped seared his throat, even as the image of his beautiful young wife seared his mind.

An hour passed. Or was it two? Halfway to oblivion, Simon wasn't really quite sure.

His mood as dark as the night, he stared into the bottom of the glass. Drink wasn't what he needed. What he needed was Anne.

Under him.

Around him.

Beneath him.

Bloody hell, he thought. If Anne was willing, why was he so reluctant?

Almost before he knew it, his hand curled around the door handle. He thrust it open. Moonlight spilled across the floor, flooding the way to Anne's bedside.

So much for resolve, jeered a voice of dark, brittle humor.

She was lying on her back, the covers tangled around her waist, her expression one of peaceful repose.

Simon had never felt less like smiling in his life. And it was everything but peace that roiled in his chest.

Smoldering—inside, outside—his regard swept over her. His throat grew parched and dry. The gossamer-sheer nightgown she wore hid nothing. With each breath, the cloth trembled beneath breasts that jutted high and round, her nipples rosy against the cloth. A white-hot shaft of longing pierced his middle. He wanted to see them, washed shiny and wet from the heat of his tongue, feel them thrust into his mouth, and hear her moan with need.

All at once he froze.

An acid darkness crept over him. A scathing self-disgust. Sweet Christ, what the hell was he doing? Had he sunk so low that he allowed his lust to cloud his judgment?

He couldn't do this. By God, he wouldn't.

* * *

The sound of a crash splintered the night.

Anne's eyelids snapped open. She woke with jarring awareness.

The sound had come from Simon's room.

Throwing back the sheet, she ran through his door.

"Simon? *Simon!*"

Strong fumes of spirits assailed her. It took but a glance to glean the situation. A lamp atop his desk burned low. It cast a tiny sphere of light. A circlet of deep ruby liquid stained the wall to the right of the desk, still trickling to the painted white molding beneath. On the floor were shards of crystal.

Simon sat in front of his desk, his legs sprawled out in front of him. The sound of his name seemed to startle him, but then he leaned back.

"Sorry," he said. "Did I wake you?"

"I heard something." She moved toward him, careful not to step on the glass. Her gaze slid over him. "Are you all right?"

"All is well and good. No cause for worry."

No cause for worry? Anne didn't share his opinion; despite his inebriated state, his speech was as articulate as ever; his focus on her, as steady as ever. But his eyes were bloodshot. Deep lines scored his cheeks. Her heart knotted. An incredible weariness etched his features.

On the desktop, his journal lay open, the quill poised across the pages. Anne knew what it held . . . what it meant. It was filled with his heart. His life.

His very soul.

And yet . . .

He had seen the way her gaze dwelled long and hard on the journal.

"Why do you keep it?" The words welled in her throat. She couldn't contain them. "Why . . . when it torments you so?"

Something bleak chased across his face. It was as if, for one awful moment, she saw clear inside him—and what she saw made her heart bleed. She could have cried out for his anguish . . . and her own.

Then, all at once, everything changed. In that very same instant, she saw him retreat. Sealing away his heart. Sealing *her* away.

He reached toward the corner of the desk— the other glass upon the tray.

Anne was quicker. Her palm came over the top of the glass. "No," she said.

His gaze sharpened, his shuttered mask fully resurrected. Anne was both exasperated and furious.

And all the more determined.

Her chin came up. She was well acquainted with the iron lock on his control. When he willed it, it was a formidable, unreachable fortress.

Perhaps it was time she acquainted him with her own.

Simon's gaze swiveled from her face, to the glass—and back again. "Anne—"

"No," she said again.

Simon glared.

Anne refused to be quelled. She refused to be swayed.

Simon's eyes narrowed. He was drunk—more than a little drunk, to be precise. He was both incensed—and aroused. A part of him wanted to remove her. Physically, if need be. The way he'd wanted to remove her from the library that day. She prodded, she probed, she pricked him. She knew precisely where to jab.

Still another part of him wanted to drag her down and kiss her until they were both delirious.

"My dearest Anne"—he was glacially polite—"I appreciate your concern, but rest assured I am capable of deciding on my own—"

"You don't need it, Simon."

"Don't I?" He released a brittle laugh. "It's the only way I can fill my nights—"

"I will fill your nights."

Something fierce leaped in his eyes, an emotion he couldn't suppress. Just that quickly, between one single heartbeat and the next, a silence of a very different sort presided. The air was suddenly ripe with expectation. Sizzling tension arced between them, a pulsating awareness, as if the air came alive with currents. She knew from the way he gritted his teeth that he was fighting it.

"You leave me no peace."

"You leave me no *choice*."

His jaw knotted. His gaze trickled slowly down to her lips—and stayed. He wasn't nearly so aggrieved as he pretended, she realized. Nor was he as immune to her presence as he pretended.

A hand on his chest, she anchored him to the seat. Sinking down, she perched herself on one long, hard thigh, settling into her role as seductress with startling ease. His entire body was taut beneath her. Yet this time, nothing had ever excited her more. Burning silver eyes skimmed slowly over her cheeks, her jaw—then settled on her mouth.

A steely arm curled around her waist. His grip tightened. Reckless abandon swept over her. Perhaps he intended to lift her away, but it was just as she said—she allowed him no choice.

"Kiss me, you fool."

Her whisper inflamed them both. They were both breathing hard when his mouth released hers. Desire flamed in his eyes, a fevered heat that made her dizzy and weak.

He shifted, fumbling with the buttons on his trousers. Anne's eyes trickled down, just as he wrenched them wide . . .

Just as his rod sprang free.

Her eyes widened. Her heart lurched. Simon caught her close. His eyes pinned hers.

"Tempt me," he said thickly. "Touch me."

And she did. She touched him there where he'd not been touched in so long . . . Simon's breath hissed in; it was an exquisitely painful pleasure.

Her fingertips hovered, discovered his organ swollen and thick, feathering over the rigid upsurge of his sex, up one side, down the other.

He muttered a dark encouragement.

Her stomach clenched. Heat stole into Anne's cheeks, her entire being, despite all the ways he'd touched her last night. The sight of her hand on that part of him made her quiver. There had been no modesty between them last night.

There was none now.

Her fingertips, wet with a milky heat, curled around and over the straining head, wringing forth a sound low in his throat.

He caught at her hand, molding her against his shape. Curling her fingers beneath his, curling them against him, around him. One by one, clamped tight around his burning member. Engulfed by his hand, engulfed with *him*, he dragged her hand down to his very root . . . and back up. Again—and yet again, faster and harder, rocking into a shockingly bold rhythm—

an explicit caress, so blatantly sexual, so raw and explosive, her throat locked tight.

His breath grew labored. He was trembling, she realized shakily. A sweet, dark thrill shot through her. *She* made him tremble. She couldn't tear her gaze from his face. His features were tense and strained, the cords of his neck standing taut. His eyes were silver-bright, a molten reflection of sheer, mind-numbing desire.

The rhythm quickened, apace with her heart.

"Oh, Christ." With a gasp, Simon jerked back. But he didn't release her.

He swept her gown to her waist. His eyes were hot and brilliant. Strong fingers cupped one buttock, trailing down . . . hooking behind one knee. She felt herself turned. Lifted, ever so slightly. Anne drew a long, fractured breath. Oh, Lord, she had never imagined . . .

Her thighs imprisoned his. She was above him, astride him, cradled *around* him. Her nightgown was bunched about her waist. She was naked above and beneath. Simon's hands encompassed her hips.

Stunned, her eyes flew wide. Her lips parted, even as his thumbs parted *her.*

"Simon—" His name emerged in a desperate rush of air.

"Open for me, Annie," came his sweltering,

scorching whisper. "Yes, sweet, just like that . . ."

Their eyes collided, then lowered. So did her body. Lean hands came up to snare her hips. He brought her down . . . inevitably down. Inch by inch, he lowered her onto his thickness.

Her feet left the floor. Her thighs tensed. Tightened. It only made them both more searingly aware of how deep he was buried. Deep as a man could go. Deep as *he* could go.

Anne gasped.

Simon groaned.

His mouth closed over hers . . . as she closed over him.

Awash in sensation, a thousand firelights danced in her blood.

Awash in ecstasy, a thousand flames lit his.

His hips began to rise and fall, slowly . . . oh-so-slowly at first.

"God," he whispered hoarsely. "God."

It was as if a fever broke inside him. He pumped hard, driving deep—and Anne was plunging and churning, a wild, frantic union that left them both blazing. A cry tore from deep in his chest. Anne's eyes squeezed shut, for it was almost more than she could bear. One last, desperate thrust, and he exploded inside her. At that very instant, the walls of her cavern contracted, again and again.

Anne collapsed against him, her head pillowed on his shoulder. Awareness crept back, little by little.

"My word," she said weakly.

Simon gave a rusty little laugh. "Well," he murmured, "that isn't quite how I would have put it, but it will do, I think."

Anne blushed fiercely.

He chuckled again.

Shortly before dawn, Anne found herself installed back in her own bed. She had a vague memory of Simon carrying her there, depositing her beneath the covers and pulling up the sheet. She stirred sleepily.

"Simon?"

"Shhh. Go back to sleep." The tender sweep of a hand lingered on her cheek. Turning into it, she felt a fleeting wisp of a kiss breathed upon her lips. Smiling, she turned her face into the pillow and slept.

At breakfast, he was crisply polite. An elusive hurt tugged at her breast, swiftly suppressed. She took her cue from him, but she was stung. Duffy came to him with some business or other, and after landing a perfunctory kiss on her forehead, Simon strode from the room.

Anne sizzled. Her lips compressed. Her gaze drilled into him. If it could have bored a hole in his back, it would have. She couldn't banish the sensation that he was relieved—the cad! She didn't see him again until supper.

By then—oh, by then!—forged deep in Anne's

soul was a vow. A vow that she would not go to him. If he wanted her, then he must come to her.

A part of her didn't expect that he would . . .

He did. That night, and nearly every night thereafter.

At times his lovemaking was slow and mellow. At other times passion raged between them like wildfire, torrid and fierce and uncontrollable.

His possessiveness thrilled her. His touch melted her. He shared his body. He whispered how much he craved her. But in the light of day, they did not speak of all that passed between them in those hours after midnight.

He came to her only in the dead of night. Only in the dark.

As if he were ashamed.

He was not a selfish lover. He saw to her pleasure . . . then denied himself his own. Anne was no fool. Nor was she blind. It was there in the tautness of his body over hers, the crushing tension of his arms around her back. She saw it in the torture on his features—half pleasure, half pain—the way his breath scraped harsh and labored against her ear.

He brought her to climax—at peril of his own.

Why did he deny himself? Why did he deny her? Yet when morning came, he was gone. And Anne was left alone.

Confusion reigned. She was alternately both angry and despairing. Simon cared for her. He couldn't hide it. Whether he knew it or not, whether he willed it or not. But did he care enough? Would he *ever* care enough?

Anne wanted more. She wanted everything— all he could give and more.

The way he'd given himself to Ellie.

Was that so wrong? To covet—to capture— his heart? Was she so selfish?

Never would she deny him. Never would she refuse him. Desire disguised her love, however. If he guarded his heart so fiercely . . . then she must guard her own.

The cornerstone of their marriage had been based on so little . . . in all honesty, on nothing but a fleeting moment of ardor.

Six weeks had passed since they had wed. Six long weeks of both ecstasy and torment. Oh, but they had come such a long, long way!

But now . . . now she feared they had reached a stalemate.

Perhaps, Anne speculated several days later, the strain was taking its toll more than she realized. In the mornings, she woke abysmally tired. It was all she could do to prod her eyes open. She longed to roll over and go back to sleep. By day's end, she was exhausted.

She dismissed it, for she was not one to fret unduly, nor was she given to bouts of sickness.

But only this morning, immediately after breakfast, her stomach pitched like a ship in the seas. In fact, when she looked over the menus for the next day, she mentioned to Mrs. Wilder that perhaps the milk had soured.

She had just left the kitchen when she saw Simon in the hallway. "There you are," he said lightly. "I'm just on my way into the village to see Vicar Townsend. Will you come with me?"

Normally Anne would have relished the opportunity. On numerous occasions now, she'd accompanied him on visits to his tenants, or to the village. Perhaps it was silly, but she quivered inside when he lifted her from the curricle and tucked her hand into his elbow. And it sent a thrill all through her when he introduced her as his wife.

She shook her head. "Not today."

"What! Am I such poor company then?"

"Not in the slightest! Actually, however, I think I shall take a nap."

Simon cocked a brow. "Not even halfway through the morning"—a smile twitched at his lips—"and you're anxious for a nap?"

His crooked smile made her toes curl into her slippers. He was so tall, so strikingly handsome, he made the breath stop in her lungs.

"Perhaps you might bring me back one of those lovely plum cakes from the confectionary. The one with the delicious icing."

"Done. But we'd best not tell Mrs. Wilder you prefer those to hers." His eyes twinkling, he lowered his voice to a conspiratorial whisper. "Else we may be searching for another cook in very short order."

We. She hadn't known what one word could do to her . . . A vast swell of emotion surged inside, so vast she could barely contain it.

"Is there anything else you'd like?"

Just you! she wanted to cry. Her throat suddenly hot, Anne shook her head. Damn, she thought helplessly, what was wrong with her? She watched as he turned and strode down the hall.

"Simon!" she blurted.

Simon swung around. His boot heels echoed very distinctly as he retraced his steps.

He stopped before her, some nameless emotion kindled in his eyes. He captured her chin—and her mouth—in a soul-stirring kiss that made her sing inside.

Anne didn't stop to think. Winding her arms around his neck, she clung. She hadn't realized she was going to do it until it was done.

Simon's laugh was husky. But he was startled too by her impulsiveness. His gaze scoured hers. He frowned. "Are you all right? I'll stay if you want me—"

If she wanted him . . . Oh, Lord, she would want him for all time. She would need him for all time.

"I'm fine," she said breathlessly. "A trifle tired."

The gaze he fixed on her was rather thoughtful. Yet within his eyes was a glimmer of something that turned her inside out—and made her long to pitch herself back into his arms. He ran his thumb along her lower lip, an unmistakable caress. "Have a rest then. I'll be back soon."

When he was gone, Anne made her way upstairs and lay down. She was exhausted, but she discovered she was too restless for sleep. Finally she rose. She tugged a paisley shawl over her shoulders, for the chill of autumn now lingered in the air. Already the leaves turned golden and russet.

Sighing, she started toward the writing table in front of the fireplace—a lovely piece fashioned of rosewood, edged in tulipwood. She'd dispatched a letter to her mother yesterday, but it had been nearly a week since she'd written to Caro.

Halfway there she remembered she'd used the last of the paper when she'd penned the note to her mother. Perhaps there was some in Simon's desk.

She felt a trifle guilty rummaging through the top drawer, but yes, there it was. She retrieved half a dozen sheets, started to leave, then paused.

Simon's leather-bound journal lay open on the corner of the desk.

Something fluttered inside her. For one perilous instant, the urge to pick it up and read governed all else. Her good sense—and her conscience—quelled it almost in the very same moment. It would be an intrusion, one she could neither permit nor allow herself.

Despite her best intentions, Anne couldn't resist a glance. A sudden shaft of sunlight wheeled through the window, as if in invitation.

The date leaped out at her.

28 September 1848.

Yesterday's date. Nothing unusual about that.

Yet a faint consternation puckered her brow. Her mind counted back—groped fuzzily—then foundered.

Her heart lurched. Her mouth grew dry.

Her free hand came to rest upon her belly.

In that instant, Anne was struck numb. Struck dumb.

But in the far distant reaches of her being, the certainty thundered through her.

She was going to be a mother.

And Simon was going to be a father again.

Was she elated? Shocked? Perhaps a little of both, she decided shakily.

How long she stood rooted to the spot, she

didn't know. The clatter of wheels rumbling up the lane reached her ears. Anne stepped to the window and glanced out.

She blinked—and blinked again. She didn't need to write Caro at all, she realized numbly.

Caro was here—here at Rosewood.

Nineteen

I cannot deny my faith has been tested and tried throughout the years. Yet in sending my dearest Anne to me, I cannot help but wonder . . . Is this God's way of punishing me?

Simon Blackwell

"Hellooo!"

Anne raced down the staircase. She tore open the front door to the bubbling sound of Caro's greeting. It registered vaguely that Simon was helping Caro from the carriage—she didn't know he was back from the village. Then everything else was forgotten as Caro looked up and saw her.

Clutching her bonnet, a rainbow of ribbons

streaming out behind her, she ran up the wide stone stairs.

"Annie!"

They tumbled into each other's arms. Anne was half laughing, half crying. "Caro! Oh, Caro, I can't believe you're here! I thought you were staying in London until after Christmas! Oh, I was just about to write you!"

"Oh, were you now! I declare, I've had but . . . what? . . . two letters in all these weeks? I had no choice but to come and see for myself how you are!"

Anne was still half dazed. They hugged once more.

"Are you off to Gleneden?" Anne asked. "Or Lancashire?" Lancashire was where Caro and John maintained their primary residence.

"Gleneden," Caro said. "Alec's been there for nearly a month, you know. John left last week to join him for some hunting. Aunt Viv received an invitation to Bath from her friend Susan. Oh, and Aidan is thinking about resigning his commission. Won't it be grand to have him home after so long? It seems he's been in India for years, doesn't it? Well, actually he has, hasn't he—"

Caro was going on in her usual vivacious fashion, veering in all directions at once.

"So there I was, left in London on my own. I decided the children and I might as well join John and Alec in Scotland. And since Yorkshire is on the way—well, somewhat on the way—and you know how impetuous I am . . ." She gave an exuberant laugh. "At any rate, I thought it would be divine to see you again. So I do hope it's not altogether too presumptuous of me if we stay the night."

Finally she stopped. Her smile took in both Simon and Anne. "It isn't, is it?"

"Not at all. We're delighted you're here." Simon had been looking on, one side of his mouth curled up in a faint smile.

Pure, sweet pleasure flooded Anne at his ready reply.

Until now, Izzie and Jack stood on either side of their nurse, grasping her hands. Anne turned to them and held out her arms. They sped forward. Anne snatched them up against her.

Izzie smacked a wet, noisy kiss on Anne's cheek. Jack dropped his head against her shoulder.

Anne laughed delightedly, burying her nose against Izzie's soft, plump neck before pressing a kiss on Jack's little nose.

"They've been so excited all day." Caro chuckled. "They couldn't wait to see you!"

The driver fetched a valise from the boot, carrying it inside. Anne instructed the maid to show them to a room, and Caro and the children followed the maid.

Lingering at the foot of the staircase, Anne turned to Simon once they were alone. She hesitated, then laid her fingertips lightly on his arm. "Are you quite certain you don't mind if they stay?"

Simon's gaze rested for a long moment on her mouth before he answered. A faint smile curved his lips. "A silly question," he admonished. "You needn't seek permission, you know. Any of your family—all of your family—is welcome for as long as they please."

Reassured, Anne smiled up at him—a smile that caught at his heart.

A short while later, they gathered for tea in the drawing room. Anne sat next to Simon, near, but not touching him. A maid produced the treats he'd bought. Two pairs of blue eyes immediately sparked. Jack seized a slice of the plum cake Anne loved. Izzie let out a squeal and grabbed a lemon tea buscuit in each fist.

"Izzie," said Caro, "one is quite enough, dearest."

"One for me and one for Dolly," Izzie declared. She glanced at her doll, perched next to her on the settee. Such earnest logic nearly sent Anne into gales of laughter.

"I don't think Dolly is hungry just yet." Caro quirked a brow. "Why don't you set it on my plate and I'll hold it for you," she suggested.

Izzie pursed her lips, but deposited the treat on her mother's plate. Caro glanced at Anne and Simon. "Izzie and Dolly are inseparable," Caro explained with a straight face.

They chatted for a few minutes. The children

glanced at Simon every so often, but they said nothing, clearly shy around the stranger. Setting her teacup on her saucer, Caro glanced around the room, then addressed herself to Simon. "You have a lovely home."

Simon crossed his booted feet at the ankles. "Thank you. I confess, it's mostly due to Anne's influence."

Anne flushed with pleasure. She ran a finger around the rim of her teacup, hoping she didn't read more into the words than was really there.

Jack crammed the last bit of sweet into his mouth. His lips and cheeks were smeared with icing.

Anne set aside her tea. "Jack. Come here, pet." Jack glanced at Simon, then apparently decided it was safe to clamber onto her lap. Anne blotted his mouth and wiped his hands with her napkin.

Snugly ensconced in her arms, Jack peered up at her. "Annie," he said.

"Yes, sweet?"

Blue eyes gleamed. "Did you know Mama has a baby in her tummy?"

Caro's eyes rounded. Her mouth formed an "O," her expression utterly mortified—and utterly precious.

"He climbed inside," Jack said before either of them had a chance to respond.

Caro sputtered. "Jonathan Sykes!"

Jack was all innocence. "Yes, Mama?"

Caro caught Anne's eye. Anne's shoulders heaved with silent laughter. It wasn't often that Caro was rendered speechless, and Anne savored it!

"Jack, you—you really shouldn't say that."

He sighed as if he possessed the wisdom of the ancients. "Mama," he said sagely, "Papa told me."

Caro's tone was weak. "Did he now?"

Jack nodded. He'd warmed to the subject. "He did. And when he is born," he boasted, "we will have a brother."

Izzie erupted, scrambling to the floor. "No, Jack!" She planted a fist on her hip, her little mouth puckering fiercely. "We shall have a sister. Her name will be Dolly."

"Jack! Izzie!" Caro spread her hands, trying hard not to laugh as well. "Do not argue, dears! I promise, it shall be one or the other. And Papa and I shall decide the baby's name, darlings, and I'm sure you'll love it."

Caro hadn't noticed that Simon had suddenly disappeared for a moment. Anne bit her lip when she saw him reappear behind her. Caro's face was crimson, and, she was certain, so was hers! Had Simon heard the exchange? She wasn't sure if she should be mortified or amused!

Rescue came from an unexpected source. From his pocket Simon produced two candy sticks. That dispensed with Izzie and Jack's shyness. He eased down on his haunches and offered one to each child.

Jack reached for his. Izzie grabbed hers eagerly, popped it into her mouth, and sucked on it a moment. All the while her eyes moved curiously over Simon's face. Anne held her breath, for Simon wore an odd expression. Then, suddenly, the stick popped free of Izzie's mouth. "What's your name?"

A faint smile rimmed Simon's lips. "My name is Simon."

"Do you have a puppy?" she asked hopefully.

"No," he said. "But we have woolly sheep, and cows, and a stable full of horses. Oh, and two goats that are not averse to a little petting."

Izzie's eyes rounded. "A boy goat?" she breathed. "Or a girl goat?"

Anne's eyes met Caro's. Both stifled a laugh.

"A boy *and* a girl. Fred and Libby. Mrs. Wilder, our cook, makes cheese from Libby's milk. Would you like to see them?"

Izzie's eyes went wide. "Fred and Libby! I want to see Fred and Libby!" She hopped up and down, barely able to contain herself.

Simon got to his feet. He appeared to hesitate, then extended a hand to the little girl. Izzie wasted no time latching on. Simon glanced at Jack. "Would you like to come along, Jack?"

Jack's head bobbed up and down. He grabbed

hold of Simon's other hand. In her excitement, Izzie even forgot Dolly.

Anne let out her breath, unaware she'd been holding it. She couldn't deny the relief that poured through her. She'd been rather uncertain—perhaps even a little fearful—that Simon would be dreadfully uncomfortable with Izzie and Jack. Oh, she knew he would never be deliberately rude. But the reticence she'd feared he might feel around the children—particularly Jack—did not appear to be present . . .

Anne's gaze followed the trio as they left the room. It was a moment before she realized Caro was talking.

"Since Jack now has a pony," Caro was saying dryly, "Izzie has decided her most dire need is a puppy. And John has promised she shall have one."

Anne laughed. "She reminds me so much of you when you were young."

"Odd." Caro chuckled. "I was just about to say the same thing about you!"

Caro went on to tell her about the goings-on in London. Anne listened with half an ear. Her mind was still on Simon and the children. Finally she set aside her cup, brushing the crumbs from her skirt.

"Perhaps we should check on Izzie and Jack." Thankfully she managed to mask her anxiety.

"Excellent idea," Caro observed cheerily. "I expect they're in good hands, though."

It wasn't the little ones Anne was worried about. She kept her opinion to herself, however.

Simon and the children were coming up the drive as Anne and Caro stepped outside. Simon led Lady Jane by the bridle; Jack was atop the mare.

Jack let out a whoop. "Mama! Annie!" he crowed. "Look at me! I'm riding Lady Jane!"

Izzie had been sauntering alongside Simon, kicking the gravel, her hand snug in his. Upon spying her mother and Anne, she turned and stretched her arms high toward Simon. "My turn! My turn!" she cried.

Simon swung her up behind Jack, careful to keep a hand on her lest she tumble.

Izzie beamed. The most unexpected thing happened . . . Simon gave a low, unmistakable rumble of laughter.

Anne's heart surely stopped in that instant. This was how she yearned to see him—relaxed and carefree and laughing.

The three of them stopped in front of the portico. Simon swung the children down from Lady Jane's back.

"Mama!" Izzie shouted. "We petted Fred! But Libby wouldn't let us. Simon chased her around the pasture. But he couldn't catch her!"

Anne laughed hard as she imagined Simon chasing the goat around the pasture. Caro's lips quirked. Simon frowned over at them.

Izzie danced before Simon. "May I pet Fred and Libby again?" she begged. "Please?"

"Perhaps before dinner. If your mama doesn't mind, that is." He glanced at Caro with a smile. "I should imagine they're chafing a bit after all that time confined in a carriage."

"You don't know the half of it! I declare, every few minutes either one or both of them inquired how much longer before we saw Annie. I daresay, you've been missed, Annie!" she grinned at her cousin, then glanced at Simon. "Truly, though. I should hate for them to be pesky."

"They're not. Really."

Caro arched a brow. "A nap, Izzie. And Jack, you too. Then you may go."

Izzie threw her arms around Simon's legs and squealed.

Late that afternoon, Simon, Jack, and Izzie led the way toward the pasture. Simon soon picked up Izzie and carried her. Jack paused every so often to pick up a stone and fling it with a grunt across the hedge that meandered along the lane. Caro and Anne sauntered behind at a more leisurely pace.

"He's good with the children."

"Yes," Anne murmured. "He is, isn't he?"

It was that very thought that dwelled in Anne's mind later that evening. Jack and Izzie had been tucked into bed after dinner. Simon excused himself to his study. Anne and Caro wandered onto the terrace; twilight was nigh. The scent of roses lingered in the air, for they were just outside the rose garden. It wouldn't be long, she thought vaguely, and the roses would die off for the winter.

Anne was aware of Caro's eyes on her profile. "I'm pleased to see you looking so well," Caro said softly.

Had someone else been listening, it might have appeared an offhand, even obligatory remark. Anne detected the underlying inquiry beneath.

Her smile tripped. She drew her shawl more tightly around her shoulders.

And now Caro was staring.

"Annie?" she whispered. Then: "Annie! Oh, I'm so sorry. I didn't mean to distress you—"

"You needn't worry, dearest." Anne rolled a pebble beneath the toe of her boot. She made a valiant, plucky effort to sound normal. But all at once her throat clogged tight. Her control was rather precarious. She had the most absurd desire to break down and weep.

For this was Caro, in whom she had always confided everything. But Anne couldn't— wouldn't!—divulge the true state of affairs between her and Simon. She certainly couldn't divulge what she had only guessed today—that she was expecting his child. Especially when Simon had yet to be aware of it.

Most especially when she couldn't predict
what his reaction might be.

That might well be a brutal truth she must
confront. No, Anne couldn't pretend that all
was right in her world. She couldn't hide it.

Caro took her hands. "Do you remember what
I said to you in London before you left? That
above all, I should like for you to have what I
have," she said softly.

How could she forget? "I remember."

"I haven't forgotten your reply, Annie. You
told me that someday you would."

So she had. And then—then she hadn't
doubted it.

The breath Anne drew was painfully acute. "I
don't know that it will ever happen now." Her
tone was very low. It hurt to say it aloud.

Caro squeezed her fingers. "Annie! Don't
look like that. You must believe it."

"I want to. I want to so desperately. But it's
not so simple. Simon"—unwitting tears spilled
into her voice—"he had a wif—"

"I know," Caro said quietly. "A few days after
you and Simon left, John recalled something
vague—and so I asked Alec." There was a
pause. "Things have changed, Anne. He's different. I can see it. *You've* changed him."

Anne's mouth was tremulous. "Perhaps you
see more than I."

"Perhaps," Caro said with a faint smile. "But

you and Simon belong together. I said it once and . . . well, I stand by my opinion. So dry your eyes, love. Dry your tears. I know you," she said simply. "You'll find a way."

Anne failed to meet her regard. Caro sighed. She began to say something, then abruptly stopped.

"Look!" Caro said suddenly. She pointed over Anne's shoulder. "Look there!"

Anne twisted around, followed her gaze to the purple haze that floated on the treetops— followed it to the west, far to the horizon . . . where an evening star began to flicker. Even as they stared, it twirled and flared bright.

"The night's first star," Caro breathed. "Make a wish . . . Make it quickly!"

"Caro—"

"Annie!"

"It won't come true if I tell you—"

"Then don't tell me!" came Caro's fervent whisper. "Make a wish, Annie. Make it now!"

Anne closed her eyes, lifting her face to the heavens . . .

When she opened them, a soft smile rimmed Caro's lips. Ah, but Caro was such a romantic! And yet . . .

Hope stirred. Strength returned.

Anne gave her cousin a lopsided smile. "Somehow whenever I need it, you always manage to make me feel better."

"Well," Caro said lightly, "thank heaven it isn't often you need it. But I do try."

Reaching out, Anne hugged her fiercely.

Caro had decided to make an early start for Gleneden the next day. The following morning, they gathered outside the front door to say their good-byes. Caro and Anne hugged once again. Izzie slipped her hand into Simon's. He bent over, and she flung her arms around his neck and aimed a sloppy kiss at his cheek. Jack then shook Simon's hand like a proper little man.

On her knees, Anne embraced the little ones. Jack began to cry.

"I liked it when you lived with us, Annie. I don't want you to live here anymore."

His woefulness tugged at her heartstrings. "Jack, I'm married now. Like your mama and papa, love. I live here now. With Simon."

He clung to her. "I don't care. Come with us, Annie. Come home with us."

Anne smoothed the hair from his brow. "Love, I'll come visit soon. How will that be?"

Pink, pouting lips thrust out. "Do you promise?"

Anne ran a finger down the tip of his nubbin nose. "I promise."

Caro was last. They were each misty-eyed, each reluctant to let go.

It was Anne who finally drew back, laughing

shakily. "Would you look at us? Veritable watering pots, the both of us."

One last, quick hug all around, and then they were off. Anne waved until the carriage rumbled from sight, unwittingly reminded of their poignant, sentimental parting on her wedding day, when she and Simon left London for Rosewood.

It was just as she'd told Jack. This was her home now. Her life was here, with Simon.

Things had changed, Caro said. *He* had changed. That he had changed was Anne's most wistful, ardent prayer!

If only she possessed Caro's faith.

Twenty

It seems like a lifetime has passed since I've courted a woman. How odd it seems to even think of such a thing. I fear I no longer know how ... For it's not just any woman I must court. It's my wife! And I cannot help but wonder—it's been so long. Is it too late?

Simon Blackwell

Anne had yet to tell Simon of her secret.

Her pregnancy was a thought that rarely left her mind. She was elated. Awed. Perhaps even a little humble. Boy or girl, she didn't care. She could hardly wait to feel that small, slight weight settled in the crook of her elbow, for she knew it would feel right and so very perfect!

Would Simon feel the same?

It was a question that gnawed at her endlessly.

She told herself it was caution, not cowardice, that compelled her silence on the matter. First off, she wanted to be absolutely certain. And as she anticipated, her monthly time did not arrive.

Secondly, there was the matter of *how* to tell him. Anne pondered long and hard how to give Simon the news. Thirdly, she wanted the time to be right. She didn't want to just blurt it out—that might prove horridly awkward for both of them!

She prayed it would be a time of tenderness and peace, of gentleness and gladness. Yet Anne was wholly unsure how Simon would take the revelation.

Simon's behavior with Jack and Izzie was encouraging—yet was it encouragement enough?

She couldn't forget Simon's reluctance the night they had first made love. He'd cited how it would change everything—indeed, that was what lay behind his reluctance! Her thoughts gave her no peace. Was it still his intention that they should part after a year?

Nor could she forget his flat denouncement that very first night at Rosewood . . . that he wanted no children.

And it was that which frightened her most of all.

She must be honest with herself. She didn't

know what Simon wanted from her—other than her body. If he was not content to continue as they were, then it appeared he was resigned to it. The passion that flared between them was real. It left them both breathless and desperate and wanting. Yet there was a part of himself he withheld—withheld fiercely!

Anne wanted this baby—*his* baby. This might well be the chance to truly begin their life together. To share their lives, their hopes and dreams.

What held her back, she wasn't quite certain. Somehow the right time to tell Simon just didn't seem to come.

For this might well be the turning point of their marriage.

If only she could be certain *which* way their marriage would turn!

She longed for Caro's staunchness. Caro's faith, for when it came to this, her own deserted her.

One week to the day after Caro and the children left for Gleneden, Anne found herself in Simon's study. She dropped the day's post atop his desk, glancing outside. Dawn brought with it a dreary covering of leaden gray clouds. Perhaps it was the weather that kindled a slight melancholy.

For whatever reason, she found herself lingering. The scent of Simon's cologne still swirled in the air. It was somehow comforting, and she found herself lying down on the chaise, her fist tucked beneath her cheek. She would lie down. Just for a moment.

The house was very still and quiet. Anne suddenly remembered how lively it had been with Caro and the children here—and one memory in particular stuck in her mind.

The morning of their departure, Anne accompanied them downstairs to the entrance hall. While they waited for the carriage, Izzie wanted to be held. Anne lifted her high, holding her close, relishing the feel of her small, warm body.

"Dance," Izzie commanded. "Dance, Annie!" And so Anne dipped and twirled, waltzing around and around, faster and faster until they were both dizzy and laughing. Whirling to a halt, she stumbled. A pair of strong male hands closed warm about her waist in rescue . . .

"Careful," Simon had murmured.

An indulgent, almost lazy smile had curled his lips—she recalled thinking how devilishly attractive he was.

Anne never expected to sleep, but sleep she did. And she dreamed—dreamed once more of dancing and whirling across the floor. But the child in her arms was not Izzie, but a beautiful little girl with shining blond curls and rosy cheeks.

"Dance," the child commanded. "Dance, Mama!" Her face lifted, a delicate, miniature version of her father's bold features. And once again, Simon reached out in rescue. But this time he was laughing too . . .

It was a lovely, lovely dream—one that Anne hated to relinquish. Rising through the clouds of slumber toward wakefulness, she clung to it. Sighing, still smiling, she opened her eyes.

It gave her a start to see Simon seated behind his desk. His ledger was open, his quill in hand. Something lurked in his eyes; something that made her feel suddenly breathless. Curling his lips was the promise of a smile.

She had the unmistakable feeling he'd been watching her for some time.

"Oh, hello."

"Hello." That smile widened ever so slightly.

Anne sat up slowly. "How long have you been here?"

A brow quirked. "Long enough to discover you have an adorable snore."

Anne frowned at him good-naturedly. "It's quite horrid of you to sit there and watch me—"

"Snore?" he finished blandly.

Anne blushed.

Simon laughed, then crossed his arms and regarded her.

"What were you dreaming about?"

Feeling rather rumpled and disheveled, Anne raised a hand and smoothed her hair. "What?"

"You were smiling in your sleep. Dreaming, I think."

Anne busied her hands, replacing a pin in the heavy mass of her hair. "I—I was thinking about Caro." Her hands lowered. "And—the children."

"They're quite enchanting, aren't they? Your dream must have been quite enchanting too, the way you looked."

And so it was, she thought wildly. Her mind began to race, and so did her pulse. Should she tell him? Oh, but what was she to say?

By summer, the house would no longer be so empty. By summer, Jack and Izzie would have a new cousin.

He cocked his head. "Anne? Is something the matter?"

This was absurd, really. He was her husband. So why couldn't she say a word? All at once her tongue felt absurdly clumsy.

Something must have given her away. His eyes flickered. His smile withered.

"What," he said faintly. "Have you . . . conceived?"

Anne knotted her fingers in her lap. She neither denied nor confirmed it. Instead she countered his question with one of her own.

"I remember the night we came here, you said you didn't want children . . . You still don't, do you?"

There was an awkward—an endless!—pause.

He didn't say anything. He didn't have to. His silence said it all.

Anne resented him. She resented him bitterly in that instant. Granted, theirs was no ordinary marriage. Children were a natural consequence of marriage. It was natural—expected!—that a woman—a wife—would want children to nurture, to love and cuddle and watch grow. And men . . . men wanted children to carry on their blood and their name.

Every man but Simon.

There was a ringing silence.

Frost settled around Anne's heart. This was everything she had dreaded. She knew then . . . knew he didn't want a child. She couldn't convince him. She couldn't reach him. She'd thought she could make him love her. She'd thought she could make him care.

She thought only of the future.

While he thought only of the past.

She couldn't tell him about the baby. She simply couldn't.

"So," she said quietly. "That's why you refuse to take your pleasure, isn't it? Why you pull from me before you can spill yourself."

His features seemed to freeze over.

Bitterness twisted inside her. "What," she said, "did you think I wouldn't *know*?"

Inside Anne was stricken, stunned, but she wouldn't show it. "You may recall," she said very deliberately, "that on several occasions you were careless."

"Once." His voice was very low.

"Twice, Simon. *Twice.*" Anne took an almost perverse pleasure in reminding him.

A telltale color seeped up his neck. "I believe I was quite inebriated," he said coolly. "My recall is rather limited—"

"Liar," she said softly. *"Liar."*

His eyes grew chill. "My dearest Anne, the subject of bed play is hardly a matter that should be discussed—"

Anne was suddenly on her feet. "I beg to differ with you, sir! Is it to be done—and never spoken of? You are my husband. I am your wife. I've felt you tremble with want. I've felt you tremble in passion, but you refuse to let me close. You lie with me at night. You lie *inside* me. But in the light of day, it's all you can do to look me in the eye. It's as if you—you pretend it didn't happen. You share nothing with me, save your body—no, not even that!"

Tiny white lines appeared beside his mouth. His lips compressed. Very deliberately he shut his ledger—but he would not shut her out.

Her steps carried her forward, directly in front of his desk. Was he truly so blind? Or was he simply so blind to her? "Look at me, Simon."

He clasped his hands atop the ledger. "My dear, you have my undivided attention."

Anne took a sharp, agonizing breath.

"I know you, Simon. I know what you hide. I *see* what you hide. You deny me your seed. You deny me yourself. Have you any idea how that makes me feel? You cheat yourself. And you cheat *me*."

Simon's jaw clamped tight. It was true. She did know him, he acknowledged furiously. She threatened him. She exposed him. She'd found the chink in his armor, and she attacked precisely where it would do the most damage.

His fingers drummed on the journal. "Damn it, Anne, what the hell are you doing? You know damned well I would never hurt you—"

A cry broke from her lips.

"How can you say that? How?" Her eyes went dark. "My God," she whispered, "you're breaking my heart . . . Do you even care?"

His jaw tensed. "I know what you think." His tone was very low. "That I don't know how to love."

"Oh, I think you do, Simon. I know you do. I think you *won't*."

Simon took a breath. He felt . . . oh, oddly out of step. At odds with the world and everyone in it.

His gaze slid away, to a point just beyond her shoulder. He swallowed. "I can't, Anne." It was a crippling, brittle truth. A brutal truth. "You don't know what it's like. You don't understand. Children are so fragile. Life is so fragile—"

"And what about me? Are you so selfish then? Do you think you're the only one who's ever lost someone you love? The only one who's ever lost a child? My mother lost three, Simon. *Three.* And my father—I sat at his bedside for nearly a year watching him die, little by little. Day by day. My mother rarely left his side. When he died—when her babies died—she didn't run away. She didn't hide. So do not dare to tell me I don't know what it's like."

Her fingers curled into her palms. "I do not mean to be cruel. But they're gone, Simon. Ellie and your boys are gone. You've punished yourself all these years. How much longer will you continue to punish yourself? How much longer will you punish me? I want a husband. I want children. Children of my own. Children of *you.*"

Anne was relentless.

"Your pain is still alive. Bury it, Simon. Bury *them.*"

Simon felt as if he'd been struck. His head was spinning—the world along with it. "That's enough," he said sharply. "Stop this instant."

"And if I don't? You can't send me to my room like—like a child. And you certainly can't punish me like one."

"Then don't punish me!" His tone was like ice.

He was still fighting her, she realized. She

hadn't known it would hurt so much. It was like a knife lacerating her heart. It sliced her in two. Everything inside her cried out. Would he be forever lost to her?

It was as if she'd been caught in a stranglehold. He would safeguard his heart at the risk of her own, and it was more than she could bear. Inside she was bleeding. He was tearing her asunder. She couldn't tell him about the baby. Not now. She didn't want him out of a sense of guilt or duty.

She didn't want half measures. She didn't want scraps. She wouldn't take them. She would salvage her pride and she would not yield it.

She longed to lay her head against his shoulder—lie with him the night through! Rest her hand above his heart, in utter safety and trust.

And know that when morning broke, he would lie beside her.

She wanted him next to her. Each night. Every night.

It was all or nothing. She would take no less.

But his expression was inscrutable. She could see him pulling back. His defense was like a war. Parry and retreat. Duck back where he thought he couldn't be seen. She wouldn't let him. Not this time.

Lodged in her breast was a whirlwind of pain—a whirlwind of impotent fury.

She slapped her palms on the desktop. "Why are you like this?" she cried. "Why do you shut me out?"

He said nothing, merely sat back in his chair and surveyed her coolly. "Anne, you are over-wrought. When your mind is clearer, we can continue this discussion."

Pure, unbridled rage shot through her. "My mind has never been clearer."

"For heaven's sake, Anne, please listen . . ."

His irritation merely fired her outrage. Her wedding ring all at once seemed an oppressive weight. Her fingers were on it, twisting and dragging.

"No," she said fiercely. "You listen. I won't be half a woman. I won't be half a wife."

Her wedding ring scraped free. With all her might, she flung it—straight it at his chest. Straight at his heart.

"If you do not want me, then by God, I don't want you."

The ring bounced from his chest, then rolled across the floor.

Simon emitted a curse. "Anne, what the devil! *Anne!*"

But Anne had already turned a deaf ear. It was with no little amount of satisfaction that she did what he had done to her . . .

She turned her back and stalked away.

* * *

Anne didn't go down to dinner that night. She didn't have the energy—or the will—to face Simon just now. She didn't regret it. Any of it. She was tired of struggling. Frustrated with his resistance. She'd thought it would take nothing but persistence and patience to bring him around. She never dreamed it would be so hard. There was little point in wishing on stars, in spinning daydreams that would never come true.

What a fool she was.

Audrey brought her a tray in her room. Anne picked at the meal. Audrey helped her undress; she dismissed the girl and sat down in front of the dressing table. Faith, but she was pale! Tugging the pins from her hair, she dropped them in a pile. A tug of the ivory combs that secured her chignon sent the heavy curtain of her hair tumbling around her shoulders.

Picking up a silver-handled hairbrush, she pulled it slowly through her hair. The monotony of the movement was somehow soothing. The confrontation with Simon had left her drained. She didn't want to think about the consequences of the day. She didn't want to think about tomorrow. She didn't want to think about anything.

So distant was she that she didn't hear the connecting door open.

But she heard it close.

Anne went completely still, the brush still

poised in her hand. Her senses were suddenly screaming, her throat suddenly parched.

She couldn't see Simon, but she knew he was there. He stood in the dark. He stood in the shadows, his heart in shadow.

Then all at once he was behind her. Anne stared at his reflection in the mirror. She sucked in a breath.

Then she felt his hands on her shoulders, strong and warm.

Slowly he pushed down the straps of her nightgown, baring her to the waist.

Paralyzed, Anne couldn't move. Her heart tumbled to a standstill.

His hands slid down, closing around her breasts. His fingers splayed wide, filling his palms with firm, jutting flesh, as if staking his claim. Anne couldn't tear her gaze away from the mirror, riveted by the sight of his hands on her—his fingers so brown, her flesh so fair—a sight that was almost unbearably arousing. He toyed with the tips, deliberate, tantalizing play that sent a tremor all through her. Her lips parted; her hairbrush was still suspended in midair.

The brush was plucked from her hands. Anne had one single, mind-spinning glimpse of his eyes, silver and glittering. Without a word he caught her up, turning her in his arms. Anne's first thought was that he'd been drinking.

He hadn't.

"I need you, Anne," he whispered in an odd, strained voice. *"I need you."* Within was such despair that she could have wept.

His mouth closed over hers; he pulled her tongue into his mouth, a kiss as starkly erotic as his hands on her breasts. It obliterated her will, that kiss, eroding any protest she might have made. Her knees turned to pudding; she would have fallen if not for his almost crushing hold. Trapped not by him, but by her own desperate desire. Everything inside her ignited into a raging conflagration.

All that mattered was Simon. All that mattered was now.

She gave her mouth with a strangled, half-stifled moan. Her arms crept around his neck. Reason was forfeit; her heart was forfeit. She didn't submit, didn't surrender. There was nothing of triumph or victory in his embrace, just a wild desperation that equaled her own.

Powerful arms swept her high. She was dimly aware of the door between their rooms bucking wide. She felt the mattress beneath her, then Simon alongside her, as naked as she. His mouth captured hers. Anne's fingers scaled his back. Her fingers ran over the ridges of his scars. He stiffened, but he didn't gainsay her. With the pressure of her palm, she pushed him down. Her lips brushed over the uneven boundary of the scars, then kissed every inch of those horrible scars until a low, muffled exclamation broke from his lips.

Borne back to the pillow, he feasted on her breasts, dipped his tongue into her navel. With one hand he dragged his fingers through the furrowed valley of her sex, driving her half mad. Fiery shivers coursed the length of her. Just when she thought she could bear no more, one sleek, hard shoulder nudged her thighs apart. Her eyes flew wide at the sight of his dark head ducking low.

It was beyond bliss, beyond imagining. With his thumbs he widened her cleft; with his tongue he played her, plied her, pleasured her beyond anything she'd ever imagined. Anne fell back beneath the delicious onslaught, writhing against his mouth—his tongue—until at last she exploded.

When she surfaced, Simon was on his knees between her thighs. Parting her with his knees, he pushed his rod inside her, stretching her to the brink, sealing her mouth—sealing her body. Anne moaned. He pierced deep. With every driving lunge, he touched the gate of her womb, entered her soul. She yielded all; he withheld nothing. A hand beneath her buttock, he urged her against him, then held her tight, spewing inside her again and again almost violently. It was like a tempest, the furious rise of a storm that left them both gasping.

Little by little, the strength seeped from Simon's limbs. His fingers slid through her hair. He rolled to his side, a long, sinewed arm sprawled across her waist.

He slept within minutes.

 *Twenty-one*

I shall never forget the first day I saw her . . . my darling Anne. And I shall never forget the moment when she came back to me.

Simon Blackwell

This was the first time they had slept together—all the way through until morning.

Simon slept heavily, not rousing even once.

It was a far different matter for Anne, however. Carried along by the tumult of the day, she barely closed her eyes that night. Her mind twisted and turned first one way, then the other—in much the same manner as her feelings!

Eventually, daybreak sent its first pale fingertips into the room.

Simon lay sprawled on his stomach. Holding
her breath, she extracted herself little by little,
easing herself away. One last tug on a chestnut
skein of hair from beneath one sculpted biceps,
and she was free. It had been like that throughout the night; he'd wrapped himself around her
body, twisted his hand around a lock of her
hair, as if to capture and hold her bound to him
forever.

Anne wasn't quite sure she could have explained it, but she didn't want to be with him
when he woke. She wouldn't be in his bed—
and not his heart.

By morning, she had come to a decision. And
she was going to do something she'd never
done before . . .

She was going to run.

She was, she realized a while later, relieved
when Simon didn't show for breakfast. She was,
in fact, already back in her room when she heard
him going down the hall toward the stairs.

It wasn't long before she heard a knock.
"Come in," she called.

Simon stepped inside. He took in at a glance
the trunk half filled with clothing, the neat little pile of stockings laid on the bed.

Anne's pulse was suddenly thudding. Her
demeanor, however, was calm. "Good morning," she greeted. She finished folding the
nightgown in her hands and placed it on the
bed.

Simon's gaze slid from the nightgown to her face. "What's this, Anne?"

Guilt flashed through her at his quiet tone. She thrust it aside. Smoothing her skirts, she cleared her throat, praying for a calm she hoped wouldn't desert her.

"I'm just packing up a few of my things."

He glanced at the trunk. "More than a few, I'd say."

Anne cleared her throat. There was little point in prolonging this. She might as well just come out with it.

"I thought I'd join Caro and Alec at Gleneden."

Simon's gaze sharpened. "This is rather sudden."

"Yes. I suppose it is." Through some miracle she managed to sound normal.

Simon gave her a long, slow look.

Anne clasped her hands before her to still their trembling. Doubt and despair suddenly crowded all through her. Damn it all, why did he have to look at her like that? He made her feel almost guilty!

He stepped close. Anne was aware of his gaze moving over her face.

"Shall I come with you?"

"No!" That was the last thing she wanted! But she'd made it sound like a condemnation . . .

Frustrated, Simon looked at her. He took a breath.

"This doesn't have anything to do with wanting to see your family again, does it? It's about last night."

Anne's control was suddenly tenuous, her mouth tremulous. It was folly to love him. Folly to remain here. Now that she loved him, well . . . the stakes were too steep.

I need you, he had said. But Anne wanted more than need. More than passion.

She wanted more than he could give.

She swallowed. "I can't do this, Simon. I can't go on like this. It's too hard. It hurts too much. I—I have to go. I *need* to go. We need to be apart. It's best for both of us, I think."

If it's best, then why does it hurt so much? Anne ignored the nagging little voice in her head.

Silence, thick and despairing, hung between them.

"How long will you be gone?" he asked.

The question tore at her conscience. Anne fought it off. There was so much turmoil churning in her breast, she could barely stand.

"How long, Anne?"

Her throat constricted. "Must you make me say it? I don't know when I'll be back, Simon. I don't know *if* I'll be back."

His gaze snared hers. "I don't want you to go," he said.

"You give me no reason to stay!"

The words slipped out before she could stop them. Something sped across his features. Pain?

Regret? She wasn't sure. Her vision was misted so that she could barely see.

His eyes bored into hers. It spun through her mind that he saw so much . . . he saw *too* much.

"You can't go, Anne. You can't. I—" His tone was taut, his expression almost gritty. "I don't want you to."

Anne couldn't say a word. His declaration made her ache inside . . .

"Damn it, Anne. You—you love me." His tone was barely above a whisper. "Your eyes give you away every time you look at me . . ."

No, she thought brokenly. No.

The agony she heard in his tone pierced her to the quick. He caught at her hand—he caught at her heart.

Anne broke away, trembling, her eyes filled with tears.

"I—I don't know where I belong anymore. I don't even know why I'm still here . . ." The admission came low and choked. "Everything's been said. So please don't stop me. Please don't make it harder than it already is. If you care for me even a little, then . . . just let me go."

His eyes captured hers. His long, scraping silence nearly shredded what little remained of her composure.

"Perhaps you're right," he said finally. "Perhaps it's what's best." He paused. "But I'm afraid you'll have to wait until tomorrow. Duffy told me this morning there's a wheel on the carriage that's being repaired."

Anne gave a wooden nod. "I'll leave in the morning then."

Simon headed from Anne's room to his study. There he headed straight to the bottle of whisky. The bottle and glass in hand, he sank down into his chair.

An hour later, the bottle and glass—half full of the brew—sat before him on the desktop.

He hadn't touched it.

Just let me go.

Anne's plea played through his mind, an endless litany. He couldn't forget her expression today—and last night. Her face was so pale, her beautiful blue eyes tear-bright and wounded. It was like a brand on his soul, that look, like a driving blow to the heart.

Her finality pierced him to the quick.

Her tears had said so much . . . all that she could not.

His heart squeezed. Was she so unhappy then?

You're breaking my heart . . . do you even care?

He'd robbed her, he realized. He'd robbed her of so much! Anne needed to be surrounded by those she loved—and those who loved her. But the one thing she needed was the one thing he would never allow himself to have.

Oh, God. He'd been so selfish. She gave so much. And he gave so little.

To return to a life without Anne ... the thought made everything inside him cave in.

He'd been lost for so long now. But Anne ... she was like a candle in the night. A beacon in the dark. She lit his way ...

She lit his life.

There was a terrible tightness in his chest.

When had he become such a coward?

How could he let her go? *How?*

The thought thundered through him, taking hold, until it beat like a drum in every pore of his body.

A rending pain tore at his insides. He couldn't stand to think what life would be like without Anne. And if he lost her now ...

Then he would know what it was like to be *truly* lost.

Then he would know what it was like to be *forever* lost.

Mid-afternoon, Anne changed into a walking gown and sturdy boots. The house seemed so somber. She felt suddenly stifled. A breath of air would do her good, she decided.

The weather was lovely, rather warm though it was early October. High overhead, the sun played games; it sneaked behind puffy white clouds, then slipped free.

Her path took her along the ridge to the north
of Rosewood. She walked and walked, her head
down, her thoughts a rather lonely companion.
She hadn't figured out how—or when—she
was going to tell Simon the news of his im-
pending fatherhood. It wasn't her intention to
keep it secret. Even if she wanted to, she knew
she wouldn't. It wouldn't be right. Simon might
not want this baby, but he still deserved to
know of its existence.

Lightly she touched her belly. As much as it
pained her to admit the child she carried might
grow up without his—or her—father, an un-
swerving certainty filled her breast. She would
love this child enough for both of them.

As for what the future might hold for both
her and Simon . . . she wouldn't speculate. She
wouldn't hope. As much as it pained her, the
future would simply have to play out. Perhaps
they would divorce, scandalous though it was.
Perhaps they wouldn't. Either way, Anne knew
she would never marry again.

And she was reasonably certain that Simon
wouldn't either.

At Gleneden, perhaps, the answers she sought
would come to her.

A puff of wind snatched at her hat, loosening
the ribbons. Anne caught it and looked up.

Dark, boiling clouds had smothered the sun,
she saw. Ahead of her, the moorland lay covered in shadow. Glancing over her shoulder,

she saw that the house was but a speck in the distance. She hadn't realized she'd come so far.

A sudden eddy of the wind made her shiver. She wore neither shawl nor wrap, nor did she carry a parasol. It was no longer a question that it might rain—but when. Even as the thought sped through her mind, she felt her head pelted by raindrops. The wind whipped her skirts. Lightning split open the clouds ahead.

Oh, dear. Simon, she suspected, would not be pleased if he discovered she was out in such weather.

Indeed, Simon wasn't.

Back at Rosewood, Simon entered Anne's room. Her maid stood near the armoire, her arms full of Anne's gowns.

"Aggie . . . Audrey," he corrected, "where is your mistress?"

"I believe she was headed out for a walk, sir. It's been quite some time now. I don't believe she's returned yet." The girl's eyes flitted toward the window, where clouds had suddenly blotted out the sunlight.

Simon had already whirled, bolting headlong down the stairs. He was in a dead run when he clamored into the stable. A mighty crack of thunder shook the ground.

Ice ran through his veins. He rode from the stable at breakneck speed. To say he was perturbed to discover his wife caught out in such weather—again—was scarcely an exaggeration.

But far stronger was the choking fear that swept inside him like the blackest cloud. He wasn't sure he could ever be rational. Not about this—

Indeed, it was quite odd the way it happened . . . At the crest of the hill above the manor house, he stopped. The curtain of rain was so thick and gray, he could barely see. Then, suddenly, lightning flashed. And then he saw her in a blaze of light . . .

His darling Anne . . . Framed against the sky, against the storm, a sodden little figure trudging up the hill toward him, the wind whipping her skirts. Raw emotion seared his soul at the sight of her. She gave a wave . . .

He gave her his heart.

She was waiting when he leaped down to the ground.

"I know what you're going to say." She had to shout in order to be heard above the storm. "I promise you I shan't go out again without—"

That was as far as she got. An arm snaked around her waist, he'd already seized her and dragged her up on tiptoe against him, his mouth on hers. On and on he kissed her; Anne's hair was streaming, their clothing dripping. And all the while the wind wailed and thunder raged and the skies wept . . . as he wept.

He was still kissing her when the winds lost their fury and blew calm and peaceful, when the air began to warm and sunlight splashed the earth below.

When he finally summoned the strength to release her mouth—and it did indeed take every ounce of willpower he possessed—he discovered his wife's arms still linked around his neck, her eyes closed.

"Simon?" she whispered.

He nuzzled her cheek. "Yes, sweet?"

With a breathy little sigh, she opened her eyes. "May we go now?"

He kissed the corner of her mouth, his own curved up in a faint smile. "And where would you like to go?"

"Home," she said simply.

"An excellent choice, my love."

Once they were home, Simon saw Anne safely to her room to bathe and change. Audrey was there, waiting. But before he left Anne, he ran his knuckles over her cheek.

"When you've finished," he said quietly, "we need to talk."

Anne bit her lip. "I know."

He took quiet note of her anxious uncertainty, but Audrey had stepped up. Lightly he touched Anne's hair.

In his chamber, he shed his wet clothing and changed into breeches and a clean white shirt. Anne was still closeted with her maid. He heard the splash of bathwater, so he went downstairs to his study.

Before long, he went back upstairs. But Anne

wasn't there. And, he discovered, she was no-where in the house.

Puzzled, he stepped outside. He wasn't quite ready to let his concern give rise to full-blown alarm just yet.

As so often happened, the storm left in its wake a glorious, golden day. The late afternoon sunlight left the outside world alive with color, gilding the leaves of the trees. Raindrops shim-mered like jewels. The air was damp and tangy with the scent of grass and earth.

On the terrace, he paused. A second later his steps carried him down the path toward the rose garden. Exactly why, he couldn't say, for he ventured there but rarely. Yet he found himself lured by some strange, indefinable force.

He peered down the pathway, only to be brought up short by the sight that met his eyes.

His heart stilled.

Anne was kneeling on the ground in front of the three white rose bushes where Ellie and the boys were buried.

She was talking . . . talking to Ellie.

"He loved you so, you know," she was saying. "And I've thought—oh, perhaps this is silly!—that if I were more like you, that he might come to love me too. Would you have liked me, I won-der? I should like to think you do. That you would have. I love him too, you see. I—I love him rather desperately . . ."

At the wobble in her voice, Simon felt his

throat constrict. God. Oh, God. He didn't mean to eavesdrop. He truly didn't. Yet no power on earth could have stopped him from listening.

"My cousin Caro says that love will happen when and where it will and there's not a thing we can do to stop it. And in much the same way, I suppose, I know that I—I can't make him love me back. But he needs to be happy again, Ellie. I think you'd want that—to see him happy again . . . So I've decided I must try . . ."

A moment later, Simon retreated, as quietly as he'd approached. By the time she came down the path toward him, Simon stood on the terrace. His hands clasped behind his back, he turned.

"Come here," he said quietly.

Anne hesitated, then crossed to where he stood. She held perfectly still as he trailed a finger down the line of her jaw.

"You do know that I would have come after you, don't you? There's nowhere you could go that I wouldn't find you."

Judging from her expression, he had the feeling he'd shocked her.

Catching her hand, he slipped on her wedding ring. Carrying her hand to his lips, he kissed the circlet of gold.

"Never take this off again. Never."

For the space of a heartbeat, he caught it up tight against his cheek.

There was an uneven catch in his voice.

Anne was stunned to feel a damp, peculiar warmth . . .

Yet when he raised his head, his eyes were shining and clear, a soft, pure gray. There were no shadows, no darkness, no doubts, no emptiness. Instead they were filled—filled with a wealth of tenderness.

It proved her undoing. Anne burst out sobbing.

Simon closed his arms around her and wrapped her close. Drawing back, he slipped a finger beneath her chin, bringing her eyes to his. His voice was very soft.

"You told me that everything's been said. But there's one thing that hasn't." He bent so that their lips just barely touched. "I love you, Annie. I love you."

Anne began to cry all over again.

"Hush, sweet." He rocked her back and forth against him. "I've hurt you so much. I only hope that you can find it in your heart to forgive me."

Her fingers on his lips stopped the words. She shook her head, her mouth turned up in a crooked little smile. "Simon," she whispered, "this is what is in my heart . . . I've never loved you more than I do at this moment. And I'll never *stop* loving you."

Their kiss was long and lingering. Reluctantly Simon released her mouth, then rested his forehead against hers.

"Anne," he whispered. "My Annie . . . I'll give you everything I have, Anne. My heart. My home." He kissed the corner of her mouth. "My baby . . ."

Her smile was dazzlingly sweet, dazzlingly bright. "Simon," she said softly. "You already have . . ."

 *Epilogue*

Their daughter arrived the following May.

It was just after midnight when Simon helped Anne into their bed. She'd had a nagging back-ache throughout much of the day, but it wasn't until evening when her belly began to draw and cramp that she realized what was happening. Simon had a feeling throughout the day that her time was near. Just before dark, he sent for Dr. Gardner.

It was a good thing, too, that they decided not to wait.

Shortly after midnight, clouds began to smother the light of the moon; they gathered in wait to release their fire and fury. And indeed, it was a night such as they'd not seen for quite some time. A night when thunder raged, and the wind blew wild and fierce and seemingly never-ending. It was a night when the very walls of Rosewood Manor seemed to shiver and shake— and all the earth for miles around.

It was easily the most vicious storm of the year.

And this was the night their daughter chose for her arrival.

But when the storm was over . . .

Ah, but when it was over!

Simon held his daughter for the very first time.

Wrapped in a delicate lace blanket, she was the most enchanting little creature he'd ever seen—with the exception of her mother, of course. She had fine, delicate features that were a miniature of his own—a tiny little button of a mouth, a dusting of sun-drizzled hair, and a pointed little chin that made both mother and father eye each other and laugh, wondering where on earth it came from!

Simon had stayed with Anne throughout— where else would he have been? Anne held the baby and cradled her close, then gave her over to her father. Simon kissed Anne with a fervor that had poor Dr. Gardner clearing his throat and turning away—then settled in to inspect his daughter.

It was precious, that moment when she was laid in his arms, and one he knew would stay with him forever. Anne was beaming as she eased the babe into his arms. A powerful surge of love and protectiveness shot through him.

Anne smiled mistily, her heart in her eyes, as always.

Simon wanted to shout to the world that all was *right* in his world. Instead he laughed and traced a fingertip over the babe's cheek. He glanced at the first faint glimmer of sunlight peeping through the curtains, then back to his daughter. He pressed his lips to the golden down of her scalp and smiled.

"Welcome to the world, sunshine."

They named her Katharine—or Katie—not for anyone in particular, but just because they liked it. And because it somehow suited this tiny little girl who slept blissfully in her father's arms.

Four years later, it was somewhat different story, for Katie was a bit of a whirlwind. Among a slew of other things, she loved nothing more than whirling around the floor with her mother.

"Dance," Katie commanded. "Dance, Mama!" Anne swirled her around and around until they were both dizzy and breathless. And if they chanced to stumble, there was always a pair of strong male hands there to rescue both mother and daughter.

And when Katie was joined by her cousin

Margaret—Maggie, as she was called (and who was a scant four months older than Katie)—the two were a veritable tempest.

They chattered. They squealed. They chased after the sheep in the pasture—and chased after Izzie and Jack.

At least, as Caro laughingly commented to Anne one day, they always knew their whereabouts when the girls were together.

There was no doubt the two would be as close as their mothers had been . . . and still were.

On this particular summer day, Katie and Maggie had been into both of their mothers' trunks. They'd decided to put on a play in the drawing room. They paraded and pranced, necklines hanging, hems dragging. Katie's younger brother Jameson dragged across the floor in his father's boots. Izzie was declaring herself "Mama" to all present. Jack was busy trying to restore order among his siblings and cousins.

Katie had gone to change into yet another outfit. There was an eruption of giggles from behind the divan where Simon and Anne, Caro and John were seated.

Katie rushed out before them, flinging up her arms. "Mama," she crowed. "Look! Papa, look!"

She had decided to don her mother's corset over the rest of her costume.

Simon leaned over. "An adventurous girl, I daresay."

Anne wasn't sure whether to convulse into laughter or tears. She settled for a moan.

Later that same night, Simon had to shoo Katie and Maggie back into their bed at midnight.

Yet both Simon and Anne thought the house dreadfully quiet when they packed the children off to Caro and John's home in Lancashire for a week.

It was, however, an opportunity both decided should not be wasted, particularly when a wet drizzle began to fall that evening.

Climbing into bed that night, Anne ran a hand over Simon's naked chest. "I do believe," she announced blandly, "that it shall rain at least another three days."

Simon slipped a hand beneath her nightgown. "Mmmm," he said with a wicked grin. "We can only hope, can't we?"

Anne pursed her lips, in utter innocence. "I suppose," she murmured, "we shall simply have to find something to occupy ourselves indoors. Oh, dear, whatever shall we do?"

Simon's grin was utterly wicked. "Ah," he said. "Leave that to me."